TWISTE FLOWER

Book Two
DUPLICITY
MARIE CARR

| Page

Table of Contents

Chapter 1

I AM NOT A MURDERER! I promise. I'm a good person. I mean, yes... I *have* killed someone... but, damn it! I didn't mean to! It was an accident! I didn't plan any of this! I was the victim that night... but, I also did something bad— really bad. And I can't take it back. I promise, I will regret it every day for the rest of my life.

FOUR MONTHS AFTER THE worst day of my life, and I still can't sleep through the night. Of course, the accidental death of your lover— a death that you are responsible for is no small thing, especially when you didn't call the police.

That was the thought that didn't just disturb my sleep, but it consumed almost every waking moment— the fear of that knock at the door; the police finally figuring it out and arresting me for murder. *It was an accident!* I reminded myself of that constantly, but the accident wasn't the thing that really scared me. Keeping my mouth shut and allowing someone to get rid of his body was what made me envision handcuffs clicking into place over my wrists.

I spent every day trying to forget what happened to Mark. He was gone and nothing could change it. I hadn't seen or even spoken to Joseph, my partner in crime, since the night after it happened. Joseph was Mark's best friend and it was as hard for him as it was for me.

It was hard not talking to Joseph. He and I had grown close during my time when I was with Mark. I missed him, but it was a decision we both made, to go our separate ways. It was for the best. Too much had happened. I thought of him often, really as much as I thought of Mark, but I stayed away. Those eight months with Mark, although filled with excitement, were the darkest and scariest of my life. It almost destroyed me. And the terrible truth is, if I had never met him and planted myself in his life...he would still be alive.

"Well, at least I got an extra hour," I thought, flipping the covers off and dropping my feet to the cold floor. I knew there was no hope of getting back to sleep, at that point. I looked over at my clock, which was glowing— two minutes after four. Usually, when I woke up calling his name it was around three in the morning, so this was a small improvement.

Every morning, as I showered and got ready for work, flashes of the recent past consumed my thoughts. It would send a jolt through my stomach— the images of Mark and Joseph; the sex— the crazy fucking sex, the people, the parties. It was all still there, filed messy into my memories and bursting into my mind's eye at unexpected times, like scenes from a dirty movie. Sometimes I would be startled by visions of Mark standing in my kitchen or sitting on my bed, as I walked around my house. It was like he was really there, for a moment... a ghost haunting me. I knew I could benefit greatly from therapy, but when you've covered up a crime, it makes it kind of hard to share your thoughts.

I had to be at work at eight o'clock, so I had plenty of time to sit and drink my coffee. I tried to do what most people do and scroll through social media on my phone, or watch the news, but most mornings I just sat at the table, staring at nothing—thinking.

Suddenly, a knock at the door startled me out of my thoughts and I looked at the time on my phone. It was seven o'clock. I knew exactly who it was—Linda, my quirky neighbor. She and her husband Paul had moved in next door a few months ago and Paul left for work promptly, at seven, which left Linda alone all day, bored out of her mind the second he pulled out of the driveway. My kitchen window looked right into Linda and Paul's kitchen, and Linda knew I was an early riser, so she had begun the habit of popping up very early, most mornings. I slid out of my chair and opened the front door.

"Morning Kathren, am I too early?" Linda asked, her blonde hair pulled into a messy ponytail. She tightened her robe around her as she came in, just like she did most mornings when she dropped by unannounced. "I saw you through the window. Thought I'd come say hello."

"No. You're not too early, Linda. I'm just having my coffee before I head out. Grab some if you'd like," I offered, sitting back down.

Linda had made herself at home weeks ago, so I didn't go out of my way to play hostess. Linda got her coffee and began rambling about what she had picked up at the store the day before and bickerments she'd had with Paul the day before. I didn't really know Paul; he'd waved hello a few times from their driveway, but Linda popped in shortly after they arrived, determined to make a new friend. From all the stories Linda had shared already, I knew Linda didn't work because Paul wanted a perfectly spotless home and dinner on the table when he got there. A bit old fashioned, in my opinion, but that was Linda's marriage— not mine. Who was I to judge, after all my terrible choices. I was far from perfect— miles from it.

"I swear that man is never happy. I spent all day preparing that dinner. He gets home late and then complains about the chicken being dry. Well, it wasn't dry when I took it out of the oven. If he'd give me some notice I could plan a little better, ya know what I mean?" Linda rambled on. I smiled and nodded, trying to act interested. Finally, after Linda had talked through two cups of coffee, I saw that it was time to leave.

"Well, I hate to cut you off, but I have to get to work," I said, taking my cup to the sink.

"Of course you do. I've talked your ear off. Let me get out of your hair," Linda acknowledged, chattering all the way to the car.

"Well, have a good day, Linda." I hesitated shutting the car door, since Linda was still mid-sentence. Finally, she took a breath and waved goodbye allowing me to close the door on my old, red Honda. I didn't mind Linda most mornings. She was sweet, but sometimes her excessive jabbering gave me a small headache, especially in the mornings. Pulling out of the driveway, I gave Linda a short wave back, and I thought about what her reaction would be if I told her some of the stories of my adventures with Mark and Joseph, the sexiest and most troublesome men I'd ever known. Linda would probably pass out at the stories of orgies, sex clubs, drugs and the covering up of Mark's death.

It was a short drive to the office of Jake Lewis, CPA. I was thrilled to have a secure position as his secretary. I spent my days answering phones, gathering files for Mr. Lewis, typing up letters and keeping his schedule straight. He spent most days in his office with the door closed handling reports, checking transactions, and doing audits of the many companies he had as clients. His work was tedious, in my opinion, but luckily my job was pretty simple. Sometimes Mr. Lewis went out to his clients locations and I would spend the afternoon alone, in the office. That was perfect for me, since I found myself daydreaming so often and occasionally drifting into a quick cat nap.

On one morning, Mr. Lewis informed me he would be out most of the day, "I should be back around three-ish, Kathren. Call me if I'm needed," he said, heading out the front door. The glass door looked out onto the parking lot, so I had a clear view of him getting in his car and driving away.

I sat back in my chair, took a deep breath, and let out a long sigh. As usual, my mind floated back to Mark. When I met him, I was captivated by his good looks and sexy swagger. He was tall, dark, and handsome, with piercing blue eyes and an angular jawline covered by a five o'clock shadow. He just looked like a bad boy. After I had sex with him for the first time, I became infatuated. Sex with Mark was like nothing I'd ever experienced. He left me trembling and exhausted every time. One orgasm was never enough. All I ever wanted was for him to love me and when he made it clear that he didn't due exclusive relationships or love, I still couldn't give him up.

Then, when he began sharing me with his friend, Joseph, you would have thought that would have ended it, but I was still obsessed. And what I never expected was that I would begin to have feelings for Joseph too. I began to enjoy the relationship I had with both men. The way they shared me— it made me feel dirty, but so desired.

When I first met Joseph, I hated him— absolutely hated him. He was pompous and sarcastic, but over time I began to appreciate his honesty and I started to see another side to him— a kinder, warmer side. The friendship developed between us after we had slept together, at Mark's request— or maybe his demand; I wasn't sure anymore. It was hard to remember exactly how Mark always talked me into doing the most unconventional sex acts and always made me think it was my decision. I was deep in a flashback of a night spent with both men, visions of Mark standing behind me and Joseph in front, when the front door bell jingled. *Thank God for the small bell hanging from the top of the door.* I sat up quick and poised myself. There was a short, gray-haired man standing there, in a cheap, navy-blue suit..

"Hello. May I help you?"

5

"I'm looking for Kathren Thompson," the man said, looking around the wood paneled room.

"I'm Kathren. And you are?"

"Detective Pete Casteel." He reached into his suit coat and presented a badge. My mouth went dry and I swallowed hard. *Oh shit! It couldn't be! Had they finally figured it out?*

"What can I do for you, detective?" The words shuddered from my throat.

"I'm investigating a disappearance. Do you know Mark Sanders?" *Oh God! Here it is!*

"Yes— Mark? I knew him."

"*Knew* him, ma'am?"

"Well, yes. I haven't seen him in months." I tried to steady my tone.

"I see. Well, his family hasn't heard from him in months, either. No one has."

"Oh wow! Well, I can't say I'm totally surprised." I raised my brow and widened my eyes.

"Oh? Why is that?"

"Well, Mark had a tendency to disappear for days or weeks at a time. He was always disappearing on me, leaving town, without so much as a word."

"Well, he kept in touch with his brother, Mason. Mason heard from him every week, but there's been nothing since May. It's been four months. And I've checked in with friends and no one seems to know where he is." I wondered if he had spoken to Joseph. "Can I ask what your relationship with him is?"

"Was!" I corrected him. His brows lowered. "We were dating, but that ended."

"May I ask what happened?" He sat down in the chair across from me.

"Not much of a story. Mark wasn't big on commitment and I think he got bored. I was one of many women in his life, I'm sure. It was never that serious."

"Oh, I see." He wrote on a notepad he had pulled from his pocket. The scratching sound of the pencil dragging across the paper was making me cringe. I tried to act calm, but mildly concerned. I never knew that Mark kept in regular contact with his brother. I wondered where the detective had gotten my name. I took quick, shallow breaths, trying to stop fidgeting, which I'd been doing since the detective introduced himself. I looked into his eyes, trying to hide my alarm. "He never mentioned leaving town for good or someplace he may go in the future?" he asked.

"He didn't share details like that with me."

"How long did you date?" he asked.

"Maybe six months, off and on. Like I said, it wasn't that serious."

"No? I thought you spent quite a bit of time together," he said, watching my reaction. I was stunned. *Who was talking about our relationship?* I was about to say something else when Detective Casteel rose from his seat. "So, you didn't know him that well. I guess that's all I need for now. Thanks for your time, Ms. Thompson." He handed me his card and turned to leave. I stood. "Oh…" he turned before reaching for the door. "Do you know Joe Brooks?" he asked. I paused. I realized at that moment that I'd never known Joseph's last name.

"Joseph? I'm not sure of his last name, but I know Mark's friend, Joseph." The detective flashed a tight, thin smile and continued out the door. I watched him head into the parking lot. My stomach was doing cartwheels. It was short and simple. *Do you know Mark? Do you know where he might be? How well did you know him and do you know Joseph?* I walked to the door and peered out to make sure Pete Casteel had gone. I watched his navy-colored Buick pulling out of the lot. I turned and stood frozen against the door. I chewed my lip, trying to calm myself, but I'd seen too many police shows. The detectives were always smarter than they seemed and knew more than they let on. *Did he already know I was involved and was he testing me? Who would talk to a detective about my relationship with Mark?* Joseph was the only one I could think of, but it was hard to imagine Joseph sending the police my way since he was always uneasy that I might tell someone our secret, in a weak moment.

I couldn't concentrate for the rest of the day. This was what I'd been dreading for months. *Damn it! I knew you couldn't just disappear a body and expect no one would inquire, even about a lone wolf, like Mark.* That was how Joseph had convinced me to go through with it, after all. No one would be looking for Mark cause he was always disappearing and he was so private about his life. I needed to talk to Joseph, but it had been months and I was nervous. How would he react to me showing up on his front step after all this time? A phone call would be easier, but it didn't seem right. He hadn't called me, yet, after all.

By the end of the day, I was exhausted from the anxiety. I drove home in a daze. Pulling into my driveway, I screeched to a halt! Linda! I almost ran her down. *Why was she standing in the middle of my driveway?* Linda had one hand on her chest and the other out in front of her, as if that would stop my car from plowing into her..

"Oh my goodness! You didn't see me," Linda said, as I jumped out of the car.

"What are you doing, just standing in my driveway like this? I could have hit you!" I slammed the car door and hit the button to lock it. Linda followed me as I walked past her to the door. I was in no mood to talk.

"I'm sorry. I wanted to make sure I caught you." Linda tripped, trying to keep up with me. "Someone was snooping around your house today!" I stopped, my key already in the lock. I turned and glared at her.

"What? What are you talking about?"

"Yes. I was busy cleaning the house. Paul says I've been slipping on my house work. I don't know how. I spend three hours a day..." I held my hand up, stopping Linda mid-sentence.

"Linda...Please!"

"Oh, of course. Sorry." Linda shook her head, obviously aware of her bad habit of going off topic. "So, anyway, I was vacuuming the living room, when I got a glimpse of a man in your backyard. I went to my window and opened it to get a better look. I guess he heard me cause before I could ask him what he was doing, he darted to the other side of the house, out of my view. I waited to see if he'd come back around, cause you know there's a fence over there and... well, any who, I heard a car and when I went to the front, a car was heading down the road. I assume it was him leaving your driveway." I looked around nervously, as if he might still be there.

"What did he look like?"

"I couldn't really say. Tall, dark clothes— I think dark hair, but he had a hat on." Linda wrinkled her nose and squinted her eyes as she tried to remember details, but offered nothing else.

"That's it? You didn't see anything else?"

"Sorry, hun." Linda studied my reaction. "Something to be worried about? Should I have called the police?"

"No— no. It's ok. The car—was it a dark blue Buick?" I immediately thought of the detective.

"No. A light color. Silver, I think— maybe light blue. I couldn't tell the make or model." Now I was really confused. If not the detective, then who?

"Thanks Linda. I appreciate you letting me know. I've gotta get inside. I have a call to make." I wanted to get rid of Linda. I needed to figure out what was going on. After a quick goodbye, I went in and locked the door behind me. I went to the sliding glass door in the back of the house and looked out. The curtains were open. Anyone could see in. I checked the lock and closed the curtains. I walked around checking all the windows. I closed the blinds, including the one that looked into Linda's kitchen. I was uneasy. I couldn't imagine who would be lurking around my house.

As the evening went on, I tried to relax and distract myself with a book I'd been trying to get through. After reading the same page a half a dozen times I put it down. I began to pace, peeking out the windows, through the closed blinds, repeatedly. Linda's story of the man in my yard had me on edge. I knew it was going to be hard to sleep. Just the same, I headed to bed earlier than usual and tried to get a head start. As I lay there, worrying about the man outside my house and the detective asking questions, visions of Mark danced through my mind. Then worry melted away and the past entered, as usual. I replayed the first night he shared me with Joseph. I liked that memory. It was quite an experience, Joseph watching as Mark fucked me and then Mark watching as Joseph joined us in bed and took his turn. As the memories frequented my thoughts I found myself slipping from arousal to shame, sometimes blushing and covering my face, although there was no one to hide from in the solitude of my bedroom. Some nights, a memory like this would be the only tool needed to inspire an orgasm while touching myself. Of course other nights, I would jolt awake from flashes of other events during that time— events I didn't want to remember—horrible acts that plagued my mind and my soul. This was one of those nights.

Bang! Bang! Bang! My eyes opened. How long had I been sleeping? I scanned over to the clock— 12:16am. I sat up. *What was that? Was I dreaming? Surely, someone wasn't banging on my door at this hour!* I waited and then another bang. This time further away followed by a dog barking. I jumped to my feet. That first noise was much closer. I may have been sleeping, but it was loud. Three bangs, I was sure of it. I went to the front window and peaked through. I searched everywhere, the street, the yard, around every tree and car. *Where did it come from? What was going on?* I was seriously scared. I didn't sleep the rest of the night.

Chapter 2

THE NEXT COUPLE DAYS were uneventful. I was still on edge, but my nerves were starting to settle. I was sitting at my desk one afternoon, going through some files, when the phone rang.

"Hello. Thank you for calling Jake Lewis' office . Can I help you?"

"Kathren?"

I knew this voice. It was quiet, but I knew it.

"Hey. It's me... Joe— Joseph." Everyone called him Joe, except me. I always called him by his full name. My stomach fluttered at the sound of his smooth voice and, to my surprise, my eyes tear.

"Joseph! How are you?"

"Good. You?"

"Okay." A warm tingling filled me.

"It's been a while," he said, his voice becoming stronger— less timid. And the more it sounded like Joseph, the more the muscles, between my thighs, squeezed. I was always turned on by Joseph and we had quite the past, but I usually had control over myself, with Joseph. It was Mark that always caused me to lose all self-control. But Mark and Joseph were connected in my mind— like two halves of the same force.

"Yes it has," I said, looking over my shoulder to make sure my boss's door was still shut. His phone would glow green when a line was in use. Most calls ended up being forwarded to him within a minute. "I'm at work, Joseph. I can't talk for long."

"I know. I couldn't find your number and I didn't want to just pop up at your house. I remembered you got hired at a CPA's office, so I figured I'd call around. I got lucky. I found you on the third call. I need to talk to you. Can I call you later, or maybe... I could swing by your place?" My whole body trembled and I gasped. *Oh God, I hoped he didn't hear it.*

"Kat?" There it was. *Kat!* He was the only one who called me that and it took me right back to the days when he was my lover.

"Yes. Sure. Maybe around seven?" I tried not to sound too eager. "Do you remember my address?"

"I know where you live," he said, "So... seven then."

"Yes."

"See you then. Bye Kat."

I said goodbye and hung up. I took one more look at Jake's office door. I sat back in my chair and looked down at my hands. They were shaking. It had been months since I'd seen Joseph and not only that, I hadn't seen him since everything happened. The rest of the day I was a basket case. I tried to stay focused, but it was practically impossible. I knew he wanted to talk about the detective investigating, but I couldn't help wondering if we'd be able to control ourselves, when we finally saw each other again.

Five thirty finally came and I rushed home. Thankfully, there was no sign of Linda. I hurried in and locked the door behind me. I jumped in a quick shower and made sure I smelled good. I blow dried my hair and put on a little make up. I slipped into a tight pair of jeans and a white tee shirt that hugged my breast just enough to show the outline of my bra and possibly my nipples if they chose to pop out.

"Casual, but sexy!" I mumbled, as I tousled my hair in the mirror. As I rushed around picking up the messes in each room I wondered how long it would take him to make a move. *Would the night end with Joseph in my bed?* It had been a while since I had been touched by any man, but Joseph wasn't just any man. He was a masterful lover, just like Mark and incredibly gorgeous. He was used to women chasing him and he knew how to talk any woman out of her panties.

Finally, lights in the driveway shined through the front blinds. It was 7:05. I didn't rush to the door when he knocked. I didn't want to seem too eager. I waited a few seconds and then, I calmly walked over and opened the door. There he stood, hands pushed into his pockets, staring down at me. He was gorgeous as ever; that tall, fit body, sexy hazel eyes, and dark hair. He wore jeans and a black button up shirt, untucked, sleeves rolled up to the elbows. He had a slight gruff on his face—that was new. Joseph usually stayed clean shaven, but he looked even better with a little hair on his face. We just stared at each other for a few seconds, then Joseph's eyes scanned up and down. I felt heat low in my belly.

"Hey Kat." His lip curled up on one side. *Oh my God... That smile!*

"Hi." I swallowed hard.

"Can I come in?"

"Of course." I moved to the side and Joseph walked in. I got a whiff of his cologne as he passed— a familiar scent. "Can I get you something to drink?"

"Got a beer?" he asked, looking around the room.

"Sure." I pulled two beers from the fridge and handed him one. I noted the edge of his index finger grazing my pinky as he took it. I was hypersensitive to his touch and to his presence in the room.

"Have a seat." I stuck out my hand and directed him to the sofa. He sat down on one end and I took the other. My eyes drifted to his legs and I recalled the feeling of his warm, strong thighs pressing against the back of mine as he thrusted into me. It really wasn't that long ago, but it felt like years.

"So how are you?" he asked, taking a sip of his beer.

"Good, I guess. I mean, it's been an adjustment," I said. I gazed at him, wanting to move closer. "How about you?"

"Just trying to move forward and get back to my life, ya know."

"Sure. I understand." I did understand, but something in his tone seemed distant.

"You look good." He seemed a little hesitant to pay me the compliment.

"Thanks. You too."

"So, have you talked with the detective, investigating?" I noticed how he didn't use Mark's name.

"Yes. He surprised me at work a few days ago. It was pretty alarming, to tell ya the truth."

"And what did you tell him?"

"Nothing really. I dated Mark off and on for a few months. I said he was a private person and I didn't know anything."

"That's all?" Joseph looked me in the eyes, like he was searching for deception.

"Yes. That's all. What was strange, though. He seems to know more than he should. He questioned me about how much time I spent with him and insinuated that he'd heard it was more serious than I was suggesting. I was wondering who would have spoken to him about our relationship. Who even knew about our relationship, outside of you. "

"Well, it wasn't me. The only time he mentioned you was at the end. He asked if I knew you."

I gasped.

"What is it?"

"Nothing. It's just, that's what he did to me, on his way out the door, actually. He asked if I knew you. Well he said Joe Brooks. I assumed that was you."

"What did you say?"

"Just that I knew you. He didn't ask anything else."

"Yeah, same here. At the end he asked if I knew Kathren Thompson. I said that I thought so. I told him that he had so many girls it was hard to keep track." I knew that was the right answer, but the words still stung, especially since there was truth in it.

"Do you know who else he talked to?" I asked.

"Mason." Joseph said, as he took another swig of his beer.

"His brother?"

"Yeah."

"I never knew his name."

"Well, you may get to know more than his name. He's coming tomorrow."

"He's coming here— to Fairlawn, from California?"

I was bothered by the idea of meeting Mark's brother, the one who raised him, who was, apparently, so worried about his little brother that he was flying across the country to look for answers. The idea of it filled me with dread. Joseph put his beer down on the coffee table and turned his body to face me. He scooched a little closer.

"Listen Kat, I know that you know how bad this will be for us if anyone finds out what happened. We will go to prison! Both of us!" He was clearly expressing the real reason he came to see me.

"I know that," I said. I realized Joseph was worried. Somewhere in my stupid fantasies, I imagined Joseph was coming because he missed me and couldn't wait to see me any longer, but he didn't trust me to stay quiet. That's why he was really there. "I know my story, Joseph. You just stick to yours. We both have a lot to lose. Me more than you. You don't have to worry about me." I stood up and took Joseph's beer bottle from the table. It was still half full. I took both bottles and poured them out in the sink. Joseph watched me, as I dropped the bottles in the trash.

"Well, I guess that's my que," he said, rising from the couch. He walked to the door and turned to face me. He just looked at me for a few seconds. "It really is good to see you, Kat. I *have* missed you." He reached out and touched my cheek, gently. I closed my eyes, longing for more than the caress of my cheek. But he didn't offer anything more.

"I guess our five minutes are up," I said. My disappointment was obvious. Joseph lingered for a few seconds more and then turned and walked out. He didn't even try to hug me. I couldn't believe it. That was not the reunion I had expected. All that time we spent together, not just the sex, but the conversations, the joking and laughing. We had become friends during those months we spent together. And— we had incredible sex, too. He acted like he barely knew me anymore. I was crushed by his lack of interest and embarrassed by my presumption that Joseph still wanted me. I felt like an idiot. The truth was, there was serious stuff going on and I was fantasizing about him, like a silly girl wondering if the boy I liked still liked me.

I was about to head to the bedroom when something caught my attention. I felt a breeze. A window was open! *No! It couldn't be!* I closed every window and locked them three days ago and I hadn't opened anything. Then I noticed it. The window in the dining room was open, just a few inches. I remembered locking it, though. A chill ran up my spine. I looked around. I'd been home for a while already. I took a shower and cleaned the house. *No one could possibly be in the house! What the hell was happening?* I went to the dining room window, shut it, and locked it. I went around the house checking the windows, again.

My house was small. The front door opened to a small area that connected the kitchen on the left, with the dining area and living room straight ahead. A short hall on the right led to two bedrooms, a bathroom and laundry closet. It wasn't much, but it was perfect for me. It would be hard for someone to hide. Just to make sure, I grabbed a bat I kept behind the bedroom door and looked in all the closets, behind the shower curtain and under the bed, all the places the killer hides in the scary movie. All clear. It took me a long time to go to sleep that night. The bat stayed by my bedside.

The next day at work, I got another phone call from Joseph. He wanted me to come to his house. Mason had arrived and wanted to meet me. I didn't want to go. It had been months since I'd been in Joseph's house. I hadn't been there since that horrible, awful night. And I really didn't want to meet Mark's brother. *What the hell was I going to say to him? Why would he want to meet me, anyway? I wasn't anyone special, just one of Mark's many playmates.*

"I don't think I'm up for that, Joseph. I don't think I can come to your house. I don't know if I can even walk inside."

"He really wants to meet you, Kat. What do you want me to tell him? I mean, shit! Don't you think that might seem suspicious?" I sighed hard and dropped my head into my hand, massaging my temple in the spot a headache was beginning to throb. I just knew this was all leading to something bad, but I gave in.

"Fine! I'll come. What time?"

"He's staying with me while he's here, so any time after work is fine," he said.

"He's staying with you? Do you even know him?" I asked, surprised by the arrangement.

"Yes. We know each other."

"Oh, I didn't know that."

"There's plenty you don't know, Kat." *What the hell was that supposed to mean?*

"Apparently. I'll see ya later," I said and hung up.

I drove straight over after work, gripping the steering wheel so tight, I could have torn it off. I really didn't want to go. I was already flashing back, as I turned onto Joseph's street. Memories of riding in Mark's truck, heading to Joseph's house, the parties, the sex— it all flooded my mind. I pulled up in front of the house and slowed to a stop. It looked the same. I mean, it had only been a few months, but it felt like years. I was nervous to get out of the car. I just sat there...frozen... remembering everything. My hands were soaked in sweat. Then, after a few minutes, the front door opened. Joseph was standing in the doorway; the light from his foyer shone around him, almost beckoning me in. He didn't motion; he just looked at me... waiting. I took a deep breath, turned off the engine and got out of the car. I rubbed my sweaty palms against my skirt as I approached. I smoothed my hair and adjusted my blouse.

"You look great, Kat." Joseph said, noticing me fidgeting. "Good to see you."

As I got to the door, Joseph stood in my path, staring down at me. He was so sexy, in his tee shirt and jeans.

"Can I hug you?" he asked. Inside I was screaming, *Yes—Please—God—Can't you see how bad I want you?* But I simply nodded my head. He wrapped his long arms around me and pulled me close. He scooped me up off my feet and it felt amazing. I wrapped my arms around his neck, feeling the warmth of his neck against my cheek. "I really missed you," he whispered.

"Me too."

"He doesn't know we've seen each other already," he breathed into my ear. I let go and he lowered me back to my feet. He gave me a look, letting me know he wanted me to be careful of what I said. Again, he was worried I would make a mistake and say too much. I tilted my head and scowled at him. He really didn't trust me and that agitated me, immensely. He moved to the side and projected in a louder voice, "Please come in."

As I walked in, images of the past were everywhere. It was like Mark was standing there, beside me. I was slightly nauseous. Even the smell was familiar. I tried to stay calm, but once inside I wanted to turn around and run back to my car. So much had happened there. As I turned the corner into the living room; the room I'd spent so much time in, months ago, my eyes glanced around until I focused in on him.

I gasped and instantly felt faint. *Mark!* Joseph put his hand on my back to steady me. He could see it in my face. *Why hadn't he warned me?* Mason was a spitting image of Mark. It took my breath away to look at him. He was obviously older and his hair was longer, pulled back into a man bun, but the resemblance was uncanny— and disturbing.

"Hello Kathren," he said, walking toward me, reaching out to shake my hand. Even his voice was similar, deep, and smooth, like the first time I was introduced to Mark. "I'm Mason."

"Hi— Hello," I stuttered. "So glad to meet you. I'm so sorry," I said, shaking his hand.

"Sorry?" His expression turned to confusion. Joseph also looked at me, from over Mason's shoulder. His look was different. It was more of a "What the Fuck!" kind of look.

"I mean—I understand Mark's missing, I've been told. I'm sure he's fine, but you must be so worried." Joseph turned, rubbing his hand over his face, and crossing his arms. He was so on edge.

"Yeah. It's not like him not to call me. When was the last time you saw him, if I may ask?"

"Oh gosh! I'm not exactly sure. It's been quite a while. We were never really exclusive. He came and went a lot."

"Yeah, that sounds like Mark," he said, almost sympathetically.

"Sure does," Joseph added. "Why don't we all sit." Joseph stretched his hand toward the couch. As I headed to my seat, I couldn't help thinking of all the things that happened on that couch. I felt like someone else, as I sat down, not the same dirty girl who fucked all over this house. I wondered if Mason knew about that part of his brother and if he did... What must he think of me? I blushed at the thought, and suddenly, I was embarrassed.

"Do you have any idea about where he may have gone?" Mason asked. His eyes were wide and curious, looking for answers.

"No. I really don't. I wish I could help, but Mark and I really weren't that close."

"Really?" Mason looked surprised. "I had a different impression." *There it was again! Someone with a different impression of our relationship.* "I thought you *were* close."

"Really? What gave you that idea?" I asked.

"Mark did."

I felt a lump in my throat. *Mark talked about me to his brother? And he told him he felt close to me?* Sadness crept in. The whole time I dated Mark I was desperate for him to love me. I wanted him to feel close to me, but he never really gave me any indication that he did. Even though he spent several nights with me, sleeping in my bed, he was always an arm's length away, emotionally.

"To be honest, I'm kind of surprised by that, Mason. He made a point to let me know, from the beginning, that he didn't do relationships and he dated other women the whole time, so...." Mason stared at me. I tried to read his eyes, but I was unsure of what he was thinking.

God, it was hard to look at him. He looked so much like Mark. His eyes were so familiar. Mark's were an intense crystally blue, whereas Mason's were more gray, like little oceans shining out at me. I didn't know him at all, but I wanted to reach out for him. I wanted to crawl up next to him and hold him tight. He wasn't Mark, but he was the closest thing to him. I wondered if he'd smell like him: soap, leather, and vanilla. I missed that smell. I tried to look directly at Mason, but my eyes drifted over his shoulder to the bottom of the stairs. The last place I had seen Mark, lying on the floor.

I really didn't mean to push him down the stairs. I was just so angry and I wanted him to let me leave. After what he did, I couldn't stand for him to touch me. I didn't notice how close he was to the staircase. I would have called the police. I tried to talk Joseph into it, but he insisted we didn't. Joseph wasn't even there when it happened. He showed up shortly after and he was heartbroken, just like I was... but he was scared. I never knew what all went on behind the scenes at Joseph's house, but I knew he had drugs and shady characters around sometimes. He convinced me that it wouldn't be cut and dry for the cops. He said we had no choice. I went along with it and it's haunted me ever since. So, as I sat in front of Mark's brother, staring into his eyes, forced to lie, I felt even more terrible and I didn't think that was possible.

" Did anyone check his house?" I asked.

"Yes. It's cleared out. All his stuff is gone," Mason said. I looked over at Joseph. *My God! How did he do all this?* Joseph just looked back at me and then dropped his eyes to the floor. He never mentioned clearing out Mark's house. Mason continued, "I mean, I guess that's good. It looks like he moved. It's just so odd. He doesn't do this. I know he's spontaneous and does his own thing, but he always calls me. This is bullshit. If he's ok, I'm gonna kill him!" Mason was so clearly worried and confused. I could barely stand the shame. I wanted to help him, but I had to play stupid.

"Well, as much as I'd love to help, I don't know how I can," I said, standing up. I wanted to get out of there. Mason stood up too.

20

"Oh, you're leaving? I was hoping to get to know you a little, since you and Mark were close."

"We weren't!" I said, with frustration in my voice. I Immediately saw the look on Mason's face. He caught my tone.

"I'm sorry. I didn't mean to..."

"No! I'm sorry!" I said, quickly. "Forgive me. I've had a rough week at work and something is going on at home that's got me on edge. I shouldn't be snapping at you, especially at a time like this." Joseph stood up and moved toward me.

"I'm sorry. It's my fault. Kathren mentioned she was tired and I kind of insisted she come tonight. I was just hoping she may have some helpful information. We all just want to make sure Mark is okay," Joseph said. "Maybe we can get together for dinner one night... the three of us."

"Sure. That would be nice," I offered. I didn't really want to, but I tried to make nice.

Mason smiled. "Sounds good." His voice was uncertain. Damn it! Why did I respond like that?

"I'll walk you to the door," Joseph said, putting his hand on the small of my back.

"Goodbye Mason. It was wonderful to meet you. We'll see eachother soon, I hope."

"Yes. Have a good night, Kathren." He sat back down as Joseph led me out of the room.

When we got outside Joseph pulled the front door closed and grumbled in a low voice, "What the hell was that?"

"I'm sorry. I'm a nervous wreck!" I said. "It upsets me when I keep hearing how close Mark and I were. And I do have other stuff going on in my life, believe it or not."

"Something more important than this?" he asked, folding his arms.

"Actually— someones been lurking around my house and it's freaking me out!" I told him, looking around as if the lurker could be there watching me that very minute.

"Wait! What! What do you mean someone's lurking around?"

"My neighbor saw someone in my backyard while I was at work."

"Maybe it was a utility worker," he suggested, holding his hands out as if it was the obvious explanation.

"Yeah, but they took off when she tried to ask what they were doing there, and my window was open after I locked it."

He looked concerned. "Are you sure it was locked?"

"Yes. I'm sure."

"How would someone open a locked window?"

"I don't know... I... I don't know. I heard something at night, too. It woke me from my sleep. It sounded like it was right outside my window."

"Kathren! This doesn't sound good!" His eyes were big. There was worry on his face. "What are you going to do?"

"I don't know. Keep my doors locked and keep my bat close," I told him. "I don't know if it's smart to call the police right now, ya know."

"Yeah, I don't know. Maybe you should, though. You don't have any idea who it could be?"

"None."

"Well, let me know if you need me," he said. I stood there, the words on the tip of my tongue. *I need you, damn it!* But, I just smiled. Joseph stepped down and walked me all the way to my car. It was getting dark. As we got to the car, I turned and looked at his house. Joseph looked at the house and back at me. "Lots of memories, huh?"

"Yeah." We looked at each other and I wondered if he was thinking of our nights together. Did he miss touching me, the way I missed touching him? For a second I thought he was going to kiss me, but he didn't.

"Good night, Kat."

"Good night, Joseph." I got in my car and drove away, leaving his gorgeous image in my rearview mirror.

Chapter 3

A COUPLE DAYS WENT by with nothing out of the ordinary. I was starting to feel more at ease when I got a call on a Saturday morning. It was Detective Casteel. He wanted to know if I could come into the station. It was the last thing I wanted to do, but I had to be cooperative and act concerned. So I headed down to the police station. As I walked in, I noticed a man sitting on a bench, waiting and a couple speaking with an officer behind the counter. There were other officers walking by, and as they glanced at me, I felt guilty. I imagined being cuffed and everyone looking at me as I was taken into custody. I felt like a criminal. *Could that be my future?*

"Ms. Thompson!" Detective Casteel emerged from a door in the back corner of the waiting area. He waved me in. I smiled and headed for the door. I followed him down a long hall into a small room with a table and two chairs. There wasn't one of those two-way mirrors like you always see in the movies. "Can I get you anything? Water? Coffee?" he asked.

"No thank you. I'm good right now," I told him, sitting in the gray folding chair across from him. The room felt cold, but that wasn't why I was shaking. He removed his gray suit jacket and folded it over his chair before sitting down.

"Well, like I said on the phone, I just have a few more questions for you, if it's alright."

"Of course. Anything I can do to help."

"Great! So, going back to our first conversation, you said that you were not that close to Mark. Is that accurate?" He looked down as if he were reading from notes and then looked up at me, his pen tip pressed against his notepad, ready to write.

"Right. Well, I guess that's all a matter of opinion. I didn't feel that he considered me someone he was close to, but it's possible, I guess." This issue kept coming up about how close we were. Detective Casteel scratched a quick note on his pad.

"Uh huh. And there isn't anything that you think you could tell me that might shed some light into what kind of man Mark is?"

"Well, I could tell you my opinion, but again, he was so private. He was a confident person. I know that much. I've never met someone so sure of themself. Our relationship was more— physical, than anything. We didn't talk a whole lot if you know what I mean," I told him, blushing.

"I see." He cleared his throat. "Did Mark use drugs?" The question popped out and I was instantly concerned. I wasn't sure where he was going with it.

"Well, he drank and I know he smoked weed," I answered.

"And what about you?"

"Do I use drugs?"

"Yes."

"No, sir."

"No?" He lowered his notepad and leaned forward. "So you never used drugs with Mark?" I just stared at him— frozen. "I was told that you lost your job at Kilmore construction, where you worked with Mark, for drug use." He smiled the tiniest bit, waiting for my response.

"Oh... well...yes. That's true. But it was only a couple times. I'm not a drug user. I never have been. I smoked weed a couple times and took an ecstasy pill once and that just so happened to be right before a new drug testing policy started at work and...well... It was bad timing." I swallowed hard. My palms began to sweat. Mark did smoke weed and drink a lot, but I never knew him to use harder drugs. He did encourage me to take drugs, though, in an effort to loosen me up. That was the cause of me losing a job that I loved. I was always ashamed of that.

"I see. Yes, that *is* bad timing. And were those drugs used with Mark?" He looked me right in the eyes, as if he were seeing my thoughts. The room was starting to feel hot and small.

"Yes sir."

"And did you party with Mark at Joseph Brooks' home?"

"Yes."

"And were drugs used there?"

"Between Mark and I? Yes. I'm not sure about anyone else," I told him, squirming in my chair.

"Were you also involved with Joseph Brooks?"

Oh dear God! What is happening? What does he know? I was terrified and embarrassed by the questions he was asking. It felt like he knew the whole story and was just letting me hang myself. That was impossible, though. He couldn't know everything. I couldn't even understand how he knew what he knew.

"Not really involved. We partied a couple times, if you know what I mean."

"No, Ms. Thompson, I don't. Why don't you explain to me what that means." He stared, stone faced, now, and I stared back. After what seemed like a long silence, he continued, "Ms. Thompson, let me be clear. I don't care what kind of life you lead. I don't care who you sleep with or how well you get to know your lovers. I don't care about your drug use. What I do care about is getting to the bottom of Mark Sander's disappearance and any bit of information can be helpful. I need to find him. Do you understand?"

"Yes of course." I took a deep breath and smiled at him. "I'm sorry. Some of this is a bit embarrassing and out of my normal character. I'm trying to tell you everything, it's just..."

"What about altercations?"

"Altercations?"

"Yes. Mark was known to get into altercations. Apparently he was quick to throw a punch. Can you tell me about the fight between him and Frank Garza?" *Frank! Oh God! How did he find out about that? They didn't even get arrested!*

Frank was my oldest friend and first real boyfriend. How did this cop know about Frank? He had left over a month ago, with his new girlfriend, to look for work near her home. Frank had been crazy about me for years and wanted us to be together. He saw my bizarre behavior when I was seeing Mark and I ended up telling him a lot—too much. Frank met a woman at a work conference a few weeks after Mark died and sparks flew. It was love at first sight, I guess and Frank followed her to her hometown, right outside of Chicago, a few hours from Fairlawn. I encouraged him. He knew I didn't want to be with him romantically and he needed to have love in his life. We've only talked a few times since he left.

"Oh geez, I forgot about the fight with Frank."

"Yes, according to Frank..."

"You spoke to Frank?" My surprise was obvious.

"Yes. And according to him, you were in love with Mark and Mark was forcing you to do all sorts of things that you didn't really want to do, but you were obsessed with him. According to Frank, Mark was destroying your life. He claims he begged you to leave Mark but you repeatedly told him you couldn't. He seems to think you and Mark were pretty serious even though Mark treated you terribly. He claims Mark got you to start using drugs so you could— well, handle some of the difficult things he was making you do." He was reading from notes on his notepad and only looked up occasionally to see my expression. "Frank claims you were in tears a lot, over Mark, and he had never seen you so taken by any man, including himself. I understand you and Frank dated for several years. Frank says he cared for you deeply and was so hurt by what Mark was doing to you that when Mark approached the two of you one afternoon, at a restaurant, it ended with the police being called. They had a physical altercation." He paused for a few seconds and then continued. "He also says that when you finally did end it with Mark, you were so upset that you couldn't speak about it. You told him to never mention Mark's name to you, ever. He'd never seen you so devastated."

I didn't know what to say. He knew way too much. Frank told him everything. When Mark died, I couldn't tell anyone what Joseph and I had done, so when Frank asked, I just told him I finally ended it. I told him to never mention Mark for two reasons: One, I didn't want to think about it. And two, I didn't want to accidentally say something I shouldn't. I just sat there for a minute, my mind frantically searching for the words, something that would not make me look like a huge liar.

"Ms. Thopson, it feels like you are keeping some aspects of your relationship hidden, and I'm not sure why." He waited for me to respond.

"Detective, Please understand, I loved Frank. He's a good friend, but his view of things is a little tainted by his feelings for me and frankly— his hatred for Mark. See, Frank was trying very hard to rekindle our relationship during that time and I used Mark as an excuse to keep Frank at a distance. And there were some moments when I did cry, but some of that was out of sadness about hurting Frank. He was so heartbroken that I didn't want a relationship with him and I hated hurting him like that. Plus, I had lost my job around that time and I was upset over that. It was a stressful time. But, he makes it sound way worse than it was."

"So, it *was* bad, then, Just not that bad?"

"No! That's not what I meant. I did do some things with Mark that were out of my comfort zone. I mean, I experimented. But Mark never forced me. He encouraged me to try things, and sometimes I felt a little— out of sorts. The drugs were a mistake." I folded my hands in my lap and squeezed my sweaty palms together. He wrote on his pad. "I'm not trying to hide anything. I promise."

"I need to know everything, Ms. Thompson. Do you understand?"

"Yes. I'm trying to think if there is anything else. I just can't think of anything," I said. "Mark was a good guy. He was honest with me about who he was. I was very attracted to him and honestly, I was bored with my life at the time. I dated Mark, but I never thought of myself as his girlfriend. Never. He was clear that he didn't do commitments. I accepted that. We had fun together, but he did live a very different life than I was accustomed to and after a while, I realized I couldn't keep up, if you know what I mean. There were a lot of parties and— honestly, a lot of sex. When I lost my job for drug use..." I looked down in shame, "It was a big wake up call. I let things fade out between us and after a while he just didn't call anymore and that was that. I've just been trying to get my life back on track, ever since. Back to boring, I guess." I smiled and sighed.

He wrote on his pad for a few seconds and then looked up and smiled. " So— nothing else you can think of?"

"No. Not that I can think of."

"Ok." He stood up and I followed. "Well, if you think of anything else..."

"Of course. I will call," I told him. I couldn't wait to get out of there. I moved toward the door.

"Oh, Ms. Thompson, one more thing," he said. I turned, my hand holding the door knob. "Do you know Ronald Holt?"

"No. Never heard of him," I said.

"He goes by Rex."

I felt my stomach turn and my heart climb into my throat! I don't know what my face must have looked like, but it was almost impossible not to react. I couldn't just say I didn't know him. He would know I was a liar. "I'm familiar with him. He was a guy who I saw at Joseph's house a couple times. He was a rough looking guy. I don't actually know him, though."

Detective Casteel just looked at me for a few seconds. I tried to look blank, trying not to let him read the horror on my face. After a minute he smiled and said, "Have a nice day, Ms. Thompson."

"You too. Bye." I stepped out and hurried down the hall. Walking out of the station, I felt a sick feeling rising up from my stomach. I had to get out of there, but I wasn't going to make it. I saw the restrooms to my left and made a quick turn into the ladies room. I rushed to an open stall and before I could close the door I started vomiting into the toilet. *Thank God I made it to the toilet!* I cleaned up as fast as I could and got the hell out of there.

When I got to my car, I sat in the police parking lot for a few minutes, trying to calm myself. Flashes of the violent attack exploded in my mind. *Rex! How the hell did he know about Rex?*

Rex was someone I tried to forget. He was the reason for all of this. The rapist— *my rapist*— that night— that horrible night! This detective was smart. He knew way too much. I had to talk to Joseph. I called him and told him to meet me at my house. He didn't want to, but I insisted. We needed to talk.

When I got home, I hurried to the door, anxious to get inside and have a drink. I started to put my key in the door, but I stopped. My door was open! It was cracked! I looked around, scanning my surroundings. It wasn't dark outside yet. My street was quiet and calm, nothing out of the ordinary. I pushed the door open, but didn't walk in. I just stared into the space I could see and listened. It was silent. I stepped inside, but not past the doorway. I just listened for a minute. My bat was in the bedroom. I positioned my keys so that the sharp edges were sticking out between my fingers; I'd seen it in a movie. "Hello!" I called out, into the empty darkness of my house. All the blinds and curtains were closed, so it was dark inside. "Is someone in here?" I hollered.

There was no response. I took a small step and then another. I didn't close the door, just in case I needed to turn and run. I moved slowly, trying to step lightly, not to alert an intruder of my position. I stretched my neck to look around the corner. The main area of my house was clear. Nothing appeared to be moved. I gently set my purse on the kitchen floor, next to the wall. It ran through my mind that it could be Rex. Having Detective Casteel mention his name shook me. *Did he speak to him? Does Rex know who I am and how to find me?*

This Detective had a way of telling you small pieces of the story he already knew. He was putting it together, and it was hard to tell how close he was to the truth. What if he had told Rex about Mark's disappearance? Maybe he told him that he suspected Mark was dead and that Rex had something to do with it. Maybe Rex had figured it out and thought he had to get rid of me because I was talking to the police. My mind was racing, but everything going on was crazy. I moved toward the hall and peaked around the corner, my eyes moving from door to door: the bathroom, first and then the bedrooms. The bathroom door was open. I looked in. Empty! Then I turned to the other side of the hall and I pushed the ajar door open and looked into my spare room. The cluttered mess looked untouched. I had purposely left the closet doors open the last time I looked for an intruder, so no one could surprise me. Then I turned toward my bedroom. *Did I leave that door half open?* I couldn't remember. I took a deep breath and pushed the door. It creaked so loud! I didn't remember it ever creaking that loud! I could see half the room. My bat was still there, leaned against my bed. I tried to lean forward without moving my feet. I listened for any shift in the room. Then I took another step and the open closet door came into view.

"Kat!" A voice rang out! My heart jumped out of my chest!

Joseph! Oh thank God! I turned and hurried back to the kitchen. He was standing a few feet into the kitchen, looking uneasy.

"Why is your door wide open?"

"It was cracked open when I got here," I told him.

"What? Did you lock it when you left?"

"Of course I did!" I moved around him and shut the door.

"How would someone get in, then? Who has a key?" he asked, looking around.

"No one! I don't understand what's going on. I'm about to lose my mind."

"Have you looked through your house, in your closets?" he asked, walking to my hall, and looking around the corner.

"That's what I was doing, just now." He walked through the house with me and helped me double check everything. It was empty. We went back to the living room and sat on the couch. We both took a deep breath and looked at eachother. We were both obviously stressed.

"You need to tell the cops, Kat. This is fucked up."

"I know. I just came from the police station," I told him. "That's why I asked you to come. That Detective Casteel. He knows stuff."

"What do you mean? What stuff?"

"He knows about drugs and parties and Mark's fight with my friend, Frank. He spoke to Frank. Frank told him everything."

"What the hell does Frank know? What did you tell him, Kat?" Joseph was alarmed. He rested his hands on his knees and his stare was hard.

"When all that was going on, I confided in Frank— a little."

" Confided in him about what! Shit! Kat, I told you not to talk to anyone!" He shook his head and looked up at the ceiling.

"I didn't talk to anyone after that night! This was before that!" I stood up and folded my arms. "Look, I'm not an idiot! I didn't tell Frank what happened to Mark. I told him we split up. I was obviously upset and I told him it was because we broke up, but he was around during that time. He knew I lost my job. He knew about the drugs and the sex. He knew I was really into Mark. The detective talked to Frank and probably to my old employer. That's it— as far as what Frank knew. But that's not all the detective knows." I turned and started to pace. Joseph stood up and put his hand on my arm, turning me to face him.

"What else?" he asked, his voice low. I took a deep breath and looked at him. "What?"

"He asked me if I know Rex." I looked up into Joseph's beautiful hazel eyes, that seemed so worried. I waited for him to speak, but it took a minute. He let go of me, folded his arms, and began walking around the room. He took a deep breath and stopped.

"What did you say?" he asked, calmly.

"I said I knew who he was, that I'd seen him a couple times, but I didn't know him."

"What did he say?"

"Nothing. That was it." I stood there biting my lip waiting for his response. He was looking at the floor, trying to process.

"Why would he ask about Rex?" he mumbled to himself. Then after a minute he looked at me. "It's ok. I don't know why he would bring up Rex, but he can't possibly know anything about that night. Rex isn't going to admit to what he did. Rex was gone before Mark died. He doesn't know what we did. Rex is a criminal and he probably has warrants and stuff. Maybe this cop connected him to Mark in some other way and he's just fishing for connections, ya know. Mark was involved with Rex in ways that have nothing to do with you or me. We need to stay calm. No one knows anything."

"Joseph, I know you told me not to ask you what happened to Mark's body..." Joseph started to cut me off, but I continued, "I'm not asking where Mark is! But what I need to know is who helped you? I know you didn't do it alone."

"You don't need to know that!" Joseph said, firmly.

"I do! I need to know if I need to worry about..."

He cut me off again and moved toward me, "You don't! You don't have to worry about what happened after you left that night! There is nothing and no one to be worried about. Trust me when I tell you, we are all good! I was careful. You have deniability. You're protected. I promise."

He was standing right in front of me, staring down at me. I could smell his cologne. "Do you still trust me?" His voice was quiet— seductive. I stared up at him, studying his face: his eyes, his jaw, his lips. I wanted to touch him. Our eye contact began to feel intense. "Do you?" he asked again. His eyes traveled around my face and then down to my body. The sound of our breathing began to sound amplified and it filled the room.

"I do," I whispered.

He raised his hand, slowly dragging the back of his finger against my arm. His touch sent shockwaves through my body. His fingers crawled all the way up my arm, to my shoulder and over to my collar bone and then continued up my neck, to the side of my face. I quivered and the muscles between my legs began to throb. He lowered his head and lightly brushed his hair against my forehead. As he cupped my face, I felt his fingers wander through my hair and then he took hold of it in his fist and pulled my head back hard, raising my lips to meet his. I opened my mouth and my breath was heavy against his. His gaze was intense, searching me for the hunger required for what was coming next.

"I miss you, Kat," he said, grazing his lips against mine. He brought his other hand up to my mouth, running his thumb across my lower lip. This wasn't the first time he'd done this. "Do you miss me?" he asked, dipping his thumb into my mouth. I sucked it and his breath quivered, as he moved it around my tongue.

"Yes," I breathed, as he pulled his thumb out, wetting my lips with my spit. "So much."

He dropped his hand to the bottom of my shirt and his fingers slipped under and found my trembling flesh. He still hadn't kissed me, yet. He was staring into my eyes, inches from my face as he circled my belly button with his touch. His seduction was slow and agonizing. I was already so wet, and the heat between my thighs was begging for his fingers. He found the button on my pants and unfastened it. My whole body shuddered and jerked. I could barely wait to feel him touch me there. I tried to press my mouth to his, but he backed away only allowing the slightest touch. My eyes closed, as I felt him tug at my zipper. Then he reached down with his other hand and slid my pants over my hips. They dropped to the floor. He dragged his finger tips back up my thighs. The edge of his nails scraped my skin. I'd been waiting so long. I pulled the bottom of his t- shirt up, exposing his lean, chiseled abs. He pulled it the rest of the way, lifting it over his head, giving me the enticing view of his perfect torso. I touched his chest and that familiar feeling rushed over me. I could have bitten a chunk out of him, I was so desperate for him. He reached down and grabbed my shirt. He pulled it over my head. I stood there in my panties and bra, thankful I had chosen a matching lacy white set. He ran his hands down my back and over my ass, scooping me off the ground, wrapping my legs around him. I was glad because my knees were about to buckle. He was strong and sexy and I wanted him inside me. I couldn't wait. He carried me to my bedroom and dropped me onto the bed. He stood above me, unbuttoning his jeans, pushing them down, as he devoured me with his eyes. He was fully aroused, his huge cock pushing out through his black boxer briefs. He looked me up and down and shook his head, as if he was thinking "oh man, what I'm about to do to you." He leaned over, grabbed the edge of my panties, dragged them down my legs and tossed them across the room. He stuck his thumbs under his boxers and slid them off, causing his rock-hard cock to spring up and bounce in front of me. My breath shuttered from the sight of him.

"You want me?" he asked.

It was obvious. I was dying for him. He knew it and he enjoyed the dance: teasing and enticing me, making me wait— making me soaked. I just nodded, my teeth tearing into my lip. He lifted my leg and kissed the inside of my calf slowly. He moved up my leg, to my thigh driving me wild with anticipation. Then he was there, his mouth on my pussy, opening me with his tongue. My body jolted and shook as he moved his tongue, slowly swirling it around my clit. I moaned and panted, already feeling like I could come any second. He held my legs tight to control his play area. His tongue and lips were soft and warm. My whole body was vibrating. His mouth felt like heaven. Then his finger was inside— first one, then two and three. They curled, hitting that place, as he licked my clit.

Shit, I had been waiting for this for so long. After a few minutes of his head between my thighs— tasting me, he moved up to my stomach and then lifted my bra and kissed my breasts. He took his time, squeezing my breast and pinching my hard nipples. And then, just as he reached my mouth and his tongue found mine, finally, he slid inside of me, making me grab hold of him and cry out, but his mouth was on mine now, kissing me hard, stealing my breath. He thrusted into me deep and my pussy squeezed and gripped, pulling him in. I missed the feeling of him fucking me and his strong, hot body against mine. His rhythm was perfect, as his hips curled and made circles, touching every part of my insides. I held on to him, my orgasm building. I listened to him moan and pant. His sounds excited me even more. And then, as he pushed into me again and again, my mind pulled at memories of Mark; not Mark instead of Joseph, but Mark and Joseph. I remembered what it was like when they were both sandwiched around me, touching me, kissing me, and fucking me at the same time. It was like nothing I have ever experienced— the pleasure and the pain. They were my drug— my addiction and as I held on and Joseph fucked harder and harder, Mark was there, both of them working together to please me and use my body for their own pleasure. I could hear Mark, in my ear, asking me if it felt good, ordering me to come for him. Then, I was there, exploding in a fierce eruption . Joseph followed me, thrusting harder and pulling me against him tight as he came, moaning in pleasure and total release. I could feel the heat of both of our fluids forcing their way out as he kept moving, allowing the aftershocks to finish us off.

"Finally!"

Joseph laid on top of me, catching his breath and started laughing. "It's been a while, huh?" he chuckled.

"Did I say that out loud?" I asked. I was in such a state, I didn't even realize.

"You did. But I agree. Finally!" he said, sliding off me and pulling me into his arms. I wanted to say so much, but I didn't. I just laid in his arms, enjoying the warmth and comfort. I slept peacefully that night, with no worry and no fear.

Chapter 4

"I DIDN'T TELL MASON I was coming here, so let's not mention it, ok?" Joseph said, finding his shirt in the living room. The sun was shining through the edges of my closed blinds, as the sun came up.

"That's fine. Isn't he probably wondering where you are, though?" I asked.

"I told him I may not be home last night."

"You assumed you would stay here?" I smiled. He just smiled back at me and didn't respond. He came over and wrapped his long arms around me, squeezing tight. He nuzzled his face into my hair and made a growling sound, then nibbled at my neck. It tickled and I pulled away, giggling.

"You were fucking amazing, last night. I really did miss you," he said, kissing me and biting my lip. Then as he turned to leave, he said, "Oh, we need to plan that dinner with Mason."

"Do we really need to?" I asked. "I feel really uncomfortable around him."

"I think you need to. You need to give him peace of mind that he's investigated everyone."

"Investigated? See, that's what I'm nervous about. I don't want to be investigated," I stressed.

"He just wants to ask questions. I think we owe him that. And if you can handle that cop, you can definitely handle Mason."

"He just makes me feel so guilty."

"I know. But, we need to try to ease his mind and cover ourselves. too. I know it sucks, but..."

"Okay," I said, "Maybe tomorrow night?"

"Sounds good. My house at eight?"

"Okay."

After Joseph left, I floated around for a few hours as if nothing bad was happening. Joseph had a way of making me feel like everything was okay. He made me feel safe and I really liked that. When I was with Mark and he introduced me to Joseph the first time, I hated him. He came on to me, with Mark just rooms away and I didn't understand how their relationship was, so I was very offended. It caused the first fight I ever had with Mark. Mark and Joseph were like brothers, almost extensions of each other. They shared everything, including women—including me. At first, I did it to please Mark, but after a while Joseph and I began to bond and sleep together when Mark wasn't around, not that Mark minded. I started having feelings for Joseph. I had romantic feelings for both of them and they were both fine with it.

I look back, now, and I think I was selfish, in a way. I wanted Mark and Joseph all for myself, but I really didn't want them with anyone else. I wanted to be the center of their attention, all the time. I look back on everything with such delight, sometimes. Then I think— my mind is still twisted from the things Mark did and said. He was gorgeous, sexy, and wild. But there was also deception, coldness, and brutality in him. He had influence over me and I couldn't control myself. And, in the end, he betrayed me in the most horrendous way and I killed him.

The next day, I tried to focus at work, but I was anxious all day, thinking about being around Mason. I just needed to get it over with. After work, I was relieved to come home to a locked house that appeared to be unbothered. All the windows were locked.

I dressed in a casual, pink, wrap around dress and put my hair up in a ponytail. I don't know why I wanted to appear innocent; I don't know what I thought it would accomplish, but it was my plan, to seem sweet and innocent. Just before I was preparing to leave, there was a knock at the door. I peeked through the window to see Linda standing on my porch. This was not the time. I grabbed my purse and keys and opened the door. Linda looked up at me with big sad eyes.

"Oh, you're leaving?" she asked.

"Yes, I'm sorry, Linda. I have an engagement. Is everything okay?" She looked upset.

"Oh, well, yes. It's nothing. Just an argument with Paul. I don't know what's wrong with him."

"I'm sorry. Can we talk in the morning? I really need to go."

"Of course. You look so pretty." She smiled and moved off the step, as I locked the door. I rubbed her arm as I passed and gave her a consoling smile.

"Thanks. See you tomorrow, then."

"Yes. Tomorrow," she said, turning and walking back over to her house. I had never seen Linda look so distraught. It must have been a bad fight.

Arriving at Joseph's house, I was surprised to be greeted by Mason. He opened the door and like last time, I was stunned by the resemblance. Mason was very handsome. How could he not be? Mark was the sexiest man I'd ever seen and Mason looked so much like him. Mason had his own look, though. He was not as rugged looking as Mark. His face was kinder; his eyes were softer—sadder maybe. He dressed more earthy, like he spent a lot of time outside hiking. His jeans were frayed at the bottom and slightly baggy. He wore a button up, khaki colored, cotton shirt that could use ironing. His dark brown hair was long, just past his shoulders and tousled back out of his face. He was rough shaved and when he smiled, I couldn't believe it. That dimple! The same dimple Mark had in his one check. That dimple used to melt my heart and moisten my pussy. He could make me surrender to anything he wanted with that dimple.

"Hi Mason. Good to see you again."

"Hello, Kathren. Come in, please." He moved to the side and as I passed him, I noticed he looked me up and down. I looked around and didn't see Joseph anywhere. "Oh Joseph's on his way. He got hung up in traffic I think. He'll be here soon." We were alone and I was suddenly very nervous.

"Can I get you a drink?" he asked.

"Sure. Diet Coke, please."

"Okay. Diet Coke coming right up," he went behind Joseph's huge, fully stocked bar and put some ice in a glass and poured my drink from a can. "Joseph has quite a set up," he said, bringing me my drink and motioned for me to have a seat on the couch. I sat up straight and crossed my legs.

"Yes he does. A bit over the top, if you ask me."

"Yes it is, but he likes a good party. We know that, so I guess it comes in handy." He sat a few feet away and took a beer from the coffee table. "You look lovely."

"Thank you," I said, in a shy voice. I was surprised by the compliment. "So, how long are you staying?"

"Not sure. Depends."

"Any new information?" I asked, sipping my drink.

"A few things. But, nothing that helpful. I'm just trying to figure out if something happened that might have caused him to leave town fast: Did he meet someone and leave with them? Could he be hurt somewhere, unable to communicate?" He shook his head. "I just need to know, ya know?" I hated seeing his pain— the pain I caused.

"I don't know what happened, but I hope he's okay and I hope you find him." I gave him a pouty smile. I felt like a monster. The lies poured out too easily.

"Thank you." He paused for a minute. "You really are very beautiful. I see why my brother was so taken with you." I couldn't read Mason. I wasn't sure if this was flirting or just his way of being kind.

"Please! Your brother spent time with a lot of very beautiful women," I told him, blushing a little.

"He did, but many of them were— Well, I don't want to be crude." He took a swig of his beer. I was curious what he was going to say, but I didn't ask him to finish his thought.

"What are the things you found out about Mark?"

"Nothing really. I speak with Pete— Detective Casteel. He's been keeping me in the loop. I know you've spoken to him too," he said. I must have looked like a deer in headlights cause he put his hands out and waved them. "Don't worry. He doesn't tell me everything, just what I need to know."

"Oh, it's okay. I don't know what you must think of me." I said, looking down, disgracefully.

"I think you're stunning, actually," he said, quickly, as if it were on the tip of his tongue, already. I looked up. My mouth opened to respond, but then I didn't. I was speechless. He cleared his throat.

"I'm sorry! I'm making you uncomfortable. I know you're seeing Joseph."

"What? I'm not seeing Joseph! Why— Who told you that?"

"Well, he didn't come home the night before last, so, I just assumed."

"What makes you think he was with me?"

"Wasn't he?" he asked, his eyes wide and curious. I didn't want to lie. I just looked down, again. "It's okay. I know how Joseph and Mark are with women and each other. Remember he's my little brother, and I've known Joseph a long time. I don't judge. You said you and Mark weren't that close, but Joseph stayed out all night and when he came home the next morning, he said we were having dinner tonight, as if he'd just spoken to you. I figured he was with you. After what Pete told me about your friend getting into it with Mark over the way he was treating you, and you being embarrassed about the life you lived with Mark, I just assumed— I thought..."

"What? You thought what?" I asked. *So much for, "only what he needed to know!"* It sounded like Detective Casteel had shared plenty.

"I thought you must be different, not like his regular girlfriends. You don't strike me as a woman who would date a guy like Mark. I mean, don't get me wrong. He's my brother. I love him like crazy, but he treats women like crap. So does Joseph. You just seem— I don't know— better than that!"

I just looked at him, unsure of how to respond.

"I just mean, if you were mine I wouldn't share you with anyone." He looked sympathetic, but there was something more in his eyes, as well. I wondered if he'd be saying all of this if he knew what I had done. I started to feel restless and was about to tell him I needed to leave, when the front door opened.

"Sorry! Sorry! I'm here! Traffic was terrible!" Joseph appeared from around the corner, carrying bags from *"Ming's Chinese Cuisine".* He smiled and said, "Let's eat!" He headed to the dining room. Mason and I got up and followed. I was relieved to have the intimacy with Mason interrupted.

The conversation went pretty smooth while we ate, mostly small talk. Joseph led the discussion, keeping it flowing, with no awkward silences. Joseph was always good at hosting large gatherings, so just three at a dinner table was a breeze, even with the looming topic. After the meal, we retreated to the living room. We all spaced out around the large sofa, as Joseph brought more drinks. He brought a beer for Mason and a fruity looking, red drink for me. That was just like Joseph not to ask and just hand you alcohol. "Sea breeze!" he said, noticing I was examining the glass. I smiled and took a sip.

"If he would just call," Mason said, all of a sudden, as if we'd already been discussing Mark.

"I know, man. I know," Joseph said. I stayed quiet.

"I just feel like something bad's happened. It's just not like him," Mason continued. My eyes darted over at Joseph, but he was careful not to look at me and stayed focused on Mason. "Ever since he was little, he was independent and a handful, but he always checked in, just a quick *I'm ok!* He'd know that I'd be worried. And I know he can take care of himself, but he does have a habit of pissing people off and I always tell him, he's not invincible."

"He is fucking tough, though, man. He can handle himself," Joseph said.

"I know. I just don't get it. If something did happen to him..."

"Don't even say that!" I interrupted. "Don't even think it! Let's stay positive." He looked at me and smiled, sadly. I was a terrible person— giving him hope, when I knew there was none. We talked into the night, about Mark and other things. After a while, I looked up and realized it was after eleven.

"It's getting late, guys. I better go." I stood up. Mason stood up with me. His manners were charming. He looked so much like Mark, but he was a very different man.

"Why don't you stay? You can leave in the morning," Joseph offered.

"No. I can't. I need to get home."

"Why? It's late. I have plenty of room."

I didn't say it, but I wasn't sure which room Mason was staying in and I didn't want to be in the downstairs bedroom. It was hard enough being in the house at all, but some rooms held certain memories and that room held a terrible one.

"I'll just say it," Mason blurted. "I'm down here, so you can stay upstairs, and if you want to stay with Joseph in his room, don't let me stop you. No need to pretend. We're all grownups here."

I looked at Joseph. He scanned from Mason to me. "Look. Stay here. I know you don't want to head home this late." I realized Joseph was thinking of the weird occurrences I'd been experiencing at home. I was so distracted with the issues surrounding Mark, I hadn't thought much about that, but now it was in my head.

"I guess I can stay and leave early," I said. "I'll take the room upstairs at the end of the hall." I looked at both of them. They just stood there, like they were waiting for me to move. "I'm tired. I guess I'll go to bed now. Good night!"

"Good night, Kathren," Mason said.

"Let me show you to your room," Joseph offered, leading me to the stairs.

Once we got up the stairs, I exhaled hard. Although he was very sweet, I felt on edge around Mason and was glad to be away from him. I started to turn right and head for the spare room, but Joseph grabbed my hand. He didn't speak. He just looked at me and pulled me toward his room. I looked over my shoulder, down the stairs, making sure Mason wasn't in eyesight and followed Joseph down the hall. As I walked into his room, the memories hit me like a tidal wave. Joseph closed the door and walked up behind me. He put his hands on my shoulders and squeezed. I dropped my head and sighed as he massaged me.

"Feel good?"

"Yes."

"Come on." He took my hand and moved me toward the bed. The lights were dim and his bed was big and inviting. He removed my dress and bra and laid me down on my stomach. His silky, soft sheets felt amazing against my bare skin. He began to massage me; he slowly caressed my calves and the back of my thighs, squeezing the muscles firmly. It was heavenly. I hugged his big fluffy pillow and closed my eyes. He moved his strong hands over my ass and up my back, smooth and slow. He reached up and took a bottle of lotion from his nightstand. He squeezed it into his hands and applied it to my back. His fingers dug into me, kneading my flesh. It was exactly what I needed. I thought of making a joke about why there was lotion sitting by his bed, but I decided not to change the mood. His touch was soothing and erotic. I expected him to try to have sex after a few minutes, but he took his time, making sure he relaxed me completely, paying attention to every muscle. It must have gone on for twenty minutes. I almost fell asleep.

Then, as he dragged his fingers down my back one final time, he took hold of my panties and pulled them down. He turned me over. He was naked. I didn't even feel him taking his clothes off. He positioned himself between my legs and slowly pushed himself into me. A tingly warmth swept through me. I was surprised by how slow he moved. He swiped my hair from my face and looked into my eyes as he slid in and out, stirring his hips in steady circles. I wasn't used to this intimacy. He was tender. He kissed me soft, brushing his lips against mine, just barely touching his tongue to mine. He didn't rush. This felt new and it felt good; it felt— loving. Neither one of us moaned loudly or spoke; we just breathed deep. I thought maybe he was being quiet, not to disturb Mason. After a while his breathing became shaky and heavy. He closed his eyes and shuttered as he came. The feeling of his release, hot and powerful, shooting into me caused me to tingle and I came too. He collapsed. His body laid limp over me. We both lay there quietly— breathing.

He slid himself out of me and rolled off. He laid at my side, shoulder to shoulder, looking at the ceiling. He said nothing. Neither did I. I wouldn't say it out loud, but all that was going through my mind was— *Did he just make love to me?* Finally, after a few minutes he sat up on the side of the bed, facing away from me. I stared at his back. I wanted to reach out and touch him, but I hesitated. He seemed conflicted. He was unusually quiet, almost distant. Then he stood up and said, "I need a drink. You?" He didn't look at me.

"No. Thanks. You ok?" I asked.

"I'm fine," he said, still not looking at me. He put his pants on and walked out. I laid there for a while, waiting for him to come back. Something seemed to be bothering him, all of a sudden.. I wasn't sure what, though. After a while, when he didn't return, I fell asleep.

The next morning, I woke up alone in Joseph's bed. I got dressed and went down stairs. It was quiet in the house. As I rounded the corner to the kitchen, I found Mason sitting at the table, looking at his cell phone.

"Good Morning!"

He looked up and smiled. "Good morning. How'd you sleep?"

"Okay." I looked around. "Where's Joseph?"

"I think he took off already."

44

"Oh," I looked at my phone. It was 6:20 am. "Did you see him leave?"

"I heard the door shut around six," he said. "Everything okay?"

"Yes. I just wanted to say goodbye."

"Can I get you some coffee?" he gestured to the pot on the counter.

"No, I really need to get going. I enjoyed dinner last night. If I don't see you again, Mason, It was so nice meeting you."

He looked disheartened, sighed, and said, "Yeah, you too, Kathren."

I gave him another smile and walked out.

Chapter 5

WHEN I GOT HOME, MY door was shut and locked. Before I could get in the house, Linda was hurrying over. I waved at her as I walked in, leaving the door open behind me. I started the coffee and sat at the table.

"Just now getting home?" she asked, her eyes wide, as she came in and shut the door behind her.

"Yeah, it got late, so I stayed at a friend's."

"Oh, am I bothering you?" I wanted to tell her the truth. I was tired and wanted a shower, but I smiled and lied.

"So, what was up last night? You and Paul had a fight?"

"Well, maybe I blew things out of proportion. I don't know. He's just been so distant and angry lately. I can't seem to make him happy no matter what I do. Yesterday he was a bear. He wouldn't tell me why. He just yelled and slammed doors!"

I tried to listen and focus on what Linda was saying, but my mind was on Joseph. I wanted to know why he left and didn't come back to bed. The sex was different...so intimate. He'd never really touched me that way before. Joseph was always kind and a giving lover, but he was usually pretty carnal. He was sensual, but he fucked! He didn't make love.

Joseph lived the same way as Mark. When I met him, there were lots of women, orgies, drugs, and parties, but I noticed he was different from Mark. Joseph had been in love before. He had been married for a few years. He'd been hurt. That's why he lived that life. He didn't want to be close to anyone because he didn't want to risk being hurt again. Mark, on the other hand, was cold. He didn't love anyone. It was all about the sex— the experience and pushing boundaries. Mark had anger in him and was disconnected from the women he slept with.

"So, what do you think? Kathren?"

"Oh, I'm sorry. What was the question?" I hadn't heard a word Linda said in the last five minutes. She was setting our coffee on the table.

"Do you think he still loves me?" she asked.

"Of course he does, Linda. It was just a fight."

"What about the sex?"

"What about it?" I was lost.

"We don't *have* any! That's what I've been telling you. Were you even listening?"

"For how long?" I asked, trying to focus on her.

"Weeks. And the last time we did, he was so rough."

"Oh, I'm sorry, Linda. Have you tried to talk to him about it?"

"Well, that's just it. He's so distant and then when I try to talk to him, he gets mad so easily."

"Well, if this is new behavior, something must be bothering him. You need to find out what it is, before it gets worse and try to fix it, if that's what you want."

"Yeah, I know. Easier said than done— lately!" she said, scooching her coffee cup around in circles. I could tell Linda was hurting. She was so lonely. I felt bad for her, but I didn't know how to help her. I had so much going on in my own life and I couldn't share any of it with her. It made our friendship difficult.

"In my experience, Linda, some men are determined to keep their feelings to themselves. They will twist you into knots, trying to understand them. It will drive you crazy trying to figure out what you're doing wrong and how you can please them, when really— there's nothing you can do to make them happy. Even if you push yourself to the farthest edges of your boundaries, they will keep moving the goalpost— keep asking for more— keep breaking your heart! You have to know when to say enough is enough! Stay or leave! You just have to make yourself happy. Trust me. I know."

"Sounds like you've been through a rough relationship," Linda said, looking wide eyed.

"Sometimes Linda— you just need to walk away!" I told her.

"He's my husband, Kathren. I love him," she said, sadly. I just looked at her and gave her a consoling smile. After a while, Linda left and I got ready for work.

A couple days went by and I hadn't heard from Joseph. It was strange. We had slept together twice and now there was radio silence. It was upsetting. I was happy, though, that I hadn't heard from Detective Casteel. That was a plus, but I wondered when the other shoe would drop. I wondered every day if today would be the day that he would come to arrest me. Leaving work, that Friday evening my cell phone rang and I didn't recognize the number. I answered it and was surprised to hear Mason on the other end.

"Hi Kathren. It's Mason. How are you?"

"Hi— I'm good. You?"

"I'm good. I was wondering if you have dinner plans?" he asked.

"Oh, well— when?"

"Tonight," he said.

"Um, no. No plans."

"Could I take you to dinner?" he asked. I was stunned. He was talking about taking me out, just the two of us— without Joseph.

"I... um...sure. Why not?" I couldn't say no. I didn't want to go, but I wanted to seem friendly.

"Great! Can I pick you up around seven?" he asked. I agreed and gave him my address. I got home and jumped in the shower. I forgot to ask him where he was taking me, so I wasn't sure whether to dress casually. I decided to wear black slacks, black heels, and a blue silk button up blouse. I was prepared for anything.

He pulled up right on time. I opened the door, as he approached. He looked very handsome. His hair was in a sleek ponytail and he was wearing a white button up shirt, with a nice pair of jeans. We jumped in his white, Nissan Altima rental and headed for the restaurant. Mason drove as if he knew exactly where he was going.

"You like steak?" he asked.

"Love it," I told him. "There's a great Steakhouse on the North side of town. It's called..." I stopped talking when I realized where he was taking me. He was taking me to the very same restaurant I took Mark, that first night we went out— the first time he told me he was interested in me— the first time I got a glimpse of who he was and the first time he kissed me.

"Everything okay?" he asked, noticing I stopped mid sentence.

"Fine." I didn't want to tell him I had been there with his brother or that it made me feel strange to go there with him. "I just realized we are heading for another steak place."

"Oh. Yeah, I tried it when I got here and I think it's really good, but if you'd rather go someplace else..."

"No. It's fine," I told him.

We pulled in the lot and parked. As I opened the car door, I noticed Mason was rushing around the car to get my door. He reached for my hand as I stepped out. I made sure to release his hand as soon as I was out of the car. I thanked him and smiled.

"Reservation for Sanders," he said, as we approached the hostess. *Sanders!* Just hearing him say his last name made me feel sad and a little nauseous. It wasn't the kind of place you had to have a reservation, but Mason clearly wanted to make sure the night went off without a hitch. The hostess led us to a booth in the back. I was glad it wasn't the same booth I shared with Mark, but I couldn't help scanning across the room to the place Mark and I sat, getting to know each other that night.

"You look very pretty," Mason said, smiling at me. I smiled and thanked him, looking down at my lap. The waitress came over and Mason ordered a bottle of a sweet, red wine— Romance Red.

"So, how's the search going?" I asked. "Any leads?"

"No, but I don't want to talk about my brother tonight. Tell me about you."

"What do you want to know?" I asked.

"Everything," he said, revealing his dimple, as the corner of his lips curled up..

"Gosh! Everything? Where do I start?" I chuckled. Then I started talking. I talked about my job, my family, and the plans I had for my future. I talked for a while, breaking only to order our food, and then stopping only when the food arrived. "So, that's me, pretty much in a nutshell," I said, cutting into my steak. "Not very exciting."

"You're exciting to me," Mason said. "I find you fascinating."

"Mason— I think you're so sweet, but..."

"Wait! Before you say anything else, just hear me out," he said. I put my fork and knife down and folded my hands in my lap. He cleared his throat. "I haven't dated anyone in a really long time— like three years. I was in a relationship with a woman for several years. I loved her. I really thought I would marry her. I was looking at rings. Something was holding me back, though. She seemed distracted all the time. She was smart, beautiful— witty. She had so much going for her. She worked for a big advertising company. She loved it. She was moving up in the company. My job was going well, too. We were happy. Well, I thought we were happy. It took me a while to catch on..."

"Catch on?"

"Yeah— her distraction," he sighed. "Mark." My eyes were wide. I gasped.

"Oh. I see." I knew exactly what he meant. Mark had fucked his girlfriend.

"I don't know if it was Mark who started it, or her. I mean, the truth is, he always gets hit on by women— all kinds of women: old, young, smart, conservative, married, shy. He even got a gay woman to sleep with him." He laughed and shook his head as he spoke about Mark's charisma.

"I think he actually felt bad about Meagan. That was her—Meagan. But, Mark couldn't turn down any woman's advances. When I got suspicious and questioned him, he was honest. He told me flat out."

"That was Mark— always honest," I said, frowning, looking away.

"I was really angry for a while. Mark never raised his voice or responded to my insults and yelling. He just took it. He knew he'd done wrong. He just waited for me to get over it—and I did— eventually." I could tell he was going back to when it happened. He looked sad. I reached over the table and touched his hand. He looked down at our hands and squeezed mine, looking up at me.

"I'm so sorry," I said. "That sucks."

"Thanks. It was a long time ago. But, here's the thing. Maybe I shouldn't be showing interest in a woman who was with my brother. I promise this is not a pay back thing. I forgave Mark. I love my brother and I'm worried about him. But— I am affected by you. I didn't expect that." I didn't say anything. I just looked at him. "I haven't even tried to date anyone since... But, I can't stop thinking about you. I hope this doesn't make you uncomfortable, but I couldn't stop thinking from the first night we met." I let him continue to hold my hand. "I would love to spend some time with you, maybe see if there's something there."

"I don't know what to say." I pulled my hand back across the table. The crazy thing was, that was exactly what I felt when I met Mark. The first night I saw him, I couldn't get him out of my head.

"Just spend some time with me. That's all I'm asking."

" Aren't you going back to California, soon?" I asked.

"There's no rush."

"What about your job? What do you do, by the way?" I asked.

"I'm an editor, at a publishing company," he said.

"Wow. That's cool. I love to read. So, they don't want you to come back soon?"

"They know my brother's missing. This is the first leave I've taken in years. They told me to take all the time I need."

"Can I ask about your father?"

"What about him?" He looked caught off guard, by the subject change.

"Mark never spoke of him, but Joseph told me once that Mark didn't have to work because his father was well off and would send him anything he needed. But, Mark told me you basically raised him."

"My father left when Mark was a baby. He was a womanizer, kind of like Mark. As we got older, my father tried to reconnect with us. He tried to win us back with his money. I won't take anything from him, but Mark was like 'Fuck him! I'll take everything he's got and not think twice.' Our father was terrible to our mother, before she got sick and passed. Neither of us have been able to forgive him. But, Mark will use him. We deal with our feelings about him differently. I don't talk to my father, so I haven't told him Mark is missing... but, if I get news that he needs to hear, I will call him." I could tell this was a sore subject, so I didn't ask anything more.

We were both quiet for a while, sipping our wine. Then I suddenly spit out what I was thinking, plain and simple. "You look like Mark!"

It was awkward. He didn't respond at first. He took the wine bottle and filled my glass and poured the last of it in his. He took a long sip of it. I took a couple small sips of mine. I said it very matter of fact, but Mason knew what I was saying. It was freaky, thinking of dating Mark's brother, not just because they were brothers and not just because of the secret he didn't know, but he looked so much like him— the eyes, the smile. Even his small mannerisms and facial expressions reminded me of Mark..

"Is it too much— the resemblance, I mean?"

"If I'm honest— it's a little weird," I said. His lips curled at the corner a little and looked down. "I mean, you're very different, but then sometimes you look at me and it's like..."

"I'm him."

"Well—yes."

"I get it," he said. "Maybe, if we spend some time together— maybe you'll start to separate us— see more of the differences than the similarities."

"Maybe," I said. "There's just so much going on and you don't live in Illinois. Let's just see how things go." He agreed and we finished up our dinner and drinks. We talked a little longer and then he drove me home. As he walked me to the door, I thanked him for a lovely dinner. I opened my locked door, and turned to face him. I was nervous. It was that moment when a new suitor would try to steal a first kiss. I wasn't ready. I looked up at him and he stared into my eyes. I waited, trying to decide how far I would let him go— how long I would let the kiss go, but he didn't kiss me; he just stared at me, studying my face. Then he said goodnight, touched my arm and walked back to his car. I was surprised, but grateful. I didn't want to hurt his feelings. He was so sweet and very handsome, but I couldn't sleep with him. It wasn't right and it would be strange.

As I laid down to bed that night, I wondered why I hadn't heard from Joseph. It had been days now and no calls. He was so passionate that night. I wondered if he felt awkward, feeling like he was too romantic, the way he touched me... so gentle and sweet. I wanted to talk to him; to let him know I didn't take it the wrong way and that he didn't have to worry. I fell asleep thinking of him.

Chapter 6

MY EYES OPENED SLOWLY. I rolled to my back. I started to drift back off, but then I realized what I was feeling— something was touching my leg!

Am I dreaming? No!

I wasn't dreaming! I felt fingers on my leg. He came into focus, standing there at the foot of my bed—all in black, in the dark— I could only see his outline, but he was there— touching me— running his fingers down the inside of my calf to my ankle. I could hear him breathing. I jumped, pulling my legs up quickly! I screamed, scrambling to the top of the bed, reaching for my bat! I grabbed it and swung into the shadows!

"Who are you? What do you want? Get out of my house!" I screamed, swinging wildly! Then I heard noise coming from the front of the house. The door slammed open, into the wall! My kitchen garbage can hit the floor! I realized he was no longer in the room. I reached for the light. My eyes squinted as I hit the switch on the lamp. My breathing was labored; my heart racing!

"He was in here! In my room! Watching me! Touching me!" I said, out loud. I grabbed my leg, as if he was still touching it. I couldn't hold back any longer. I dialed 911!

Ten minutes later, there were two police cars in my driveway. The 911 operator stayed on the phone with me until they arrived, trying to keep me calm. It was 1:15am. I had been asleep for a couple hours. I shivered, wondering how long the man was standing over my bed, watching me sleep, touching my leg. *Had he touched me anywhere else?*

Two officers walked around my house and the neighboring yards, with flashlights. The other two came in. One looked around inside my house and checked the doors and windows, while the other sat on the sofa with me, asking questions.

"No sign of anyone outside," a young dark-haired officer said, coming through the front door.

"You have no idea how he got in?" the older officer, sitting next to me, asked. "Can't think of anyone with a key?"

"No!" I said, "No one has a key. I mean, my landlord, but he lives seventy miles away."

"There's no sign of forced entry," the younger officer said.

I looked at him and then back at the other officer. "Well, I don't know. I really can't understand it." I explained to the officer that this was not the first time someone had come into the house. I didn't tell them everything. I knew they'd want to know why I didn't call them sooner. I told them that the neighbor saw someone in the yard and I found the window open. I didn't mention the open door. I told them I didn't think much about the man in the yard and that I thought maybe I had left the window open and forgot.

"I think it's time to change the locks." The older officer said, standing up. Right then, the door opened and in walked Detective Pete Casteel. I swallowed hard.

How did he know? Do they all get notified when a call comes in?

"Ms. Thompson, I came to check on you. Are you ok?" he said, nodding at the other officers.

"I'm okay."

"Sounds like you had quite a scare tonight," he said.

"Yeah. It was pretty terrifying!"

"Any idea who it was?"

"No! None!"

The other officer spoke up, "I would say it was a random home invasion, but nothing was taken, he ran when she realized he was there and she had a couple other possible incidents."

"Possible incidents?" he asked. The officer explained the other two events to him and he looked over at me. "You should have called us, Ms. Thompson."

"Kathren is fine and I didn't know if it was anything to worry about. I thought I closed the window, but maybe I missed it— and then the man in the yard, the neighbor saw him. He was long gone by the time I got home and he could have been anyone— a utility worker, maybe. But now— with the man in my house tonight— I don't know."

The older officer who sat with me on the sofa spoke, again, "Well, like I said, it's time to change the locks, ma'am. We'll have an increased patrol in the neighborhood and maybe it would be a good idea to sleep at a family member or friend's house until you get the locks changed."

I nodded my head in agreement, although I had no family or friend's house to go to. Detective Casteel walked out on the porch with the other two officers, talking. He sent them on their way and turned back to me. He stood in the doorway.

"Can I call someone for you or take you somewhere?" he asked.

"No. I have no one to call and nowhere to go," I said. I wondered if he was testing me, to see what name I would give him. I always felt like he was suspicious of me and it made me suspicious of him.

"No one?" he asked.

"Well, my family's all up North, near Chicago and I don't really have any friends nearby, since Frank moved. There's my neighbor, but her husband is —well, I don't know him, but they are having marital problems and I don't think it would be a good time," I said.

"What about a hotel?" he said. "I don't think you should stay here till your locks are changed.

"I don't want to go to a hotel. I'm not sleeping tonight anyway, so I'll stay here. Plus, he ran when I woke up, so I doubt he'll be back tonight." He was thoughtful for a minute. I could tell he was concerned for me. "I'll be okay," I said.

"Alright. Call 911 if you hear anything or think you see something. Don't hesitate. You understand?"

"Yes. I will," I said. "Thanks."

"Sure. Goodnight Ms. Thom... Kathren." He smiled and walked out the door. I hurried over and locked the door and put the chain on. I walked through the house and checked the windows, even though the policeman had done it already. I put my broom between the back sliding glass door and the frame. I paced the house for a while. I was so tired, but I couldn't sleep.

I thought about Joseph. I thought about Joseph's bed. I knew he would let me stay over. I really wanted to see him, anyway. I was in my pajamas and robe. I changed into a pair of pink yoga pants, a smiley face tee shirt and flip flops, grabbed my purse and left. I locked up, even though it felt pointless. It was after two in the morning. Driving over, I thought about the fact that they were probably asleep and I should call first. I decided to get there and then I would call before going to the door. A knock on the door, at such a late hour, would probably scare the shit out of both of them.

As I turned the corner onto Joseph's street, I could see the lights from several houses away. Joseph's house was lit up. And as I got closer, I realized there were cars in his driveway. They filled his driveway and overflowed onto the street. A party! He was having a party. I was surprised. I didn't think he was doing that anymore. He never told me he stopped, but I just assumed. I pulled up behind one of the cars on the street. I stared into the windows. I couldn't see anything, but some moving shadows. I wondered what was going on inside and if it was the typical wild orgy that Joseph used to have. Suddenly, there was a knock at my window. I jumped, still on edge from earlier. I looked up to see Mason standing at my window. He threw his hands up and mouthed "Sorry". I sighed hard and rolled the window down.

"You scared the shit out of me!"

"I'm sorry," he laughed. "What are you doing here, at this hour?"

"Where did you come from?" I asked, trying to regulate my breathing, holding my hand over my heart, from the jump.

"I was just out walking. It's a bit crowded inside," he said, looking up at the house. "Did you come for the party?"

"No! I didn't even know there was a party. Honestly, I'm surprised. I thought Joseph was done with all this."

Yeah, me too," he said, pushing his hands into his pockets. "This is the second one this week."

"Really..." The word came out slowly, as I glared bitterly, at the lit-up house. I wasn't sure why this bothered me, but it did. I wondered how Joseph would act if I went inside. Maybe by this hour he would be locked in a room with some random woman... or two. Although there were often several people going at it in the living room, Joseph usually liked to find a quiet spot somewhere to have his fun. At least, that was my experience with him.

"So, why are you here this time of night, if not for the party? Do you realize it's 2:30?" Mason asked.

"I didn't want to be home. Something happened tonight," I said.

"What?"

"Someone came into my house."

"What!" His response sounded worrisome.

"Yeah. I woke up to a man standing over my bed. He was touching my leg." I grimaced, as I said it out loud.

"Kathren! What the hell! Did you call the police?"

"Yes. They came and searched the area, took a statement, and told me to change my locks. There was no sign of forced entry, so they think maybe he has a key— or I accidentally left a door or window open, which I didn't. I don't know what to think. This isn't the first time."

"What do you mean, this isn't the first time? Someone was in your house before?"

"Well, I think so. I came home once to find my front door open and one time there was an open window that I was sure I closed and locked," I said. His eyes were wide and his mouth hung open. "I didn't call the police before because I thought maybe it was me being scatterbrained, but after tonight— I feel more sure he's been there before. He didn't take anything, I don't think, and he ran when I screamed."

"Kathren—That's crazy. Shit! I'm so sorry. That's so scary! I'm glad you're okay. You should have called me. I would have come right over," he said. I smiled at him. I appreciated his concern. He was so kind, but I wouldn't have thought of calling him. I did think of calling Joseph. Now seeing that he was partying, I was glad I didn't.

"Do you want to come in?" he asked.

"No," I said. "I wouldn't be comfortable with the party going on."

"It's probably winding down by now," he said. "We can head straight to my room." I looked up at him. His facial expression suddenly changed to embarrassment. "Not like that! I didn't mean..."

"Oh, I know what you mean. But, I can't."

"Why? You don't want to go home at this hour— not after what happened," he said.

"Yeah, but I can't."

"Why not?"

"I can't go in that house— not right now."

"What about a hotel? I could go with you. We could get a room with double beds. I could talk to you all night till you're so bored, you fall asleep," he grinned.

"I don't want to go to a hotel," I said.

He was quiet for a minute and then said, "I could go home with you—sleep on your sofa." He squatted down next to the window, closer to my face. "I just can't send you back there alone, tonight. You came here because you didn't want to be alone."

I was about to give in, when suddenly, we heard Joseph's front door open. We both looked up. There were three women and two men stumbling out, looking like they'd partied hard. Joseph was holding the door. I could hear him offering them a place to stay for the night, not wanting them to drink and drive. They were insisting they were fine and continued to their cars. One of the men was heading for the car right in front of mine.

"Looks like you got more stragglers out here!" the man hollered to Joseph. "Coming or going?" he asked, looking at Mason. Mason didn't answer. Joseph squinted his eyes and stepped out onto the porch. Mason stood up and waved at Joseph.

"Hey man! It's just me!" he called.

"Who's that in the car? Is that Kat?" he hollered back.

"Yeah!" he said, then he held his finger up for me to wait and jogged over to Joseph. He spoke to him for a minute. Even from a distance, I could tell he was explaining to Joseph what happened to me. Joseph put his hands on his hips and then ran his hand through his hair. He always did that when something upsetting or shocking happened. Plus he kept looking over at me as Mason spoke. I could tell Joseph was telling Mason to tell me to come in and Mason was shaking his head, saying I didn't want to. Then Joseph looked at me.

"Kat! Get in here!" he called. I rolled down my window.

"I'm fine!" I hollered back. I could see his whole body rise and fall as he sighed hard. He started walking toward me. "It's fine. I'm ok," I said, as he got closer. He came to my driver's side and opened my door. Mason just stood on the porch. "I'm ok." I said again.

"Kat— Get out of the car! You're staying here tonight." He was firm about it and sexy as hell, too.

"Looks like you have a house full," I said. He just looked at me, waiting for me to do what he said. I hesitated for a few seconds, in protest, and then turned the car off and got out.

"Are you alright?" he asked, as we walked to his door.

"It scared me, but I'm okay. He ran off," I told him, noticing that we walked by Mason as if he wasn't even there. I turned and smiled at him so he wouldn't think I ignored him.

You have no idea who this guy is?"

"None. I couldn't see his face in the dark." Joseph put his hand on the small of my back and led me in.

As we turned the corner into his living room, I was pleasantly surprised to find the few people in the room fully or mostly dressed. There were a couple women scantily dressed, but all breasts and asses were covered. The men left in the room appeared to have been dressed in business attire, but were down to unbuttoned dress shirts, untucked— one with a tank top under and one bare chested. There were plenty of glasses and bear bottles sitting around and I couldn't help but notice the sound of at least two people fucking nearby— maybe in the bathroom. I looked up at Joseph— he smiled and pointed toward the bar, gesturing if I wanted a drink.

"Sure—something fruity?" I asked, the obvious Deja vu' hanging in the air.

"Of course," he said, in almost a whisper. I blushed, thinking of all the times I'd been here before, Joseph getting me a drink, as I tried to get comfortable with the surroundings. Mason stood at the doorway of the room. I gave him a tight-lipped smile. He looked around the room at the visitors and then smiled at me and shook his head.

As Joseph handed me my drink, a beautiful, Hispanic girl came bouncing from around the corner. She leaped into his arms.

"Whoa!" Joseph said, trying to keep his drink steady. "Easy, girl!"

I watched as she hung on him, clearly drunk. She was in a short black dress that looked more like a slip and no shoes. Her tiny frame made her look like a child, especially up against Joseph, who stood well over six feet. As tiny as she was, she was clearly an adult. That was one thing I never saw, dealing with Joseph or Mark, they never messed around with underage girls.

"I was waiting for you, Joe. You said five minutes," the girl whined, in a high-pitched voice. Joseph's eyes scanned over to where I stood watching. Our eyes met and then I looked away.

"Sorry doll. I was seeing to my guests. You wouldn't want me to be a bad host, now would you?" he said, playfully.

"Fuck your guest," she said, just loud enough for me to hear it. "Better yet, fuck me!"

Joseph chuckled, "You're a naughty girl."

His eyes darted from me to her. As she pulled on him, I tried not to look, but he knew I was paying close attention. She pushed up on her toes and pulled him down so she could whisper in his ear, clearly something dirty, by the look on his face. Joseph cleared his throat and whispered back to her, patted her ass and she trotted off to the stairs, making a right turn at the top, not to his room, but one of the spares. Joseph had four bedrooms upstairs and one downstairs. The one downstairs was the room I was trapped in with Rex on that horrible night. Watching the girl head right and not left, toward Joseph's room, somehow eased my mind a little.

Joseph looked uncomfortable. He came back over to where I had moved, after the girl jumped him. I took a sip of my drink and looked around the room, avoiding eye contact. "So, obviously, I have company, but I want you to stay. It's not safe at your house. My room is empty," he said.

"Thanks," I gave him a quick smile. It was awkward. He looked at me a few more seconds and then turned and went up the stairs—to the right.

A few seconds later, I noticed Mason walk past me. He shot me a quick smile as he went into the downstairs room and shut the door. I sighed and looked around. I didn't want to go to Joseph's room, but I felt awkward sitting in the living room, where two other couples were flirting and touching. I went up the stairs, stopping at the top, listening for sex noises coming down the hall. I couldn't hear anything, but that meant nothing since I knew Joseph was in the room with her, probably undressing her, as I stood there. I turned left and went down the hall into Joseph's room. I shut the door and leaned against it.

It felt strange being in his room, knowing he was just down the hall with someone else. I had no right to be mad, but I felt cast aside. I looked around the room that I'd had so many eventful nights in. His room was big and so was the bed. I went to the French doors that led out to his deck. The view was beautiful. I remembered that first night we met. Mark had taken me to Joseph's house, not telling me that they lived a different lifestyle. I had no idea that Mark believed in open relationships, threesomes, orgies and all the rest. Joseph came on to me that first night standing right there on his deck. He had taken me there to show me the view. Then he reached out and touched me, stroking his fingers against my neck, as he brushed my hair over my shoulder. I was so angry when I realized what was happening. I would have never believed that one day I would have feelings for Joseph, but I did. I would have never believed that one day I would share a bed with Joseph... and Mark... at the same time... but I did.

Although it was the middle of the night, I wasn't tired. I was wide awake, actually. I opened his closet. It was filled with blacks, grays, blues, and a bit of white, the only colors he ever wore. He had a few suits, several dress shirts, and slacks. At the back, were a few pairs of jeans, sweatpants and seven or eight tee shirts. The room was dimly lit, as usual. Joseph had a low light lamp in the corner. I looked at the oversized black leather chair in the other corner. It was the chair he sat on the first night I slept with him. He sat there and promised not to move, so I would be comfortable to fuck Mark, while he watched. I had never done anything like that before. Then, when we were done, he got up from the chair and walked to the bed. That was the first time I was with him— the first time I was with them, allowing them both to touch me and fuck me. I was so timid the first time. I shook like a leaf the whole night, but I came like I never had before, too. It was amazing. The mix of shame and thrill, there's nothing like it.

I walked over to his chester drawer. I opened the top drawer and my heart sank. There on top of some papers was a photo. It was Joseph and Mark leaning against Joseph's pool table. I picked up the picture and stared. My eyes filled with tears. I ran my finger over the image of Mark. His face— that beautiful face. He was smiling, his arms folded and he was leaning into Joseph, who was laughing, with his arm draped over Mark's shoulders. They looked so happy. They were like brothers.

"Hey there." An unfamiliar voice came from behind me.

I turned quickly. I didn't hear the door open. It was one of the men from downstairs.

"What are you doing here?" I asked.

"Looking for you," he said. "I saw you come up here. Whatcha doing?"

"Trying to be alone," I told him, closing the drawer, and folding my arms. He shut the door. "Open the door!" I insisted.

"What's your name?" he asked. "I'm Nate." He moved toward me.

"I'm not interested, Nate! Please leave!" I backed away.

"Hey, don't be so harsh. It's a party. Let's have some fun. That's what we're here for. Right?"

"Not me! I'm not here for the party. There are ladies down stairs. Find someone to have fun with down there."

"Don't act like a bitch." He stepped forward and reached for my arm.

"Get out!" I hollered. I pulled away and pushed him.

"You like to play, huh?" He grabbed me and tried to pull me toward him.

"Don't touch me, you fucker!" I squirmed away. Then, suddenly, he was being jerked to the floor. Joseph was there, instantly.

"What the fuck, Joe!" Nate said, looking up at him. Joseph grabbed him by his shirt and lifted him to his feet.

"Yeah! What the fuck, Nate! Get the hell out of my house, with that bullshit!" Joseph snapped at him. Nate straightened his clothes, looked at me, back at Joseph and then walked out. Joseph turned to me.

"Thanks. My hero," I said.

" You alright?" he asked.

"I'm fine. I think he was just drunk."

He stared at me a minute and shook his head, "Why are you always getting into these situations?"

"I don't know, honestly. It's like I got bad juju or something."

"Yeah maybe." He just stood there a minute, examining me. He looked as if he wanted to say something, but couldn't.

"You finished with your company?" I asked.

He hesitated and said, "Get some sleep, Kathren." Then he turned and walked out. I wanted to follow him and beg him to come back— beg him to fuck me. He was so gorgeous and I wanted him so badly. I went to bed after a while and when I woke in the morning, Joseph was gone, already, just like last time. It was getting harder and harder to spend time with him, since our last encounter and I hated it.

Chapter 7

I WAS GLAD THAT I WAS able to get a locksmith out to change the locks the very next day. He changed the front door locks and installed special sliding bars on all the windows and the back door.

"No one's getting in here, now, without breaking glass," the man said, dropping new keys into my hand. "And it never hurts to get a security system."

"Not a bad idea," I said, slipping the keys into my pocket. "Thank you."

He nodded, smiled, and handed him a check. "Have a great day, miss."

I closed the door and turned the new lock on the door knob, then my new bolt lock and then put the chain on. I walked through the house making sure every window had its sliding bar pushed down, a simple, but logical way to keep a window from opening. I sighed and plopped down on the couch. I was starting to feel secure, when suddenly, there was a knock at the door. I jumped— the tension from the night before seeping back in. I peeked out the window. It was Linda. I unlocked my three locks and opened the door.

"What happened? I saw the locksmith. Paul said he saw the police over here, late, last night. I was sound asleep. I didn't hear a thing," she said, walking through the door, looking at the new locks on the door.

"Someone broke in," I said.

"What! Oh God, Kathren! Are you okay?" She grabbed my arm and squeezed.

"I'm fine, but it was scary," I said. "I woke up to him standing over my bed. He was actually touching my leg." Linda covered her mouth and shook her head in disbelief. Her eyes were big as saucers. She took her hand from her mouth and placed it over her heart.

"I can't believe it! Oh Kathren— Thank God you're okay! That is absolutely terrifying. Did you see his face? Any idea who he was?"

"No! It was dark. I couldn't see. I know he was in all black and he may have had a mask on his face—I'm not sure. It was so dark and I was woken from my sleep. It took me a second to realize it was real. By the time I screamed, he was gone."

Linda wrapped her arms around me in an awkward embrace, her hug pinning my upper arms. She squeezed tight. I did my best to pat her back with the part of my arms I could move. She was a good five inches shorter than me, standing only about five-two.

"I'm okay," I said, again.

"Thank God. I don't even want to think what could have happened," she said, releasing me. "Goodness, do you think it was the man I saw in the backyard? We should have called the police right away!"

"I'm not sure. That could be unrelated. Guess we'll never know." I didn't mention the other things to Linda— the open window or the open front door. I thought most people would question why I didn't call the police then and they would be right to do so. I couldn't tell anyone, except Joseph, that I wanted no part of the police after Mark's death.

"Kathren—You have a stalker!" Linda said, as if she had just realized it. As much as I didn't want it to be true, I knew that it was... I had a stalker!

The next day, I came home to find a familiar car in my driveway— a white, Nissan Altima. It was Mason. As I pulled in next to him, he got out of the car and stood, waiting for me, a reserved smile on his face.

"I tried to call," he said, as I exited my car. "I left messages. I was getting worried."

"I didn't hear my phone ring," I said, pulling my cell from my purse. Oh, I forgot to charge it." I held it up, showing him my black screen. "What's wrong?"

"I just wanted to see if you were okay. Did you get your locks changed?" he asked.

"Yes. Yesterday," I said, walking toward my front door. Mason followed. "I feel much safer now."

"Good. I'm glad." Mason came in and I offered him a drink. "Water's fine," he said.

"Have a seat." I offered, taking a water bottle from the fridge. I sat next to him, handing him the water.

"Everything okay?" I asked, noticing he seemed troubled.

"They found Mark's truck." The words were like a bomb dropping.

"Where?" I tried to sound calm, but inside I was freaking out.

"They pulled it out of a lake, about forty miles from here," he said, his voice shaking.

"Oh my God! What... what about Mark?"

"The truck was empty," he said. "No sign of Mark."

"Oh Mason." I didn't know what to say. It was clear by the look on his face, he knew this wasn't good. "Does Joseph know?"

"I left him a message. He hasn't gotten home from work yet. He hasn't messaged me back. I've been a basket case all day. I couldn't get a hold of Joe. I couldn't get a hold of you. I've been bumbling around that big house all day, pulling my hair out."

I looked at him sympathetically. I placed my hand on his arm. He stared at the floor and then looked at me and said, "I think he's dead."

I opened my mouth to speak, but I couldn't. I wanted to say 'No, don't think that way', but I knew the truth. I couldn't give him false hope. The sooner he accepted it the better. I couldn't help but wonder, if his truck was in the lake, where were his personal things and more importantly— where was he? And would his body be discovered? I felt terrible. This man was sitting in my house, feeling like I was one of the only two people he had to confide in, desperate to find his brother, now terrified that he was dead, so full of questions and dread and I was the person who not only knew the answers to his questions, but I was the cause of all of this. I pushed his brother down the stairs—I killed him. I was so sorry. I wanted to tell him how sorry I was. I wanted to tell him what happened—the whole story, but I couldn't. I just caressed his forearm, consolingly and gave him a sympathetic look. Poor, sweet Mason.

We sat quietly for a few minutes, then he spoke. "Can I ask you something?"

"Sure."

"What's going on with you and Joe?" I wasn't expecting that question. I cocked my head and lowered my brow.

"What do you mean?"

"Are you together or... I mean, both times you slept over, you slept in his room, but I hear him downstairs late into the night. I found him asleep in his office the other night when you were there. Both times he left for work really early. I'm just trying to understand what's up between you two."

"I couldn't really say, Mason. I honestly don't know. I've been trying to figure that out myself," I told him, sliding my hand off his arm. I didn't realize he was sleeping in his office when I was there. I knew he left early both times, but I didn't realize the lengths he was going to avoid me and I didn't understand why. And he was having his parties, again. I didn't get it. Joseph had always been very open with me, in the past, but now— his behavior was baffling. *What had I done to change things?*

"Are you together?" he asked, again.

"No. We're not together. We're friends. Just..." Suddenly, without warning, Mason's mouth crashed into mine. The kiss was so abrupt, it startled me! I quickly pushed away from him.

"Mason! I'm sorry if I gave you the wrong idea."

"No. I'm sorry. You didn't. I just... I like you, Kathren. I shouldn't have done that. I'm emotional today. My mind has been racing and... Forgive me." He was remorseful. He stood up. "I should go."

"Mason! It's ok. You don't have to leave," I said, taking his hand. He pulled his hand away.

"I'm ok. Don't worry. I should go home—well, to Joe's house—see if he got my messages."

"Did they give you any other information about the truck?" I asked.

"No. But Pete said this ramps up the investigation."

"Pete?"

"Detective Casteel..."

"Oh, right! The detective."

"Well, I'm going to get out of here. Lock up behind me," he said. He smiled and touched my arm. "Have a good night, Kathren."

"You too. Keep me informed," I said, walking him to the door. He smiled, tapped his fingers over my lock, as a reminder and walked out. I locked the door and dropped my head into my hands.

"Shit!" I groaned, pressing my forehead into the door. I needed to talk to Joseph. Mark's truck had been found. The detective would certainly expect foul play. He told Mason the investigation would ramp up. I wasn't sure what that meant— maybe more people working on his case. This would only bring them closer to the truth. *And why was Joseph avoiding me? What had I done to cause him to act this way? What the hell was going on?*

Later that night, I woke up suddenly! There was a noise! I sat up in the bed and looked over at my bat, still at my side. The clock glowed. It was a little after two. I wasn't sure if it was coming from outside or in. I waited, listening to the silence. A couple minutes went by. I strained to hear anything. Slowly, I kicked the covers down to the bottom of the bed. I gently placed my feet on the floor and picked up my bat. I peeked down the hall and then creeped along the cold hardwood floor. After checking the bathroom and spare room, I looked into the living room and kitchen. It was dark and quiet. Then, I noticed the strip of light shining in from outside, at the front door. It was cracked open! I couldn't believe it! My door with brand new locks was open, except for the chain! The chain was still in place, only allowing the door to open an inch. I rushed to the door, pushed it closed and flipped on the light. I inspected the rooms. I wondered if someone was in or out. It seemed to be empty. I locked the bolt and door and peered through the blinds. I didn't see anyone outside, either. I couldn't understand it. *How did someone get these new locks open?* I rushed around to the windows and back door, checking for tampering, still clinging to my bat. They were all still locked and secured with the drop bar. It must have been the intruder trying to come through the front door and being stopped by the unexpected chain that woke me.

I stood there, wondering if I should call the cops— wondering if they could even do anything, anyway. I found my cell phone, on the charger, on the kitchen counter, and called Joseph. It went to his voicemail. *Damn it!* Next, I called Mason. He didn't answer either. I sat on the couch and scanned around my house.

Obviously, he felt secure enough to try and come back in, after the first time I caught him. I contemplated what would have happened if he'd gotten in. Maybe he would have followed through with his plan, this time, to rape me—or kill me. After no return call from Joseph or Mason, I called the police. Fifteen minutes later, I was in the same scenario as the first time, police walking around my house and in my house. One was kneeled at the door, inspecting the locks. I noticed neighbors across the street standing on their front porch, watching the scene. I didn't know them. We waved at each other, occasionally, but that was all. One of the officers walked across the street, to speak to them. I was surprised that Linda didn't rush over to investigate. One of the officers told me they suspected that he picked the locks. It seemed to be the only explanation.

"Good thing you had the chain on," he said.

"Yeah, good thing," I said.

"We're going to have an officer sit outside your house the next couple of nights and we're going to really increase night patrols over here," he told me. "Have you thought about getting a security system... maybe cameras or a big dog?"

"I'm thinking about it, now," I told him.

"You're sure you haven't noticed anyone acting strangely: Someone at work, maybe? Someone following you around? Any bad breakups? Someone who didn't take it well?" he asked. "Think hard. Sometimes it's something little that you didn't pay attention to, at first."

"I've wracked my brain. I can't think of anyone who would do something like this." I didn't even suspect Rex anymore. After what he did to me, I felt certain he would have just attacked me, the other night; he wouldn't run away.

After encouraging me to go to a friends, they left, but one officer stayed parked out front. They assured me he would stay the night. That was enough to give me peace of mind, so I could go back to bed. I didn't sleep well, though. I tossed and turned, pulling at the sheets, in frustration. I was surprised that neither Joseph or Mason called me back. It was late, though. They were probably asleep, I assumed.

THE NEXT MORNING, MASON did call me.

"Kathren!"

"Yes. Hi, Mason—I called you cause..."

"They found a body!" he said, cutting me off. I was silent. I felt the entire world drop out from under me. "Way out in the woods, near the lake where the truck was found."

"Oh my God!"

"It's a male. But that's all they could say. The body's— the body is..." He couldn't say it, but I knew what he was trying to tell me. "I just got home from the police station. I didn't even notice you called last night. Is everything okay?"

I didn't feel right telling him my traumatic events after what he spent the night going through. "Everything's fine, Mason. I don't know what to say. This is terrible. I'm so sorry."

"A lady walking her dog found the body. Just a coincidence that it happened so close to the time of the discovery of the truck. Weird, huh?'

"Yes. Weird. But you don't know anything yet. It may not be him."

"That's what Pete said, but I know it's him. I just know it." His voice was tired and defeated. "My brother pissed off the wrong person, this time, and they killed him." He paused a minute and then I heard what sounded like sobbing. "Mark's dead. Someone killed my baby brother!" he cried. It was heart wrenching.

"Oh Mason! I'm so sorry." I tried to console him. "Do you want me to come over? I can call into work."

"It's okay. Don't do that. Maybe we can talk later. I just wanted you to hear the news from me."

When I got off the phone with Mason, I collapsed on the floor of my living room. Tears filled my eyes, thinking of poor Mark— his body in the woods for months. I didn't know if he was hard to identify because of the time he'd been out there— *had animals picked at him. Did the body decay that fast?* Or maybe whoever Joseph had to help him get rid of Mark's body, beat his face badly so that he was unrecognizable. I didn't want to imagine any of it, but I couldn't help it. I had vivid scenes of horror filling my mind. I had so much regret about what we had done— what I had agreed to. I should have demanded we call the police when it all happened. Who would ever believe that an accidental fall down the stairs would trigger us to do such a heinous thing.

Then, as usual, at this time in the morning...a knock at the door. "Don't tell me it happened again!" Linda wailed, rushing in, as I opened the door. "There's a police cruiser sitting out front!"

"Still?" I was surprised to look out the window and see the police car still parked in front of the house.

"What happened this time? I thought you changed the locks."

"I did. He tried to come through the front door. He didn't get in. I heard it and woke up."

"Oh dear God! What are you going to do?" she asked. Concern was oozing from every word.

"I don't know, Linda. I really don't know. The police are keeping a close watch on the house and the chain on the door did keep him out, so I guess I have to hope the cops catch him or he gives up."

"Right. Let's hope they catch him," she said, nodding.

"I actually need to leave, though. I'm going to have to talk to you later, okay?" I decided, despite what Mason said, I was going to call into work and go see him. It felt right. I didn't feel up for a work day with everything going on, anyway.

I said my goodbyes to Linda and headed to Joseph's house, to be with Mason. Arriving, I noticed Joseph's black Lincoln MKX wasn't in the driveway. I went to the door and knocked. It took a minute. I was about to knock again when the door opened. Mason looked surprised and exhausted. I didn't say anything. I just stepped in and wrapped my arms around him. He squeezed me tight and buried his face in my neck. We just stood there quietly embracing for a minute and then finally he released me and gestured for me to come in. I followed him to the living room and sat on the couch. He offered me coffee, since it was a bit early for the alcoholic beverage we both really needed.

"Sure. How bout I make it?" I went to the kitchen. Mason followed. After preparing the coffee and pouring us both a cup, we took it back to the living room and sat. "Does Joseph know?" I asked.

"I don't know. He's been gone a lot lately. I guess work has been busy," Mason said. I never knew Joseph's work to be busy. I actually always found it strange how little he worked and how little he spoke of work. I knew he was in finance and I was aware that he did well in the stock market. I assumed he was possibly a self-made millionaire or something. His house was large, in an expensive area and his furniture was clearly expensive, even though he was a bit of a minimalist. His car was expensive and although he seemed to spend a lot of time around the house in sweats and tee shirts— his nicer clothes were name brand and high priced. He even had a couple Armani suits hanging in his closet.

"Have you tried calling him?" I asked, taking a sip of my hot coffee.

"No. I'll wait till he gets home," he said. He leaned back on the couch. "They are going to call me when they have made a positive ID." I wondered what shape the body was in. I thought about the fact that Mark had tattoos. He was tall and very physically fit. I didn't dare mention it to Mason; I didn't want to make him think about any more terrible images.

"Did they give you any kind of time frame?" I asked.

"He just said they'd move as fast as they could." He reached up and pulled a band out of his hair that was holding it in a messy bun. He ran his fingers through his long strands, sighed and rubbed his hands over his face. "I need a shower," he said. "Do you mind if I take one real quick?"

"Of course not. Take your time." I gave him a reassuring smile. He got up and disappeared into the back room. I sipped my coffee and looked around Joseph's house. I stood up and paced. As I moved around the space I couldn't help thinking back to the different moments I had experienced there. So much sex! Before Mark and Joseph, I had only been with a few boyfriends and the large majority of sexual experiences I had were with Frank, my longest and first real boyfriend. It was never really exciting— never rough or animalistic. But when I met Mark, all that changed— and when I met Joseph my world flipped upside down. I was introduced to a whole new world of multiple partners and open relationships. Mark was gone, never having made it through his thirties, but I knew no one could say he didn't enjoy his life. He did what he wanted. He experienced everything and he never let anyone make him feel bad about it. That gave me a tiny bit of comfort. I looked at the stares, remembering that horrible night. Then I looked at the room where Mason was staying. I hadn't stepped in since that night. This was where I was the first time I was with Mark and Joseph at the same time. I was such a bundle of nerves that night. That memory made me want to go inside and look around, but there was the other thing— Rex! That memory kept me away. That was where Rex attacked me— where he raped me. I stood there, staring at the door, cracked open, envisioning being dragged in that night. I could still hear Mark telling him not to handle me so rough— but he did nothing to stop it—nothing.

Then, unexpectedly, through the cracked open door, I saw Mason. He had come out of the shower. He had a towel wrapped around his lower half. I stepped closer and positioned myself where I could see him. His dark hair was wet, hanging in his face, over his shoulders and down his back, it went just a few inches past his neck. His body was wet too and he was in good shape. He had tattoos covering his back. I was surprised. At my distance I couldn't see clear, but it looked like words across the top of his back and a bear wrapping around his lower ribs— some sort of symbols and colorful design on the other side, covering his skin down to his lower lumbar, just above his butt, that his towel was exposing slightly. He tossed his hair back and shook it, like a shampoo commercial. He had a tattoo on his chest too. I couldn't make it out. I was distracted by the line of hair from his navel running down his pelvis. Then, I was startled out of my trance by his blue eyes staring back at me. I gasped and moved out of his view. I was so embarrassed. He caught me ogling his body.

His door opened. He was standing there, still wet, in his towel, tied so low on his hips, I could see the edge of his pubic hair. I looked at him, my face red with humiliation, and then looked away.

"Kathren..."

"I'm sorry. I shouldn't have been looking in your room. I..."

"It's okay. Why don't you come over here." He sounded like Mark, at that moment. It was so much like his brother; it made me uneasy.

"I can't."

"Why?"

"It's not right," I said.

"I need you— I really need you," he said, stepping out of the room. "Please."

His words were genuine. I felt like I couldn't say no to him. Part of me didn't want to say no, but I knew it was wrong. I walked toward him. He reached out and pulled me gently to him. We were nose to nose, breathing into each other. His body was firm, pressed against me. He leaned in and kissed me, softly. I let him. I didn't just let him— I kissed him back. At first, it was just his lips pressed into mine, then he slipped his tongue into my mouth. I rested my hands against his chest. He wrapped his arms around my waist and slid his hands down to my ass, squeezing. His kiss was nice, not like Mark's, though, and I was grateful for that. That would have been too much. I felt his erection pressing through his towel, against my stomach. As his cock stretched out, his towel loosened and fell to the floor. He was naked against me. His hands roamed my body, through my clothes. I started to panic inside. I didn't want to sleep with him. It would be so wrong. He scooped me up and began to carry me to his room.

"No," I mumbled through the kiss. He didn't respond. "No!" I grunted, more clearly. Then, before he could take me into the room, I shoved away from him, hard and snapped, "No!" louder, almost yelling. I squirmed free of him and he let go. I walked away from the room, shaky and frazzled.

"What's wrong?" he asked.

"I'm sorry."

"You're obviously attracted to me. I don't get it."

"I'm sorry," I said, again, looking away from him. "I just can't."

"Why?"

"It's hard to— there's so much happening. I just..."

"I want to make love to you, Kathren." He was still naked.

"Please cover yourself."

"Why? I can see you want me," he insisted.

Without warning, Joseph's voice rang out, "Whoa! Sorry to interrupt!" He was standing in the doorway of the living room, he was looking up at the ceiling, to avoid staring at Mason's erection. Mason rushed to get his towel and cover up.

"Joe— sorry man." He headed to his room to change.

"Hey. Don't worry about me. I'll go to my room." Joseph said, looking over at me. Mason's door shut and I turned to Joseph.

"Wait! I want to talk to you! What's going on?" I asked, quickly, taking the opportunity to talk to him before Mason returned. He dropped his book bag and pulled his phone out, looked at it and typed, as if responding to a text.

"Hello?"

"Sorry. Just checking something," he said, sliding the phone back in his pocket. "How are you?" He headed for his bar and pulled out a glass.

"A little early, isn't it?" I asked. He looked at me, smirked and poured orange juice into the glass. "Oh."

"Don't just assume, Kat." Maybe that was true that I assumed too quickly, but seeing Joseph pouring liquor behind his bar was so routine, that it never occurred to me that he ever drank anything else, other than an occasional morning coffee.

"Why have you been avoiding me?" I asked. Before he could speak, Mason came back out. He had jeans and a white tee shirt on and was pulling his wet hair back into a ponytail.

"Sorry, man."

"No worries," Joseph smiled, leaning on the bar. We all stood there, awkwardly.

"Tell him," I ordered Mason. Joseph looked at me and then Mason.

"Tell me what?" he asked.

"They found a body," Mason said. Joseph scanned back and forth from Mason to me.

"Where?" he asked.

"In the woods, near the lake. They couldn't identify him. They know it's a male, though."

"Don't worry. It could be anyone," Joseph said. He was consoling, but I could tell by the look on his face there was more than that— he wasn't worried. Mason walked past me and around the bar. In the quick moment that Mason was turned away from him, Joseph looked at me and mouthed, "It's not him!", shaking his head slightly. My eyes widened. I lowered my brow at him, questioning.

He turned and spoke to Mason. "It doesn't mean anything, buddy. Don't worry."

"I hope you're right, man," Mason sighed.

Joseph came from around the bar, patting Mason on the shoulder and squeezing , as he went by and then he offered a quick hand on my back, for just a second, as he passed me. He excused himself, saying he needed to make a call and retreated to his office, closing the door. Mason leaned on the bar and looked at me.

"Sorry. That was embarrassing. I didn't hear him come in," he said, shaking his head.

"Me neither," I said.

"We need to talk."

"There's nothing to talk about. I'm not going to lie to you. You're very sweet and I do find you attractive. I was tempted, but I can't. It wouldn't be right. With everything going on— your brother missing and a body being found, his truck being pulled from the lake, plus I used to date him and you remind me of him so much. It just doesn't feel right, Mason. I know you're going through a lot right now and you could use some comfort. I want to be here for you, Mason. I really do... but, as a friend... that's it. Please don't confuse things with sex. I've let sex confuse things enough in my life."

"Can we go in my room and talk?" he asked.

"No! That's another thing. I can't go in that room!"

"What? Why?" His brow was scrunched in confusion.

"I don't want to talk about it. I just can't go in there."

"I don't understand. What's wrong with the room?" he asked.

"Please— I don't want to discuss it."

"But..." Before he could continue, Joseph came back out of his office, just in time. Mason stopped pushing it.

"So Kat— No more problems at home?" Joseph asked.

"Actually..." They both stared at me as I started to explain my situation. "I got the locks changed so that's good, but someone tried to get in last night."

"What!" Mason exclaimed. "Why didn't you say anything?"

"What happened?" Joseph added. "You said they *tried*?"

"I didn't want to bring it up, after the terrible news you were coping with, Mason, but yeah, it was a failed attempt. The chain on my door stopped him. The police think he picked my locks."

"What the fuck!" Joseph blurted. "This guy's fucking nuts!"

"Kathren— I think you should stay here for a while— if Joseph wouldn't mind." Mason and I both looked at Joseph.

"Of course, you can stay here, if you want to," he said, sounding a bit caught off guard..

"I don't need to."

"Yes, you do!" Mason insisted. I smiled at him, grateful for his kindness and sweet concern.

"I think you should, at least for a few days." Joseph said. I looked at him, trying to determine if he really wanted me to stay. He'd been so distant; I wasn't sure if he was just being polite.

"Please—stay." He sounded more sincere. I needed him to ask me, not just accept a request. He looked me in the eyes, with a clear caring expression on his face.

"Ok," I agreed. "for a few days."

"Good," Mason said, sounding eased by my choice. "You want me to go with you to get your things?" he asked.

"That's okay. I need to run a couple errands and I should talk to my neighbor. Is it ok if I come back around seven?" I asked.

"I'll give you a key," Joseph offered. I looked at him, gratefully. I tried to show my appreciation, but not the thrill I felt at the idea of having a key to Joseph's palace. At the very least, it meant he trusted me, other than that I wasn't sure, but I liked it, all the same.

"Thank you, Joseph."

"Sure." Joseph smiled at me, looked over at Mason and took a swig of his drink.

I headed out to gather my things and prepare for a few days at Joseph's house.

Chapter 8

LATER THAT EVENING, after picking up clothes, informing Linda and the police that I would be away for a few days, I arrived back at Joseph's house. I knocked before entering, and then turned the doorknob, slowly. It felt odd to just enter Joseph's house, but somewhere deep in my thoughts, I imagined doing that very thing, on a regular basis. With all that had happened, I felt connected to Joseph. I had feelings that ran deeper than attraction and friendship. Although, at the same time, I felt completely disconnected from him, as if I didn't know him at all, and sometimes I even felt like a burden to him.

"Kathren," Mason called from the stairway. "Glad you're back. Joseph has you set up with a room upstairs."

"Great." I said, following him up the stairs. Just as we reached the top, I was surprised to see Mason turn right, leading me to the spare room. I had never spent a night in that room. He always gave me his bedroom and I can't lie, I wondered if he would share his bed with me, while I was there. I followed Mason to the spare room at the end of the hall. He opened the door and walked in, reminding me of the porter at a hotel. He stood in the center of the room, smiling. I walked in and laid my bag on the bed.

"This room doesn't have a bathroom, but Joe said for you to use the one in the hall or in his room if you preferred his shower."

"Joseph's master bathroom is pretty awesome," I said, surveying my surroundings. There was a queen-sized bed, covered in a cream colored, plush comforter, and matching pillows. The room was smaller and more simply decorated than the other rooms I had been in, with pale blue walls and light oak dressers and end tables. There were fresh pink roses, in a vase, on the end table and a large bouquet on one of the dressers. I wondered if Joseph had purchased them especially for me. There was a large window that looked out to the same beautiful view as the one in Joseph's room. Only it was just a window, covered with cream-colored blinds, matching the bed. The room was definitely feminine, in its decor.

"Well, get settled and come down stairs when you're ready. We'll have dinner," he said, smiling.

"Is Joseph here?"

"No. I'm not sure where he is, at the moment." He smiled and pulled the door to a crack. I heard him heading down the stairs and I sat on the edge of the bed, looking around my room. All at once, I felt out of place.

"What am I doing here?" I mumbled to myself. I opened my bag and began to hang some things in the closet. It was empty, except for a handful of wooden hangers, a couple extra blankets and one extra pillow, on the shelf. I opened a drawer and put my undergarments away. I placed my toiletries and cosmetic bag on the top of the dresser and tossed my empty bag into the bottom of the closet. I plugged my charger for my phone into the outlet near the bed, and placed my cheesy romance novel, I was half way through, on the nightstand. I went downstairs, where I found Mason sitting on the sofa, looking at his cellphone. He looked up and smiled.

"Have you had dinner yet?" he asked.

"No. Not yet."

"I could order something, or we could go out," he suggested.

"Mason, I want to say something..."

"No need," he interrupted. "I know what you're about to say. I'm sorry about everything earlier. I'm not going to... I know this isn't a romantic weekend together. I get that. I won't pressure you or make things complicated. You can relax while you're here. You don't have to feel uncomfortable around me— even though you've seen me naked." He chuckled, playfully. I blushed.

"Thank you for saying that." I was so relieved to hear him say it and that he said it first. It had occurred to me that things could get awkward between us. I didn't want to spend the next few days fighting off his advances and as attractive as he was, I was worried I may not have the strength or consistent good sense to keep things platonic. Mason was a very sweet and very good-looking guy, but I would never forgive myself for sleeping with the brother of the man I killed. It already felt so deceptive, just being his friend and having him here, in Joseph's house, leaning on the both of us for support.

"So— dinner?" he clapped his hands together, standing.

"Let's just order in," I suggested. After a short discussion, we agreed on pizza. An hour later we were sitting in the kitchen enjoying our second slice, when the front door opened and we heard Joseph's voice. It wasn't only Joseph's. We heard several voices. We both stared at the doorway, realizing Joseph was having a get together— again. I got up and went to peek around the corner. I watched as about seven or eight people, men and women, filed into the living room. My eyes met Joseph's.

"Hey Kat. Did you get settled in okay?" he asked, pulling some glasses from behind the bar. Mason walked up behind me.

"Yes. Thanks again for letting me stay," I said, surveying the room full of party goers.

"Not a problem." He started filling glasses. Someone turned on the music and the party was in progress. I looked over my shoulder at Mason, who was studying me.

"Shall we finish our dinner?" he asked.

"I think I'm done," I said. "Let me help you clean up."

"No. You head up, if you'd like. I got this."

"You sure?"

"Go on. This will take a couple minutes. Sleep well."

I smiled and said goodnight. It was a little early, but I hadn't been sleeping well and I didn't want to join Joseph's party or witness anything that was going to cause jealousy. I knew what Joseph did at these parties, but I didn't want to have to watch it go down. I was a jealous idiot.

Joseph watched me as I retreated up the stairs. Our eyes met and there was a silent conversation happening, but this time I couldn't understand the language. I went to the hall bathroom and locked myself in. I filled the tub and took a hot bath. As I tried to focus on the soothing sounds of the water shifting around my body, I could hear music and laughter, muffled through the door. I tried to drown it out and relax. It had been a crazy week and I was stressed.

After my bath, I wrapped myself in a robe and stepped into the hallway. Joseph was in his doorway, down the hall. I looked at him for a few seconds. He didn't say anything. He turned and went into his room and closed the door. That was not an invitation. I assumed he had company. Maybe he was waiting for her to finish using the bathroom. I went into my room and shut the door. I snuggled into the cozy bed and fell sound asleep. I slept better than I had in weeks.

The next morning, I woke up and got ready for work. It was Friday morning and I had missed the day before. I needed to get things done. As I came down the stairs, the smell of coffee wafted through the air. I peeked into the kitchen, where there was a platter of croissants and bagels. There was butter and jelly on one side and a bowl of fresh fruit on the other. Mason was standing in the middle of the kitchen looking at the display.

"Wow! What a spread, Mason."

"Don't look at me. Joseph did this. He's making sure everything's up to par for his special guest."

"Who's that?" I asked.

"You, of course!"

"Me? No. I've stayed here plenty of times and never woke up to this. Maybe he has a woman up there."

"He's gone," Mason said. "And no one stayed over. He had everyone out around one o'clock last night." I was pleased to hear that tidbit.

"Well, I need to get to work," I said, grabbing a bagel from the table. "When did he do all this?" I mumbled.

LATER AT WORK, MY BOSS, Mr. Lewis stepped out and sat across from me. He had never done this before and it surprised me. Usually if he wanted to discuss something he would stand at my side or call me into his office. He looked concerned.

"Everything okay, Kathren?"

"Yes. Why do you ask?"

"You seem distracted, lately."

"Well, I've had some stuff going on— at home. Everything's okay, though."

"Anything I can help with?" he asked. I could tell he was curious. This was his way of asking me to explain.

"No. Thanks for offering. It— it sounds crazy to say it out loud, but I've had someone messing around my house."

"What do you mean? he asked, leaning forward with his elbows resting on the armrests and his hands folded in front of him.

"A stalker— I think."

"A stalker?"

"Yes. He broke into my house."

"What!" Mr. Lewis' demeanor changed immediately and he was clearly concerned. I continued to tell him the details and then I told him that on top of all that, an old friend of mine was missing and the police had been interviewing everyone he knew. I told him it wasn't looking good. He was shocked at all the chaos I had been dealing with.

I figured it was better to tell him about it. It might not look good if the detective ever decided to talk to my boss for any reason and he was clueless about the situation. It may look like I was hiding things. Mr. Lewis was very compassionate and let me know that if I ever needed to call in or go home early, I could let him know and It would be fine. He praised me on how professional I had been through all of it. He asked a few questions. I let him know I was staying with a friend and he seemed satisfied with the new knowledge he had about what had me so distracted, as he put it.

I finished my day at work and headed to Joseph's. When I pulled up at the house, both Mason and Joseph's cars were in the driveway. I walked in to find them both sitting on the couch. They looked up at me, as I came into the room.

"It's not him!" Mason blurted out.

"Oh thank God!" I exclaimed, rushing over to hug him.

"They were already able to identify the poor bastard. It wasn't Mark! Some guy who was reported missing a couple months ago." He looked like he'd been crying, as I released him from my embrace.

"Oh Mason, I don't know what to say..."

"I told you it wasn't him," Joseph said, calmly, patting Mason's back.

"You did, man— you did."

I looked at Joseph, who was staring at me. This time, I understood the unspoken message. Sometimes just a look was all it took and I knew exactly what he wanted me to know. He was letting me know that he already knew the body wasn't him— because he knew where Mark's body was. He would never tell me, but he knew.

Then, as Mason was consumed in his own thoughts, his head down, Joseph's look changed. He almost looked hurt. He got up and walked out of the room and into his office, shutting the door behind him. Mason was obviously relieved, but the stress of the situation was really starting to wear on him. He looked tired, like he was aging before my eyes. The dark circles under his eyes were not there before.

"Why don't you get a nap, Mason. You look worn out."

"I am," he said, exhaling heavily. " I think I'll get a shower first." He stood up to leave, but first he looked at me. "How was your day?"

"Uneventful, I'm happy to say." We both smiled.

"Good. That's good to hear. We'll talk more later?"

"Sure. Find me after you get some rest," I told him. He smiled and went to his room.

I walked over to Joseph's office door. I stood there quietly for a moment, leaning on the frame. There was no noise coming from the room. I wanted to knock and ask him to talk to me. I wanted to know why he was avoiding me. I thought we were starting a relationship back up— well, maybe not a relationship, a friendship, was a better word. I always felt like Joseph and I had a bond, beyond what we went through with Mark— even beyond the sex. It was all part of it, but it went deeper. At least, I thought so. When I was with Mark and I would be so confused or hurt over the things going on between us, Joseph was my sounding board. He was the one who would always tell me the truth and the one who would very often console and comfort me. We shared something more than just sex. He was my friend. He made me laugh and teased me. I enjoyed our friendship and I really missed it. I raised my fist to knock, when suddenly the door flung open. Joseph jumped, startled by my presence.

"Fuck!" He put his hand on his chest. "What are you doing? You scare the shit out of me!"

"Sorry. I was about to knock." I looked up at his stern face, now at a loss for words.

"Well— what's up?" He stood there, holding the edge of the door like a barrier to his private office. There was a pause. "Kathren, just say whatever it is you want to say."

"I'm confused."

"About?"

"The way you're acting."

"How am I acting?" He lowered his brow and folded his arms.

"Distant— like you're avoiding me— like I've done something wrong."

"I'm not avoiding you, Kat, and you haven't done anything wrong," he said, placing a hand on my upper arm— not to console me, but to move past me. He headed into the living room and to the bar. You want a drink?" he asked, making himself one.

"Sure. It's Friday night. Why not?" I said, walking up to the other side of the bar. Joseph smirked to himself, as he made me a Sea Breeze, my typical drink: Vodka, Cranberry and Grapefruit with a lime. He'd made it for me many times. I stared at him as he made our drinks, remembering how nervous he made me when I first met him. He was so flirtatious and sarcastic. He handed me my glass and stood there behind the bar, tossing his back, and pouring another. It occurred to me that he was acting uneasy. Joseph was a drinker, but he only swallowed down two in a row when he was nervous or worried, that much I knew.

"Are you okay?" I asked.

"I'm fine. Why?"

"You seem nervous."

"Nervous? Why would I be nervous?"

"I feel like I'm making you nervous or something," I told him.

"What?" He snickered. He came from around the bar and stood in front of me— right in front of me. He looked down, staring into my eyes— nothing between us, but the glasses in our hands and silent 'fuck me' hanging in the air. "You don't make me nervous." Sex radiated from him like heat and his words made me shudder a little. I was sure he could hear it in my breath—the quiver. For a moment it looked like he would kiss me and then something shifted. He seemed to catch himself, like he snapped out of it . He cleared his throat and turned away.

"What's wrong?" I asked again, reaching for his arm as he walked away. My fingertips just missed him.

"Nothing! I'm fine. Oh, just so you know, I'm having some people here tonight." He swallowed down the second glass of gin, and went upstairs. I could hear the door to his room shut. I finished my drink, huffed in frustration, and went to my ro

Chapter 9

LATER THAT NIGHT, AFTER listening to music and voices from downstairs for a long while, I decided to head to the kitchen for a late-night snack. I put on a pair of black yoga pants and a black tank top. I swiped my hair up into a messy bun and went quietly down the stairs. I hoped if I tiptoed, no one would notice me, but before I touched the bottom stair, a voice rang out from a man sitting on the couch.

"Who's this gorgeous creature coming down the stairs?" he asked loud enough for everyone to hear. There were several people in the room and most of them turned to see me. Thankfully, like last time, everyone was dressed. Joseph, who was in a conversation with a couple women, turned and looked at me. My eyes found his and I pointed toward the kitchen. He nodded at me. He watched me as I crossed the room. I heard one of the women standing with him ask who I was. I strained to listen, but I couldn't hear his response.

I went to the cabinet and found a box of Frosted Flakes. I poured some in a small cereal bowl and poured some milk over them. I took my bowl and sat at the table. After a few bites, a man came in. I didn't recognize him. I'd never seen him at one of Joseph's parties. He was a tall, handsome, black man. He had a short, well-manicured beard and short haircut with a crisp lining. Handsome probably wasn't the right word— sexy as hell might be more accurate.

"Hey there," he said, smiling— and what a smile it was.

"Hi," I answered, covering my mouth that was full of cereal.

"Sorry," he laughed. "Didn't mean to interrupt your dinner. What ya got there?" He leaned forward, looking into my bowl. "Frosted Flakes, huh? Yum. The dinner of champions."

I finished swallowing my bite. "It's okay. But, isn't it supposed to be the breakfast of champions?" I smirked.

"Yeah, you could be right." I liked him immediately. He was funny and his smile was very inviting.

"I skipped dinner earlier and just needed a little something before bed."

"You live here?" he asked, taking a bottle of water from the fridge.

"No. I'm just staying here for a few days."

"Are you a friend of Joe— or family?"

"A friend," I said and then there was an awkward silence as he leaned against the counter across from me and sipped his water.

"I'm Noah," he offered, finally.

"Nice to meet you, Noah. I'm Kathren. Not enjoying the party?" I asked.

"It's fine. I just needed some water so I came to... actually, I'm lying. I saw you come in here and, well... it made me want to get up and come in here, too." He stood propped against the counter, one hand holding the edge, the other holding his water, his eyes on me. He wore jeans that hugged his muscled thighs and a white thermal shirt that showed every curve of his deltoids, biceps and pecs that undoubtedly sat above a beautiful six pack. His smile was the kind that made you want to smile back. I knew I was blushing and wondered if it was obvious.

"So, how do you know Joseph?" I asked.

"I don't really. I came with a friend of mine once before and it was a good time, so when he asked if I wanted to come tonight, I thought 'why not'. Actually, I was getting a little bored this time, and started to regret coming. I was about to head out. Then I saw you come floating down the stairs, like a breath of fresh air, and suddenly, I didn't want to leave anymore." I felt heat filling my cheeks. "How do you know him?" he asked.

That was not a story I wanted to tell. I just gave the same answer. "Basically, the same as you. I came to a party a while back, with a friend. Actually, I came to a few and after a while, we just became friends." He nodded. I got up and took my bowl to the sink. I could feel his eyes on me, scanning my body, leaning to get a good look at my ass. I took a cloth and wiped the table.

"What do you do, Kathren?" His voice was deep, very masculine.

"I work for an accountant in town. Secretarial work. How about you?"

"I'm an electrician. I work independently," he said.

"Oh, local?"

"Yeah." He reached into his back pocket, pulled out his business card and stepped forward and handed it to me. "If you ever need anything—call me. I'll take care of you—anything you need." He had a grin that told me his statement had more than one meaning. I slid his card down a tight pocket on the side of my thigh. He moved a little closer. "So, I'm assuming you don't have a boyfriend."

"Why would you assume that?" I asked.

"Because what man would leave a woman like you, to sleep over at another man's house. And a ladies man like Joe, to boot— I know I wouldn't." He took another step, dragging his fingers along the edge of the counter. He was a couple feet away from me. He was tall, at least six feet— built so perfectly that I had to stop myself from asking if he worked out. Of course he did, but that would be corny, for me to ask.

"You're a flirt," I said, taking a step back.

"Yeah— and you're fucking beautiful." He stepped forward again. I stepped back bumping into the fridge behind me.

"You okay?" he asked, grinning at my klutziness.

"Noah, it was really good meeting you, but..."

"But..." he took another step, closing the space between us. He was only about a foot away from me. I didn't know this man, but he was standing well inside my personal bubble and I was surprised to find myself squeezing the muscles between my thighs, not wanting to get away.

"I need to..." I took a deep breath.

"Yeah. What do you need?" He was speaking in what sounded like a purr, almost. He reached up and ran the back of his fingertips across my cheek. "You're really pretty."

"Thank you," I said, staring up at him. His eyes scanned down to my breasts.

"There you are!" Joseph's voice blared into the room. He was in the kitchen, standing behind us. Noah backed up and took a sip of his water. Joseph looked at him and then back to me. "Can I speak to you for a second, Kat?"

"Sure. Excuse me, Noah."

"No problem," Noah said, nodding at me as I passed by. As I approached Joseph he turned and led the way to his office. Once we were in the room, he shut the door, turned, and glared at me.

"What are you doing?" he asked, propping his hands on his hips.

"What do you mean? I was having a bowl of cereal."

"Oh! Just having a bowl of cereal?"

"Yes. Then your friend came in and we were talking."

"Talking?"

"Yes. Talking," I emphasized. He stared at me. "Why? What's the problem?"

"No problem. I just... I don't..."

"What? You don't... what?"

"I don't understand you?" he said.

"Me! You don't understand me?" I huffed. "That's funny!"

"Why is that funny?" he asked, sounding irked.

"First of all, You have been acting strange for days. You've been distant, hiding from me."

"Hiding from you? I'm not hiding from you!"

"Oh, no? You normally get up and leave at four or five in the morning, do you? You normally sleep in your office when I'm in your bed?" I raised my brows and cocked my head forward, as I interrogated him. He was quiet now. "I texted you and you didn't answer! You barely speak to me! You find a reason to leave every time I come into the room. You seem to suddenly be back to having parties and according to Mason, you just started that again! Something's weird! I don't know what it is, but you are acting differently. That's clear!" He stepped closer to me. He glanced around my face and then focused on my eyes. He looked strained, like he wanted to say something, but couldn't. "What Joseph? What is it!"

"First, this is my house! It's not your concern or Mason's, if I have parties and..." He looked me up and down. "And second— You shouldn't be down here dressed like that! You've got enough shit going on. You don't need to add more. And third— you just...you just...just go to your room... please!" He turned and walked out.

"Go to my room? Oh, okay dad!" I replied, sarcastically. He turned and gave me a frustrated look as he disappeared into the living room. *"Dressed like this? What the heck is wrong with how I'm dressed?"*

I came out of the office and stepped into the doorway of the living room. Joseph was behind the bar, pouring drinks, again. Noah had come back into the room and was looking at me. There were about ten others I didn't know. Noah smiled. I shot him an apologetic smile back and then looked over at Joseph. He was watching me, but cut his eyes down when I noticed. A woman walked over and introduced herself.

"Hi. I'm Kendra." She was a pretty, small-framed woman with black hair in a pixie cut, wearing a short, red dress.

"Hi. I'm Kathren," I said, turning my attention to her.

"Do you live here?" she asked.

"No. Just staying a few days."

"Oh. That's cool." She paused and then asked, "Are you and Joe..." Her eyes finished her question. She was interested in him and wanted to make sure I wasn't his girlfriend. I wanted to say, *Yes. Stay away!* But I didn't.

"We're just friends. That's all."

Her face lit up, "Great! Nice to meet you." She bounced over to Joseph and started flirting, heaving her boobs into his face. His eyes glanced over at me, then he looked down at the temptress in front of him and smiled. I looked away, directing my attention to others in the room. So far this party seemed to be tame compared to the ones he had when Mark was here. Usually by this time, people were naked and fucking, but no one was undressing yet. There was a couple on the couch getting pretty hot and heavy, but everyone else was just talking and flirting.

"Everything okay?" I turned to find Noah had made his way back to me.

"Yes. Fine."

"I thought I heard you yelling at Joe in the other room," he said.

"No. Everything's fine." I said, leaning against the wall. He leaned on the wall next to me. I peeked over at Joseph. His eyes were locked on Kendra for the time being.

"You gotta thing for him, huh?" Noah said, quietly in my ear. I turned to look at him.

"What? No!"

"It's okay! It's not an accusation. But it's kind of obvious."

"Obvious?" I hoped it wasn't obvious. I wasn't sure exactly how I felt about Joseph. I wanted to be close to him, but I didn't want other people to notice it.

"Well, based on what I see, you both have complicated feelings for each other."

"You barely know him and you don't know me." I said. I folded my arms and turned away from him. My irritation with Joseph was pouring out onto Noah, but that didn't seem to deter him, at all.

"So, if you don't have feelings for Joe, prove it."

"Prove it?"

"Yeah, prove it."

"I don't have to prove anything." And then, curiosity took over. "How would I prove it, anyway?"

"By kissing me."

"What?" I gasped.

"Kiss me if you don't like Joe," he said, leaning closer to me.

"Kissing you wouldn't prove anything?"

"Well, then— kiss me anyway. I think the kiss will tell me all I need to know."

"Maybe I don't want to kiss you, ever think of that?" My anger was shifting to amusement.

"Maybe not. I'm a really good kisser, though, so I think you should go for it. Come on! Take a chance. Prove me wrong!"

"Nice try!" I tried to hide my smile. He was cute. More than cute— he was fucking hot. Joseph was across the room with his arm around Kendra. She was unbuttoning his shirt, rubbing his chest, so I turned my attention back to Noah. We stared at each other for a moment and then he leaned down and pressed his full, soft lips to mine. He slid his hands around my waist and pulled me close. He squeezed my flesh with his strong hands and pushed his tongue into my mouth, licking the inside while a moan slipped out from someplace deep. I kissed him back and rubbed my hands up his arms to his shoulders, feeling his huge, strong body. I didn't think about the other people in the room, I just enjoyed the touch of a man who was beautiful to look at and made me blush.

Then, without warning, I felt a jerk. Joseph was there, pushing Noah away from me. Noah was surprised and so was I. Noah, instinctually, came back toward Joseph, aggressively, but he stopped and backed down, raising his hands in submission or maybe just respect, I'm not really sure.

"What the fuck, Joseph!" I exclaimed. He grabbed my arm hard and pulled me. He led me up the stairs and straight to my room, slamming the door behind us. "What the hell is wrong with you?" I snapped.

"What the hell is wrong with you?" he roared back, slinging me around to face him! "What kind of shit are you trying to pull?"

"I don't know what the hell you're talking about!" I yelled back.

"Kathren! You need to stop it!" He called me Kathren. He never called me by my full name. I took this change to mean he was really upset.

"Stop what, Joseph! I really have no clue what you're talking about. What am I doing?"

"I asked you to go to your room tonight," he said.

"You were serious?" I fumed at him. "Like you're my dad, for real, now?"

"Why are you hooking up with Noah? You don't even know him."

"Why do you care? Isn't that what these little get-togethers are all about— hooking up with people we don't know? I didn't know you the first time we hooked up! And for that matter, why are you hooking up with that Kendra girl? Do you know her?"

"Yes! I do know her!" His brow tightened. "Sort of."

"So what's wrong with Noah?" I asked.

"Nothing! Nothing's wrong with him!"

"So what's the problem?" I took a step forward, standing in his space.

"What do you want, Kat? You want to be fucked? Is that what this is about?"

"Maybe— or maybe I want to meet a nice guy. Maybe it's that simple."

"You want to be fucked? I can fuck you, Kat." He moved closer, his stance was invading, almost cornering me, although I was in the middle of the room. "Is that why you're trying to work me up with your outfit and..."

"My outfit? I'm in yoga pants and a tank!"

"Do you know how fucking hot you look in yoga pants and a tank?" he asked, looking at me with hunger in his eyes. "Then you're over there making out with Noah, trying to make me..."

"Make you what?" He was jealous! I couldn't believe it. He stopped himself, but I knew that's what he was going to say. He narrowed his eyes, anger and desire pouring out of him in an intense mixture.

"You're frustrating the shit out of me, Kat." he sighed. "I'm trying to control it. I'm trying to keep things— Fuck it!" He grabbed me and kissed me hard, scooping me up into his arms. I threw my arms around his neck and kissed him back. Our tongues battled for position. He yanked my tank top up and off in one motion, letting it rip through our touching lips. I tried to unbutton his shirt as he dragged my pants down my thighs.

"Get the fuck over here!" he said, pulling me to the bed, almost dragging me. He pushed me onto my stomach and yanked my panties off. He ripped his shirt off, unzipped his pants and without taking the time to pull his pants down he pulled his rock-hard cock from his jeans and pushed into me from behind. I gasped loudly and grabbed the sheets with my fists. He wiped my hair out of his way, licking and biting my neck and the back of my shoulder as he thrust in and out of me, violently. He felt so good: his mouth, his hands, his cock. It was exactly what I wanted and everything I needed. I moaned and squealed as he moved. He grunted and cursed under his breath.

"Ah fuck—Kat!" He was as desperate for me as I was for him. I could feel it and hear it in his voice and his moans. The headboard was hitting the wall. We didn't care. We were making noise and possibly alerting everyone in the house, but it didn't matter...we were in the moment. He slid his hand under me, and rubbed my clit, as he fucked me. And that was all it took to send me over the top. Within seconds I was coming. Then a few seconds later, so was he.

"Damn it! You drive me fucking crazy," he said, laying on top of me.

"What do you think you do to me?" I mumbled between breaths. After a minute, he rose slowly and stood. He tucked himself back into his jeans and found his shirt on the floor. I turned over and laid on my side. He looked down at me, still labored a little. It was quick and hostile. There was no soft and tender this time and that was fine with me. I loved the aggression and need of his actions. It made me want to beg him to do it again.

"I wasn't going to do that," he puffed.

"Why? We've already had sex... many times. Why not now?"

"I just don't want things to be confused."

"What do you mean— confused?"

"I better go back downstairs," he said, avoiding my question.

"But..." I wanted to ask questions and understand what he meant, but I didn't. I let him go. "Okay. Goodnight then."

He walked out buttoning his shirt and closed the door behind him. I pulled the sheet down and slipped my feet underneath and then pulled it up to my chest. While I laid there it occurred to me that I hadn't seen Mason all night. I wasn't sure if he was in his room or if he had left the house. He wasn't a fan of Joseph's get togethers, but I was surprised he didn't come find me to talk. I thought about checking on him, but I wasn't going into that room. I closed my eyes and drifted off, tired from the charge from Joseph.

Chapter 10

THE NEXT MORNING I came down stairs and found Mason sitting in the kitchen. He was at the table, with his head resting on his hands, a cup of coffee in front of him.

"Hey! Everything okay?" I asked, walking in, heading straight for the coffee.

"Morning. Sorry I didn't come to find you last night. I took a bottle of Bourbon into the bedroom with me and somehow— half the bottle evaporated. I don't remember how that happened."

I laughed. "Yeah, You looked exhausted. You look better today. That Bourbon probably helped you drown out the party last night, so you could get some sleep." I sat across from him and blew on my coffee. "Seen Joseph this morning?"

"I think he's still here. Some girl just left about thirty minutes ago. She came from upstairs. His entertainment from last night, I suppose." He said it, while getting up to pour another cup for himself, so he didn't notice the look on my face. The look was disgust and annoyance . I knew Joseph and I were not a couple, but he felt the need to fuck someone after being with me. It was the kind of thing Mark would have done, but not Joseph. Even when Mark was alive and the parties were wild, Joseph would pick a woman and have fun, but he didn't typically do two in one night, unless it was a threesome. Mason sat down and looked at me.

"Did you join the party last night?"

"Not really. I came down for some food. But I didn't linger." I didn't feel it was necessary to tell him about Noah.

"I've been thinking." Mason said, looking serious. "I think I'm going to go home soon."

"What? Already?" I was surprised by Mason's announcement. "When?"

"This week. I'm looking at flights."

"Why? I mean, I know you can't stay forever, but I thought you were going to stay till you found Mark."

"Yeah. I was. But it finally occurred to me—what if we never do?" he said. "What if he's never found?" I didn't know what to say. I just looked at him with sympathy. "Joseph needs his house back. He's been great letting me stay here, but I know I'm dragging him down and I don't want to be a burden."

"I'm sure you're not a burden, Mason. He's worried about Mark too." My mouth twitched as the guilt took hold.

"I've got to get back to my life. I hate to say it— but I know he's dead. How does being here change anything? Detective Casteel can call me in California if he finds anything. I mean, I can't do anything."

"I'm so sorry, Mason. I really am so sorry." He was right. There was nothing he could do.

"Good morning," Joseph called, coming into the kitchen. He walked over to the coffee and took a cup from the cabinet. He poured a cup and leaned on the counter, facing us.

"Morning Joe. Sleep well?" Mason asked.

"I did. Thanks," he said, sipping his coffee. I rolled my eyes, doubting he had done much sleeping at all. "Morning Kat."

"Morning." I avoided looking at him.

"Everything okay?" he asked.

"I was just telling Kathren I'm thinking of heading back to California this week."

"Really?" Joe asked. "You know you can stay as long as you want, right man?"

"I know. And I appreciate it, but I'm pulling my hair out here. At least at home I have distractions, and like I was telling Kathren, they can call me if anything happens in the investigation."

"That's true. Well, I hate to see ya go, but I understand," Joseph told him, calmly. I looked up at Joseph, as I sipped my coffee. His eyes were on me already.

"What about you, Kathren?" Mason asked. I turned my attention to him.

"What? What about me?" I asked, sitting my cup on the table.

"How long are you staying?" I darted my gaze back and forth between Joseph and Mason. I didn't know what to say. I didn't want to overstay my welcome and Joseph hadn't said much about my situation.

"Um—Not sure. I'm thinking maybe through tomorrow."

"You're going home tomorrow. What are you going to do about protection?" Mason was concerned. I couldn't read Joseph.

"Well, like you said, I can't stay here forever. At some point I need to go home. What's the difference between two days or four? I've thought about getting an alarm and camera system. And of course the police are watching." I looked over at Joseph, who was busy picking at something on his shirt. His lack of interest agitated me and I blurted out, "As a matter of fact, I may go home tonight. I miss my house." Joseph looked up. He opened his mouth, as if he were going to speak, but he didn't say anything.

"I was hoping you'd stay a couple more days, so we could spend some time together before I leave," Mason said.

"Maybe we could meet for dinner before you go," I offered.

"Yeah. I'd love that," he said. I waited to see if Joseph would give me the same offer as he gave Mason, that I didn't have to rush off, but he just stood there, studying his coffee cup, as if it was a new object he'd never seen before. I could tell he was intentionally ignoring me. I got up and took my cup to the sink. I splashed the remains into the sink and rinsed it. I looked over my shoulder, at Joseph. He looked back at me and I rolled my eyes. I told Mason to have a good day and let me know when he was leaving, before exiting the kitchen.

Later that night, I gathered my things and headed home. I searched for Joseph to thank him for having me over, but he was gone. I didn't want to be rude and leave without thanking him, so I left a note. It was quick and polite. I left it on his bar, the place I knew he would see it and I headed out.

AS I APPROACHED MY front door, I felt a small twinge in my stomach. I was a little nervous to go in. I didn't expect to find someone there, but I was scared that I might find something suspicious, alluding to the fact that someone had been inside while I was gone. I just wanted my home to go back to being my safe place, a place of privacy and comfort. I started to put the key into the lock when a noise startled me. I looked toward Linda's house and was relieved to see Paul, Linda's husband. He was taking the garbage to the street. I waved as he looked over at me. He threw his hand up, as if it was the most friendliness he could possibly muster. Paul had never been friendly. He kept to himself and from the stories Linda had told, I was glad he did. He didn't seem like a person I would want to waste a minute of my time on. I was glad I saw him, though. I would have forgotten it was trash day tomorrow.

When I walked in, the house was dark. I flipped the light switch and surveyed the area. Nothing looked out of place. I walked around the house and checked all the windows and the back door. Everything seemed to be unbothered. Thank God. As I showered, I quickly poked my head out the shower curtain twice, thinking I might have heard something. Every noise made me shudder. I was acutely aware of everything: the fridge kicking on, creeks in the attic, which had been a normal thing for years, dogs barking in the distance. I got out of the shower and wrapped myself in my terrycloth robe. I walked to the kitchen, got a water bottle, and checked my locks one last time, making sure the chain was on. After reading on the couch for a while, I retreated to my bedroom, changed into my night shirt, and slid under my covers. I laid awake for about an hour, before finally drifting off. It was upsetting that I felt so on edge in my own home.

A couple days went by with no incidents. I had never been so glad to be bored. It was a few nights later when Mason called. He was booked on a flight home later in the week and wanted to have dinner. I agreed and offered to cook. He wanted to take me out, but I insisted he allow me to do this for him. After a little begging, he agreed. Luckily, I had shopped the night before and had several options. I decided on a chicken and broccoli casserole that my mom had shown me how to make, years ago. I had perfected it and felt confident he'd enjoy it. I baked garlic bread and made a big salad. I had a case of beer and a couple bottles of red wine chilling in the fridge.

I was pulling the casserole from the oven when Mason knocked on the door. I opened to see the spitting image of Mark, staring back at me. His hair was pulled back into a tight bun. His facial hair was cut and clean. He was wearing a black dress shirt and black slacks. He reminded me of Mark, the night we first slept together, after my work Christmas party. He took my breath away for a few seconds and then I composed myself and invited him in.

"Evening," he said, crossing the threshold and pulling a red rose from behind his back.

"Thank you. How sweet." I took the rose and kissed him on the cheek. "Can I get you a drink?"

"Sure. Wine would be great," he said, noticing the bottle on the table. I had already started. I poured him a glass and took mine from the kitchen counter. I took a sip and sat it on the table, near my plate. I placed the casserole in the middle of the table, next to a plate of warm bread and then retrieved the salad from the fridge.

"Can I serve you?" I asked. He agreed and I put a small helping of everything on his plate and then mine.

"This looks great." He placed his napkin in his lap and took a fork full of his salad. He ate and commented several times on how delicious everything was.

"So... Leaving us in a few days, huh?" I asked, rhetorically. "I hate that we met under these circumstances."

"Me too," he said, taking the last swallow of his wine. I poured another half glass for him, without asking. "I wanted to apologize to you."

"For what?" I asked.

"That day— when I came out of my room in the towel... and then without the towel."

"You've apologized, already, for that," I told him, blushing from the thought of his nakedness.

"Yeah, but another one is warranted. I was feeling sad and a bit desperate for affection. Plus, I really like you, Kathren. I wish we had met differently, as well. If I met you somewhere else, I would love to...well, whatever." He spooned more of the casserole onto his plate and took another bite.

"I'm glad you're enjoying my cooking," I said.

"I am. Beautiful, sweet and a great cook? Man... Mark should have married you." There was an awkward silence. He knew the remark made me uncomfortable. We both sipped our wine, feeling the tension in the air. "Sorry," he said, solemnly.

"It's okay."

"Did you ever cook for him?"

"A few times."

Mason looked thoughtful and then asked, "Can I ask you—What was it about Mark?"

"What do you mean?" I tilted my head, surprised by the question.

"He's my brother and I love him, but I never understood why the women flocked to him the way they do. He's good looking, I'll give you that, but—well, he was never faithful— like ever."

"Yeah, that's true, but he was honest about it. I don't know about how he behaved with other women, but he was very upfront with me. He even told me that he didn't think he was good for me, because I was so— well, sweet, I guess. He was like, 'This is who I am. Take it or leave it.'"

"So, why did you take it?" he asked.

"Have you seen him?" I puffed. That caused us both to chuckle. "Seriously though, he was— is... He *is* gorgeous. And he has a way about him—the way he carries himself—so much confidence—so much charisma. He was smooth—mysterious even. He had a way of looking at me and I swear I would just melt. He knew what he wanted, but if you weren't willing to give it to him and give it the way he wanted it, he was happy to move on. No sweat off his back, ya know. Kind of like, there's a million women out there, so I don't need you, but I'm choosing you, so that makes you special. You couldn't really play games with him or manipulate him. And this might be too much info, but he knew his way around a woman's body. It was like he had a masters in sex and..." Suddenly, I realized I was saying too much. Mason stared at me; his cheeks flushed his mouth slightly open. "Sorry."

"No. Don't apologize. I asked." He took a deep breath and downed the remainder of his wine. "So, all that made you okay with sharing him with other women?"

"No. I was never okay with it. That's why we eventually went our separate ways." A lie, of course.

"What about the other?" he asked, hesitantly.

"The other?"

"Joseph. He and Joseph. I know they shared..."

"Yeah. Well, That was— let's just say, Mark was very good at making things seem normal that weren't normal."

"So, you did sleep with both of them?" he asked. I looked down. "I'm not judging. I swear. I just— I don't get it."

"I was not into the idea, at first. Not at all! It caused our first fight, actually. Mark had told me he was different— not into monogamy, but the first night I met Joseph, he didn't warn me about their... well, their lifestyle. Joseph came on to me and I was surprised and super offended. I demanded Mark take me home and then, when I realized Mark didn't care, not only did he not care, but he knew Joseph was making a move that night, I was livid. But then, one night, we were all at Joseph's, just the three of us and—well, it just happened." I took another long sip of my wine. I realized I was telling Mason more than I planned, again.

"How does that just happen?" he asked. I looked at him. *Was he wanting details?* "I just can't imagine how they would go about starting something like that with a woman like you."

"I guess saying it just happened isn't accurate. It took quite a bit of talking. Coaxing is more like it. And of course, drinking and then almost begging, on his part. It wasn't all of a sudden. Mark kind of worked toward it, in conversations we had. And they both made it seem like it just wasn't a big deal. Just three friends having a fun night... making eachother feel good. Just sex."

"And was it that easy? Was it ... just sex?"

"No! Not at all," I said, scoffing at the thought. "It was very uncomfortable for me, the first time. I was terrified, to be honest. But they were slow and careful with me and... well, it happened."

Mason stared at me for a moment and then asked, "And did you... like it?" I just looked at him. "I'm sorry. I'm just curious. I've always been curious about how Mark got women to... Well, forget it."

"Yes." I answered, after a few seconds. He looked at me, sort of surprised. "I did. I was actually shocked the first time that I enjoyed it as much as I did. I felt ashamed too, though. I was confused. But, after a while, I began to feel comfortable with both of them and developed feelings with Joseph too."

"I see."

"I know this is all so crazy. Does this all sound awful to you?" I asked.

"Not awful. I've just always wanted the woman I'm with all to myself, ya know?"

"I know. That's how I always felt. It's still how I feel. Mark and Joseph were the only two I ever felt comfortable with, in that way. I never wanted to have sex with other men and I didn't want Mark to sleep with other women, but I got used to it. Plus, when Mark was gone with some other girl, I had Joseph to keep me company." I realized I was confiding my feelings about Mark more than I had and I quickly backtracked. "The thing was, because of all the sharing and multiple partners, I never fell in love with Mark. He kept a distance between us. That's why, when you suggested that we were very close, it threw me. I mean, sexually yes, sometimes...but emotionally—no!"

"I see." He looked uncomfortable. He poured more wine and stood up. He slowly wandered around my living room, looking at pictures and trinkets I had sitting around. I filled my glass and stood up, too. He was holding a picture in his hand.

"My parents."

He smiled and sat the picture back down. "They look happy."

"They are," I said. "Very. And they are wonderful parents."

"That's good." He looked around a little more and then sat on the sofa. I sat down next to him. We were quiet for a minute. He looked like he wanted to say something, but he was hesitant.

"I will miss you when I leave," he said, finally, turning to look at me.

"I'm going to miss you too." I reached out and rubbed his forearm. "We can keep in touch, you know?"

"I'd like that. It's kind of bothering me, how much I like you." I didn't know how to respond. I could feel his anxious energy. He wanted me. The thought of sleeping with him crossed my mind. He was leaving soon and he was very good looking, but his resemblance to Mark and the secret of what happened wouldn't allow me to do it. I smiled and told him I liked him too.

"I really hope you find Mark soon."

"Me too. I miss him." He looked down, staring at his lap. I put my hand on his shoulder.

"I know you do. I'm so sorry you're dealing with this."

"Kathren, would it be crazy if I asked... to stay with you, tonight?" he asked, lifting his eyes from his lap to meet mine.

The request took me by surprise. "Um—I don't think..."

"I'm not talking about sex! Seriously! It's just, I'm leaving soon and this will be the last time we're together. I just want to be close to you for a while. Not sex! I just want to spend more time with you before I go and honestly, with everything going on, it would just be nice to feel some human contact."

How could I say no? I knew it was not a good idea to lay in bed with him. The risk of something happening between us was there, but how could I deny him. He was not asking for sex. He was asking for human contact. He was asking me to comfort him. I killed his brother and he was suffering. "Sure. As long as it's clear. We're not..."

"I know. No sex." He smiled. A look of anticipation moved across his face.

We talked a while longer; he helped me clean up from dinner and soon it was bedtime. I was nervous. I showed him to my room and grabbed some modest pajamas, a tee shirt and loose-fitting pajama bottoms. I went to the bathroom to change, brushed my teeth, and pulled my hair up in a scrunchy. I hoped I was not giving off sexy vibes. You never really know with men. Anything could be a turn on. I exited the bathroom and let him go in. I let him know I had a brand-new toothbrush in the drawer if he wanted to use it.

"Thanks. That would be great," he said, as he closed the door. I hit the light switch, leaving only a dim light on my nightstand, and quickly slipped under the covers. He was in the bathroom for a while before finally coming out with nothing but his gray boxer briefs. He stood there holding his clothes folded neatly in his hands. His hair was hanging loose, and he was covered in tattoos, even a tiger crawling up his left thigh. *Damn it!* He looked sexy, as hell. I could see the outline of his dick through his boxers. I tried not to look. He put his clothes on my dresser and went to the other side of the bed.

"May I?" he asked, pointing to the bed.

"Of course," I said. He pulled back the sheet and blanket and slid into bed beside me. I looked over at him awkwardly, and said, "Well, goodnight." I reached over to the lamp and hit the switch. The room went dark as he scooched close to me. I adjusted myself, trying to get comfortable. It wasn't easy since I felt so tense lying next to him—in the quiet—in the dark. His skin was warm through the thin fabric of my night clothes.

"Good night, Kathren," he whispered snuggling close. "Is this okay?" he asked, wrapping his arm around my waist.

I laid on my back and turned my face away from him. I put my hand over his arm and whispered, "It's fine." His chin was against my shoulder and I could feel his breath on my neck. I was hoping he would just lay still. Any friction was sure to stir my desires since I was already struggling to keep dirty thoughts out of my mind. My breath was shaky and I tried to calm it. The sound of both of us breathing was so loud in the room. He smelled good. *Just go to sleep, Kathren'* I kept telling myself. I was wide awake, though. His arm moved slightly across my stomach and as it did my shirt lifted a bit, exposing a small area of flesh. Minutes passed with nothing else. His breathing was steady. I began to calm, thinking he may have fallen asleep. Then he moved his leg, wrapping it around mine, pulling it toward him, causing my legs to spread apart. I still couldn't tell if he was sleeping. His groin was against my hip and I could feel his dick. It wasn't hard. I wanted to turn on my side facing away from him, but then his dick would be against my ass and that would be a problem, so I laid still. Minutes passed again, before his arm moved, causing his hand to lay across my stomach and his pinky finger to touch my skin, just below my belly button. Just that tiny bit of flesh connecting was sending jolts of electricity between my thighs. I could feel my muscles begin to contract inside and was getting wet, already. It is almost aggravating how your mind can want one scenario so definitely. You feel so strongly that you don't want anything to happen. You know the consequences are not worth it, but just the tiniest touch...a slight movement, flesh on flesh can confuse everything temporarily and in that moment... you don't give a shit and you just want to come!

I took a deep breath and tried to sound as if I was sleeping. Surely, he wouldn't molest me while I sleep. But, over the next few minutes, it became clear to me that he was awake. His fingers were moving. It was very slow and methodical.. If you were sleeping you would never notice it, but my senses were so heightened, every millimeter felt like an inch. First there was one finger on my skin, moments later there were two and then three; his pinky was starting to move under my pajama bottoms gently and slowly.

I stayed still, trying hard to appear asleep, but I was tingling inside. I wasn't sure what to do. I didn't want to sleep with him, but my body was going in a different direction, completely. If I allowed him to make his way under my panties, he would know I was awake. There was no way I'd be that wet while sleeping. After a few more minutes, he cleared his throat, and shifted his body. As he did, he pulled my leg closer to him, opening my thighs further and slid his hand lower on my stomach, letting more of his fingers go under the cotton pajamas. The tips of his fingers were on the edge of my panties, now. I wondered if he suspected that I was awake. My clit was pulsing, by now and my body had shut my brain off. I didn't care about anything. I just wanted to feel his fingers between my folds. I wanted to come. My right arm was pinned against him, with my fist closed. I opened my hand letting my fingers slide between my hip and his dick. I felt him twitch as my fingers brushed across the shaft. I made one more slight move with my index finger, stroking it against his rising erection. His fingers inched down, lower, still slowly, touching the hair at the mound of my throbbing, wet pussy. I slowly turned my left leg out, opening up even more. His dick was hard now and he pushed it into my hand. I still pretended to sleep. I couldn't make the obvious first move.

It was a silly game that we were playing, both of us awake, pretending to sleep, while we touched each other. But, then his fingers slipped completely under my panties and his index and middle finger slid between my flesh. I couldn't help it, I gasped, and the game was over. He began to move his finger up and down in a slow circle over my clit. He moaned, as he realized I was soaked. I moved my hand against his cock and he thrusted his hips, encouraging me to stroke him. His fingers felt so good, I couldn't stop it. I was exploding with shockwaves of pleasure as he wiggled his squeezed my clit and circled his fingers around. Then he leaned in and his mouth was on my collarbone, kissing me. His cock was out of his boxers now and in my palm. I moved my hand up and down slowly and then faster, occasionally rubbing my thumb over the head. My wetness poured out of me and I quivered from the waves of sensation bringing me toward climax. My hips began to thrust against his touch and it only took a few more minutes and I was coming. I jerked and squeezed my legs together, his hand still moving as I convulsed. I didn't scream out or even moan, I just panted hard and pulled at my pillow. I continued to stroke him as he fucked my hand and came a minute later. He moaned and his leg shook as he ejaculated, shooting repeatedly.

We laid quiet for a minute and then Mason started to say something, but I stopped him. I put my finger over his lips before he could utter a word. I didn't want to talk about it. I wanted it to be as if it never happened. It was one of those things. All the sensibility and reasoning was gone, while we laid there in the dark. It was almost like masturbation. He started to pull my shirt up, but I stopped him. I didn't want to fuck him or kiss him. I wanted to go to sleep and erase it from my mind. Really, I wanted to erase it from reality because I knew it would never leave my mind. I told him I didn't want to have sex and I was clear. He started it, knowing I didn't want to do it, but sometimes arousal takes away common sense and that is what had happened.

"Are we okay?" he whispered.

"It's okay, Mason." I couldn't see his face in the dark, but I could tell by his voice he was concerned that I was upset. "I promise it's fine." I rubbed my hand across his arm and we both fell asleep.

"Kathren, wake up!" Mason said, gently rocking my leg. I opened my eyes. The sun was shining through the edge of the blinds and Mason was sitting on the edge of the bed, looking at me. He was fully dressed. I turned to face him, rubbing the sleep from my eyes. "I need to get going."

"Oh, okay. Can I make breakfast or anything?" I offered, rising to a sitting position.

"Oh, no thanks. That's sweet of you, but I need to go."

"Okay. I understand." We stood and walked to the living room. There was an awkward silence as we stood by the door. "Well, I'm glad you came for dinner."

"Me too," he said, sliding his hands into his pockets. "I'm really glad we got to spend some time together before I leave."

"Me too."

"Dinner was great."

"Thank you. I'm glad you enjoyed it." I smiled.

"Can we talk about last night?"

"There's nothing to talk about," I told him, shifting uncomfortably.

"You don't think so?"

"No. Honestly, I feel like we are attracted to each other, we were both drinking and tired and... something happened."

"Something?" He raised his brow.

"Yes. Sometimes when a man and woman are laying close, in the dark, things can happen— even if you didn't intend for it to." I swallowed hard. I didn't want to talk about it. I didn't want it to mean anything.

"Well, I'm sorry if it made things weird. I didn't mean to cause..."

"You caused nothing." I said, cutting him off. "You don't need to be sorry. It's not weird. We're okay. It happened. We were both there. It felt nice. It's okay. We don't need to discuss it."

He nodded and looked toward the door, then back at me. "Can I still call you sometime?" he asked.

"Of course. Anytime." I smiled. I felt like he wanted to hug me, but felt unsure. So, I reached out and wrapped my arms around him. He pulled his hands from his pockets and hugged me back. He squeezed me tight and held on until I let go. I took one more long look at his face, the face that looked so much like Mark that it hurt to look at him, sometimes. A face I would never see again. He stared back and then opened the door.

"Take care, Kathren. Be safe."

"You too," I said. He sighed, gave me a tight smile, and walked out. I stood in the open door and watched as he walked to his car. I waved as he gave me one more look, before getting in. I closed the door before he drove away.

Chapter 11

IT WAS A WEEK LATER when I was summoned to the police station again. I was just leaving work and Detective Casteel called me, asking me to come in. I agreed and drove over, nervously. *What will it be about this time?* I considered the idea that they might have found the body.

I went in and walked to the counter. I was told to sit and wait for the Detective. I sat on the bench near the counter and after about thirty minutes, I heard the door in the corner open. It was the same door I walked through last time when I was called in to talk. I looked over, instinctively, hoping it would be him, finally, but when I looked, I was horrified. Standing there, in the doorway, was Detective Casteel, still in conversation with a man who he was walking out. His back was to me, but I recognized him, the large stature, the long dirty blonde hair, and the biker clothing. It was Rex. I dropped my head and turned away, praying he would not see me. I could hear the voice— that eerie voice. It was deep and gravelly, as if he needed to clear his throat. I wanted to shrink away and hide. I wanted to run. There were many people in the lobby of the station at that moment, so I hoped he wouldn't notice me, but as the detective said goodbye to Rex, he called out to me.

"Ms. Thompson!" His voice carried through the room, like a bullhorn. Rex didn't know my last name and probably wouldn't remember my first, as far as I knew, but he still looked to see who the detective was speaking to and as I looked up my eyes met his. I felt sick. Luckily, this time, I was able to control the vomit, but seeing him face to face for the first time after that night— It was like being stabbed in the gut. It felt like a hand had gripped around my throat and I couldn't breathe. He glared at me, as he walked by. His expression was hard and he looked like he was possibly just as unsettled to see me, as I was to see him. He stared for several seconds, before looking forward and pushing through the glass front doors of the police station. I stood up and watched as he walked down the walkway to the parking lot. I knew he recognized me. I was sure of it.

"Ms. Thompson!" Casteel called a second time. I was so disturbed by seeing my attacker that I completely forgot, for a moment, why I was there. I was being interviewed by the detective. I turned to see Detective Casteel watching me, intently. He held the door and gestured for me to come in. I quickly shook off what I was feeling and walked toward the door and entered the hall. I stopped and looked at Casteel, waiting for him to direct me.

"Everything alright, Ms. Thompson?" he asked. "You look a bit shaken."

"I'm fine." I smiled. He guided me to the same room we went to before. He offered me coffee or water. I took him up on the water since my throat had gone dry after seeing Rex. After retrieving the water, he closed the door and sat across from me, just like last time.

"Are you sure you're alright?" he asked again.

"Yes. I'm fine." I blinked several times and tried to keep a pleasant expression on my face. He just looked at me, for a minute. I stared back. I took a sip of my water, cleared my throat, and folded my hands on the edge of the table. I wondered if Rex had been sitting in this very spot moments earlier. The thought made me shiver, like I caught a chill.

"You seemed to remember Mr. Holt, out there."

"Mr. Holt?"

"Oh, I'm sorry. Rex!" he clarified. "I noticed that you both seem to recognize each other."

"I did. I remember seeing him at Joseph's house before." I was getting better at lying calmly, although the statement wasn't a total lie.

" Ms. Thompson, you seemed very bothered when I mentioned him last time you were here and then today... Well, you seemed bothered, again. Is there something about Mr. Holt, you're not telling me?" He leaned forward and folded his arms on the table.

"No, there isn't. Honestly, he always gave me a bad feeling when I was around him, and when I saw him here, the same night you called me in—I thought maybe I was going to hear bad news. Mark's brother told me about Mark's truck being found and I thought you were going to tell me that you found him...and that he was..."

"Deceased? No. We haven't located Mark Sanders yet."

"Oh, well that's good," I said. "Well, when I saw Rex walking out, I thought maybe you were telling him you found Mark and you were questioning him."

"Is there a reason you would expect us to question Rex about Mark's disappearance?"

"Only that I know he hung around with Mark and like I said, he gave me a bad feeling." I sighed a deep shaky breath.

"I see. So, how have things been at home? Any more disturbances?"

"No. Thank God. It's been quiet for several days," I told him.

"Good. Glad to hear it. Well, the reason I asked you to come in tonight is we wanted to get a DNA sample, if you'd be willing," he said.

"DNA? From me? Why?"

"We are asking everyone who knows him. We did get some DNA from his truck. Not much, mind you, it was under water. But, we also got some prints from his house and we just wanted to rule people out."

"Rule people out?" I asked.

"Yes. We want to know who was in his truck and if we have DNA and fingerprints we can't place... well this is just part of our investigation. We're just trying to figure out what happened to the guy. Can you help us out, Ms. Thompson?"

"How will you get the sample?"

"Just a simple finger print and cheek swab," he said, standing up. He opened the door and asked someone in the hall if they could have Ms. Whitmore come in. Moments later a short older woman came in with a caddy. "We really appreciate your help, Ms. Thomson."

"Kathren." I reminded him, before opening my mouth for the swab."

"Of course— Kathren." After the swab, they took the fingerprints.

AFTER LEAVING THE STATION, I thought about heading to Joseph's house. I wanted to talk to him. He hadn't reached out to me since I left his house, which was upsetting me. We had slept together the night before and twice the week before. I needed him to explain why he was being so weird.

Suddenly, my thoughts were disrupted, as I became aware that there were lights behind me, turning every time I turned. *Was I crazy? Was it Rex?* I focused on the lights. I definitely wasn't going home. I wasn't going to lead someone to my house. I made a point to turn and turn again. The car turned every time. It had to be him! I wouldn't lead him to Joseph's house either. Even if this was Rex, I wasn't going to make the connection between me and Joseph and risk putting him in danger. I made my way back to the police station. I slowed down ten miles under the speed limit. He didn't pass me. He was definitely following me. When I got to the station and turned into the lot, the car finally drove on. I tried to turn and look at the car as it went by—light color, white, maybe gray, a midsize car. I couldn't identify it. I circled the lot and pulled back out. I drove around town for twenty minutes, watching my rearview mirror, till I finally decided I was safe. I felt certain, so I headed home.

I pulled into my driveway and sat in the car for a minute. I wondered if the police were still patrolling. I hadn't noticed any in the last few days. A light coming from Linda's house caught my attention. It was Linda standing in the door. The brightness from inside her house was shining out, from behind her. I opened the car door and got out. I waved and she waved back. I decided to walk over and speak to her. I realized, at that moment, that I hadn't seen her in a while.

"Hey! Long time no see," I said, as she stepped out onto her front porch.

"Hi. I know. I've been so busy." I noticed she turned and pulled the door so that it was cracked, but not closed. She almost seemed nervous.

"You want to come over for some coffee?" I asked, not wanting to go in alone.

"Oh thanks, but I can't. If I drink coffee this late I'll never get to sleep."

"Some tea then— or water."

"Sorry, I've got a cake in the oven. I'm just waiting for it to finish and then I'm off to bed."

"Oh— okay. Maybe some other time," I said, pretending not to notice her strange behavior. She kept looking over her shoulder, into the house, nervously. "Is everything okay, Linda?"

"Fine. Absolutely fine." She smiled, but clearly something was wrong. I didn't want to push.

"Okay, well if you want to talk..."

"Yes. Some other time. Have a nice night, Kathren," she said, stepping back into the door.

"You too," I said, out of her earshot, as I turned and walked back across the yard.

My house was dark. I really didn't want to go in. I looked around, as I put the key in the lock. I stepped in and hit the light switch, quickly. The house lit up and I scanned from one side to the other. Everything seemed okay. I quickly locked and chained the door behind me and checked all the other locks. After turning almost every light in the house on and checking all the rooms, I grabbed a wine glass from the cabinet and poured a tall, sleep-inducing glass of red. I sat at the table and thought about my crazy day, a DNA test, fingerprints, Rex possibly following me, Linda acting so strange. Maybe she had noticed how dismissive I was of her sometimes and had had enough of my rudeness. *Could that be it? I couldn't blame her if it was. And was Joseph ever going to call me again? Was he even thinking of me or was he just home enjoying his wild parties and having sex with lots of women?* Then I thought of Mason. I hoped he had gotten home okay and that he was doing alright. I drank my wine and went to bed, hoping to have a quiet uneventful night and thankfully I did.

A few nights later though, I wasn't so lucky. It was a Friday night and I was home. I sat on the couch reading a book. The house was dark, except for the lamp next to me, giving me enough light to read. I was deep in the story, when I heard a noise in the back of the house. I lowered my book, sat up and turned my head toward the back sliding door. The curtain was closed, so I couldn't see out and no one could see in, but I glared at the curtains, anyway. I sat still and quiet for a minute, waiting for another sound. It was quiet. I laid the book on the sofa next to me and stood. I tiptoed to the door as if my steps would be heard outside. My whole body was rigid. I was afraid to pull the curtain back, thinking I would see someone standing on the other side of the glass. I took a deep breath and gripped the edge of the curtain. I pulled back fast. The sound of the rings sliding across the rod screeched. I shivered, as I stared out into the darkness, realizing it was too dark for me to see anything, but someone could definitely see me. I wondered if there was someone out there glaring at me, at that moment. Maybe they were standing there, just a few feet out of my view, smirking at the look of fear on my face.

I flicked the light switch up, to light up the back porch, but it didn't come on. I wiggled it up and down and when I accepted that the light wasn't going to come on, I quickly closed the curtain and moved away from the door. I folded my arms around myself and rubbed the chill bump that had raised on my arms. Suddenly, I heard a noise outside the side of the house, to my left. It was the area between Linda's house and mine. It sounded like movement, someone shuffling through the grass. The window's on that side of the house had blinds that were closed. I stood still, now looking back and forth from the dining room window to the kitchen. I moved to the front door that was locked and stood against it, my back pressed against the cold wood. I could see into my whole house, from this position, except for the bathroom and bedrooms. I noticed my cell phone sitting on the coffee table.

I considered calling the police, but what if it was nothing? What if it was just an animal? It was so frustrating. The officers always acted as if it should be an easy choice, but it wasn't. I didn't want to deal with the glaring neighbors and underwhelmed, almost annoyed looks on the officers faces, as they walked around my empty house and yard, finding nothing— nothing but what looked to be either an overly paranoid woman or someone looking for attention. Of Course I didn't want anyone finding my dead body either... That would suck, significantly worse.

As time went by and nothing else happened, I began to calm down. I thought maybe it had been an animal. The problem was, things that wouldn't normally even cause a stir—now, they kept me on edge for hours. They disrupt my sleep. I stepped away from the door after a few minutes and stood in the middle of the space. I slowly looked around from door to window to window to door. It was quiet. There wasn't necessarily silence. Actually I was aware of every little noise outside and in, but they were normal sounds.

I picked up my cell and scrolled through my contacts. My finger stopped and hovered over Joseph's number. I took a deep, shaky breath and wondered if he would answer. And if he did, what would I say? *I need you? I'm scared? Please come over? Would he invite me over?* I wanted so badly to talk with him. It didn't have to be sexual or romantic between us, but he had always made me feel comfortable and secure. Now it was awkward and strange between us.

Then, right at that moment the phone rang, vibrating in my hand. It startled me and I almost dropped it. *Mason! It was Mason calling*! It was his first call since he had left for California. I cleared my throat and answered.

"Mason! Hi!" I tried to sound surprised and happy to hear from him.

"Hey Kathren. How are you?"

"Good. How was your flight home?"

"Good. Things are good. I'm back to work and it's good."

"That's wonderful to hear."

"Yeah. It's all...good. How is everything there? Are things... good?"

I noticed that the word good was being used quite a bit, already, which made me think things were *not good*. "It's okay. I've just been working and spending a lot of time at home, relaxing," I told him.

"Have things been quiet at your house as far as the break ins?"

"Yes. So far."

"And have you—seen Joe, lately?" he asked, almost hesitantly. I got the distinct impression he wanted the answer to be *no*.

"I haven't. Not since you left." I was pretty sure I heard a sigh of relief. Why he cared, seemed silly to me. He was a couple thousand miles away and it wasn't like I gave him any indication that we could have a relationship. Well, not in my mind, but maybe our quick frolic in my bed had him thinking there was hope. I chatted with him for a few more minutes. I didn't want to jump off too quickly. That would just be rude. I asked him if he'd spoken to Det. Casteel any since he'd been home. He had. Casteel let him know about the DNA testing. But, thankfully, Mason was told the same thing I was, that it was just to distinguish whose DNA and prints were whose and they expected to find mine. I found it odd, though, that they expected to find Rex's. I spent a lot of time with Mark, and except for one night, when I saw Rex having an uncomfortable talk with Joseph, the night he attacked me was the only other time I had ever seen him. And his name was never mentioned. They had taken Joseph's prints as well. That, I did expect. Mark and Joseph were best friends and spent tons of time together.

"Well, I would love to talk more, but I need to get to bed. I have an early morning. I still need to get a shower," I said, trying to sound truly disappointed to end the call.

"Oh, okay. I understand. I guess I did call a bit late." It was nine. It wasn't really late, but I agreed with him.

"Yeah. I'm so glad you called, though. It's good to hear your voice."

"You too," he replied and then after a short pause, "I miss you, Kathren."

I didn't know what to say. I didn't want to give him the wrong impression so I just chuckled and said playfully, "What? You miss me already? It's only been a week! You just saw me, silly!" Then I quickly said my good-byes, before he could try to get serious and talk about feelings he was having for me. He accepted my end to the conversation and stuttered a bit as he said "Good night, Kathren."

Chapter 12

THE FOLLOWING NIGHT, I was bored, out of my mind and felt the strong need to be around people. I had spent every day sitting alone at my desk, talking occasionally and briefly to my boss and I spent my nights completely alone, not including a couple trips to the grocery store. The excitement of my day, talking to the checkout lady about her work schedule, the weather, and her crazy poodle, who she loved like her child.

It was my usual life for the four months or so before Joseph contacted me. I didn't enjoy it then either, but I did have the morning and occasional evening visits from Linda. Those had suddenly stopped and I had no idea why. My sister Tammy usually called me weekly, but even that had slowed since she had met her newest boyfriend. Apparently, things were getting serious. The last time I spoke to her she had used the L word and that was something she never did. I didn't mind. I was happy for her and with everything going on in my life the last month, I was as distracted as she was.

I decided I needed some company. I was lonely and I just didn't feel comfortable calling Joseph, even though that's what I wanted to do more than anything. So I dressed up in a sexy, black dress— something sure to attract attention, I fixed my hair and makeup, and headed to Squirley's, Fairlawn's most popular bar. It was a busy Saturday night, but I found a seat at the bar, squeezed between a man and woman on one side, having a deep conversation, and a couple guys on the other, talking intensely about the latest sporting event they had seen. An obvious argument was happening over the final play of the game.

I ordered a Sea Breeze and after taking a large swallow, I turned on my stool to watch people on the dance floor. I always enjoyed watching people dance. Good or terrible, it was equally entertaining. I looked around the room, sipping my drink through the tiny straw. There were several cute guys, but most seemed to be talking to women already or engaged in talking with friends. Oddly enough, as the night went on, I felt more and more lonely. It's worse to feel lonely in a crowd of people than it is when you're home, alone. You expect to feel it then. It weighed on me that I didn't have any friends, not one friend that I could meet for a drink. I wasn't sure why that was. Was there something wrong with me? Usually, it didn't bother me. I liked keeping to myself. I liked to read and exercise. I enjoyed the quiet, but lately I was acutely aware of the solitude. Last year I had Frank. He always kept me company, but since he fell in love and moved away, I heard from him less and less. He didn't even call me to tell me about his conversation with the detective. After finishing my second drink, I was just about to call it a night and head home, when I heard a familiar voice.

"Come on now! You're not leaving already, are you?" I turned to find that the inhabitant of the stool next to me had changed and was now filled by a handsome man, who I recognized. It was Noah, the gorgeous man I had kissed at Joseph's party. There he sat, holding a beer, looking very hot in a tight black tee shirt and dark jeans. His perfectly straight teeth were sparkling through his gorgeous smile, and I thought he looked like a model in a toothpaste commercial. His body was perfect. His skin was perfect. He was almost too perfect looking? "I thought that was you," he said, leaning in close so I could hear him over the music.

"What are you doing here?" I asked, pleasantly surprised to see him. I was relieved to see a friendly face and his face was very nice to look at.

"Just meeting some friends for a beer. We are over there in the corner," he pointed to a small group of men around a pool table, "I kept looking over here, trying to figure out if it was you. I never got a chance to get your number that night. You disappeared on me." His smile wasn't just bright and perfect looking, it was sexy.

"Yeah, sorry about that." I didn't offer anything else. I wasn't about to tell him I disappeared because I fucked Joseph upstairs, or he fucked me, more accurately.

"Noah," he said, placing his fingers on his chest. "In case you forgot."

"I didn't. Kathren, in case you forgot," I said, offering the same reminder.

"I didn't." He smiled and took a swig of his beer. We sat quiet for a few seconds, smiling at each other. The silent connection was just what I was looking for. I felt a tingle roll over my body. "I like your dress."

"Thank you. I like your... shirt." I blushed, brought my drink to my mouth, and locked on to my straw, sipping nervously.

"You like my black tee shirt?" He brushed his hand down his chest and stomach, smoothing his shirt against his muscular frame. We both smiled and stared flirtatiously at each other. Noah ordered another drink and we talked and teased for another half hour or so, then he asked me if I wanted to leave the bar with him. I agreed.

"You want to come to my place? Is anyone waiting for you at home?" he asked, as we got to the parking lot.

"Right to the point, huh?" I smirked.

"Oh, I'm sorry. I thought you..."

"Why don't you follow me to mine?" I pulled my keys from my purse and gripped the fob. He smiled, looking relieved that I was thinking the same thing he was. He agreed and I jumped in my car and pulled out, Noah followed right behind me. My belly was doing flips as I drove, thinking about what was about to happen. I turned into my driveway and Noah parked his red sports car in the street.

As we went inside, I barely got the door closed and he was on me, kissing me, his hands groping me. I held on to his biceps, barely able to get my hands half way around his mass. He squeezed my ass and moved his mouth to my neck, biting and licking from my collarbone to my ear. He wasn't rough, but his strength didn't go unnoticed. His quick movements made it clear he was really anxious. I slid my hands down to his waist and began to pull his shirt up. I couldn't wait to see his amazing chest and when he reached to help me take it off, I wasn't disappointed. He was perfect; large smooth pecs sitting on top of a solid chiseled six pack. He reached for his belt, as he kissed me, but I grabbed his hands.

"Slow down," I whispered. I was a little overwhelmed by his intensity and wanted to take it just a bit slower. "Let's go to my bedroom?"

He took my hand and allowed me to lead him to my room. Once we were in the room, he started kissing my neck again and pulling my dress up. I let him strip me, removing my dress and then my strapless bra.

"You're so fucking gorgeous," he growled under heavy breathing.

"So are you," I replied.

I caressed his smooth torso, letting my fingers trace every muscle. Then I pinched at his nipples. His breathing intensified and he lifted me into the air, like I weighed nothing. His mouth was level with my breasts. His teeth grazed my nipples as he sucked and licked them. He moved me to the bed, so that I could stand on it, on display in front of him. He reached behind my legs stroking the back of my thighs, his fingers sliding in between, just barely under my panties, sending shockwaves through me. Then he reached up to my hips and hooked his fingers over the edges of my panties and pulled them down. His face was even with my tummy and he was kissing around my navel. He left one hand on the back of my thigh and reached around with his other, sliding his fingers between my folds and began to pet my clit. My knees buckled, but he wrapped his arm under my ass supporting me, as he fondled pussy. I wanted to collapse to the bed. Then suddenly, he stopped rubbing me and scooped me up in a way I'd never been lifted. Both of his arms went between my legs, spreading them as he hoisted me onto his shoulders, facing him, putting my pussy right in his face. I wobbled at first, my feet dangling behind him. I gasped and grabbed his head for balance. I couldn't believe what was happening. He was so incredibly strong. I reached up and put my palm against the ceiling for more support. Thank God my ceilings were high.

"Noah, what are you doing?" I whimpered. He didn't answer. He just held me there, high in the air, licking and sucking my clit. His hands were on my lower back and he was using his upper body strength to hold me, but I felt my weight shifting. It was hard to balance with his tongue moving against me, making me convulse. I thought he would drop me to the bed soon, since I had to be getting heavy, but he continued for several seconds. I'd never experienced anything like it, even after all the crazy things I had done with Mark. I didn't think I would be able to come, being held in that position, but he was good with his tongue and before I knew it, I felt the waves coming. That tingling and pulsing of muscle contractions that led to an explosion of orgasm.

"Oh my God!" I cried out. "Noah!" He continued until I began to jerk and smack at his back. I couldn't take it anymore. I thought I would fall. Then, he slowly lowered me to the bed and laid me back. I watched him as he removed his jeans. He was breathing heavily after that incredible workout and I was panting from the orgasm.

"Did you like that?" he asked.

"That was crazy!" I huffed. As he lowered his pants his huge cock sprung free, hard as a rock. He was very well hung and I felt slightly intimidated, but he was beautiful.

"I'm going to fill every inch of you. You ready?" he asked, taking a deep breath. I watched as his bulging pecs rose and fell.

"I'm not sure." I chuckled. He smiled. "Go easy with me."

He didn't realize how serious I was. He stroked his shaft a few times and then crawled on top of me. I spread my legs and raised my knees, allowing him to position himself. He reached down and took his dick in his hand, lined it up and pushed into me slow, but deep. He stretched me and filled my entire opening. I held my breath and prepared for possible pain. But it didn't hurt. He moved easily and smoothly. I held onto him, trying to take him all in. I think he was used to women needing him to take it slow. There weren't many women who could take his length and girth, completely, without pain.

"Oh my God! You're so big," I moaned.

"Am I hurting you?" he breathed into my ear.

"No. You feel amazing," I moaned. That excited him. His breath shook and he moved faster.

"Oh shit! Damn, you feel so fucking good," he grunted. He pumped harder. He rolled onto his back and carried me with him, so I was straddling him. He pulled me down onto him. I put my hands on his stomach, to keep him from punching a hole straight through me. Everything felt amazing, but I could tell he was just on the cusp of causing pain and I wanted to keep him from hurting me. He wasn't trying to. He was just so big. He held my hips and moved me up and down as he grinded into me. He moaned and grimaced, clenching his teeth. He handled me like I was weightless... like a doll. He was in complete control. I could tell he was about to come, hard. I wanted to slow him down. It was getting a bit uncomfortable, but it felt incredible too. I was tingling all over, but he was stretching me tight. I held on so that he could finish.

"Oh fuck! Fuck! Oh shit!" he yelled as he shot his hot seed into me. He slammed me down on him one final time and held me tight against him as he emptied himself. It practically knocked the wind out of me. I gasped and winced as he pressed against the top of me. I was relieved when he let go. I knew I was going to be sore the next day. I rolled off and collapsed onto the bed next to him.

"You okay?" he asked, again, through his laboring.

"I think I'll survive," I said, lightly. "Maybe..."

" Was it good for you?" he asked.

"Yes. That trick— putting me on your shoulders..."

"You liked that?"

"I don't know how you did that. It was crazy."

"Did you like it?" he asked again. "Did you come?"

"I did. You're incredible."

He reached for me and I laid on his chest. He was so strong— so solid. He started to talk, but I was so tired that I drifted off to sleep within a minute. It felt like a minute later that I woke to Noah leaping from the bed, putting his pants on.

"What's happening?" I asked, trying to focus.

"That's my car," he said, darting down the hall. Then I realized a car alarm was blaring. It was loud. I got up and grabbed a tee shirt and pair of shorts from my dresser drawer. I went to the front door that was standing wide open.

"Son of a Bitch!" Noah shouted, shutting off the alarm. "What the fuck!" I walked out barefoot, into the grass, and got close enough to see that Noah's car had flat tires and a broken windshield. I put my hand over my mouth and looked around. The neighbors across the street were peeking through the window. Linda's house was dark.

"Oh Noah!"

"Fuck, man! Why?" he whined. He was so upset. "Damn it!" He kicked at a nearby tree and put his hands on his hips.

"Should I call the police? I asked.

"I don't understand why someone would do this. Yeah, call the cops. Shit!"

I went back into the house to get my phone. I called the police and went back outside. Noah was leaning on his car, looking at his window. I put my hand on his back and rubbed circles.

"I'm so sorry, Noah," I said. He sighed and dropped his head.

"I can't believe this. Do you get this kind of shit in this neighborhood, usually?" he asked.

"No. Well, actually yes. I've had some problems. Some break ins."

"You have? You know your front door was open," he said, looking over his shoulder.

"What?" I realized I was so caught up in the moment with Noah, I forgot to lock up when we came in. I left the front door open. *Had he been in my house again? And if he had— when? While we were sleeping? While we were fucking? Was he watching us?*

"When I heard my alarm and ran through the house, I ran right through the open door. I didn't have to open it." He stared at me with questions.

"I'm so sorry about your car, Noah. I feel responsible."

"Why? Why would you feel responsible?" he asked.

"I think I know who did it. There's this guy—I have a stalker. He's broken into my house before—more than once. I think maybe... I'm not sure, but maybe he found you in my house tonight and took it out on your car."

Noah just looked at me, his eyes filling with anger, and then he turned and spoke into the night. "Motherfucker!" He didn't yell it, but he said it loud enough for anyone lingering around outside to hear. Then he turned back to me. "Why would you suggest we come here, instead of going to my house?"

"It never occurred to me that something like this would happen. I called the police and changed the locks. I thought maybe it was over. I guess not unless this was totally unrelated."

About that time we saw the police cruiser coming down the block. I sat on my porch as Noah talked with the officer. Then the officer came and asked me a few questions about the break ins. A tow truck came and took Noah's car. It was about two in the morning. I suggested he come in and get some sleep and let me drive him home in the morning. He agreed.

The next day, I took Noah home. He lived in the next town over, about thirty minutes from me. He didn't seem to blame me, but I could sense regret that he had run into me that night. He said he would call me soon, but I felt certain I wouldn't find myself hoisted into the air, any time soon. It was fun while it lasted.

"KATHREN!" JAKE LEWIS'S voice was loud and firm. I jolted forward in my chair and turned to see my boss staring at me from his doorway.

"I'm sorry, Mr. Lewis. Did you need me?" I quickly straightened myself, realizing he had obviously been calling me for a while. I wasn't sure how long I had been lost in my thoughts.

"Is everything okay?" he asked, a look of concern on his face.

"Yes. I'm fine. I'm sorry. I was distracted." I replied.

"You're sure? You would tell me if there was a problem, wouldn't you?"

"Yes Sir. Of course. I'm fine, really." I smiled to reassure him. He smiled back and started to head back to his office and then stopped and turned back to me.

"I wanted to mention something to you, but I'm not sure I should. I don't want to add any stress to your situation."

"What is it?" I asked, nervously. "You can tell me."

"Well. I've seen a car around."

"A car?"

"Yeah. It could be nothing. That's why I hesitate to say anything. I don't want to stress you if it's nothing, but I want you to be aware. You've been heading out before me, lately, and that's fine. I don't want you leaving here late, especially with... Well, three different times now, I've noticed a car. I don't recognize it. It's not a car that I have seen parked in this complex before. I pay attention to things like that, ya know. We must be aware of our surroundings."

"What kind of car? Could you see who was in it?" I stood and looked out the front glass door. I couldn't see anything, but I wondered if someone was out there. I hadn't noticed anyone.

"It's a black Nissan, but it looks to be a rental. I could tell there was a man in it. The last time I saw it, I approached him and when he realized I was heading his way, he pulled out of the lot. That was a few nights ago. I haven't seen him since. I've been watching for that car or any other strange person, but I haven't seen him again...yet. Maybe I scared him off. I didn't want to scare you— but I want you to be careful."

"I'm glad you told me. I am very careful. I am always checking out my surroundings," I replied. "Don't worry."

Later that night, I made a point to double check my locks. I wasn't sure if my life could be in danger. This person had the audacity to break into my house and stand over me while I sleep, even touch me, yet he ran when I woke. I wasn't sure if the damage to Noah's car was him. Maybe someone saw his fancy sports car on the street and assumed the owner was a pretentious douchebag and thought it was deserved. And I couldn't be sure about the car my boss saw in the parking lot. The car's that have been spotted seem to be different. Linda saw a light-colored car. I just knew I had to be careful, but also I had to try to carry on with my life. I couldn't let fear consume me.

As I lay in bed trying to sleep that night, I heard something. I sat up and listened. It was coming from outside of my window. I slowly slid out of bed and went to the window. I unlocked it and opened it slightly. I could hear the soft wind moving the bushes. The cool air gave me an immediate chill. I lifted the blinds. It was very dark, but I could see. I didn't see anyone, but I heard a shifting on the ground to the left of the window. I sensed that someone was there. It could have been in my mind, but I felt certain, so I decided to speak.

"Listen... If you're out there, I need you to stop this. Do you hear me? I don't know why you're doing this. I don't know what you want, but I am asking you to please stop. This is my home and I don't want to keep calling the police— but I will. I don't know what else to do. I can get cameras. I can get a gun. I just want to live my life. Do you understand? Do you hear me? I don't know if you want to hurt me or just scare me, but please—please leave me alone. Please!" I waited— and then I saw it. A figure moved in the darkness. He was there, standing in the grass, maybe six feet away. The hair stood up on my arms and I gasped. I tried to stay calm and not run. I couldn't see his face, but I knew he was staring at me.

"Say something..." I waited, but he didn't respond. "Please— tell me what you want."

He was quiet and still. I squinted my eyes, trying to see his face through the darkness, but I couldn't. The leaves rustled and I had an eerie feeling. Then he moved toward me and I panicked. I quickly shut the window and locked it. He stopped and stood, looking at me through the glass. I realized I should have called the cops, instead of speaking to him. I hurried to my phone, on my nightstand, and I dialed 911!

Ten minutes later, I found myself sitting on my couch, as the police found nothing— as usual. The officer talking to me, scolded me for my stunt, as he referred to it.

"Ms. Thompson, that was very dangerous. You should have called us right away!" he barked.

"I thought maybe I could connect with him and get him to leave me alone." I told him.

"Connect with him? You're not dealing with a rational person, ma'am. He is obsessed with you that is coming from an unstable place in this guy's mind. The only good news is when you found him in your home, he ran, but you don't know what he'll do next time. Sometimes these things escalate. If you felt like he was out there you should have called us right away. I don't want to scare you, but this guy is determined. Usually, by the time we've gotten involved and you've changed the locks, the guy will stop, but this guy isn't stopping and we can't seem to figure out where he goes. We have officers driving around the neighborhood looking for parked cars or men walking down nearby streets. We haven't been able to find any trace of him. It's like he vanishes."

"Well, I'm not making this up!" I said.

"I'm not saying that, ma'am. I just hope you are taking this seriously," he replied.

"Of course I am."

"Well, please just call us next time—first thing. The quicker you call, the better shot we have at catching him. Understand?"

"I understand. I won't do it again. I just thought maybe..." I could see that the officer was frustrated. They all were. They had been called to my home several times, asking the same questions, never finding anything. I wondered if some of them thought I was lying. It was embarrassing. I wondered if they would eventually find me dead. I morbidly envisioned them standing over my body shaking their heads. Maybe it would be my payback for what I had done. Not for killing Mark— that was an accident, but covering it up. That was my sin. That was the reason for everything I was going through now.

As I walked the police out and locked my doors, again, I began to feel angry. I started feeling like this was all Joseph's fault. I was dealing with all this, but he was giving me the brush off. He was over there just living his life, while I was dealing with everything alone. I didn't know if the stalker had anything to do with Mark's disappearance, but it was strange that it happened at the very same time as the investigation. I was mad and I thought it was time Joseph knew how I felt.

Chapter 13

I STOOD ON JOSEPH'S porch, banging on the door. It was still early for Joseph, about eleven-thirty. The light was on in his living room and I felt sure he was up. I saw movement through the frosted glass of his front door and then it cracked open.

"Kat?" His face and his tone told me he was very surprised. "What the fuck! You're banging on my door like the damn cops!" He opened the door all the way. He was shirtless, wearing only sweatpants.

"I'm sorry! But I need to talk to you!" He moved and opened the door more to let me pass. I walked in and turned to face him. "I need to know what's going on."

"What are you talking about, Kat?" he sighed, as he closed the door and walked into the living room. I followed him. He picked his drink up off the coffee table and gestured toward the bar.

"No! Thank you." I sat on the couch and looked up at him. "Joseph, please tell me what's going on. I'm so confused. You slept with me at my house, then again at your house, then you ignored me, then you invited me to stay at your house, but you avoided me while I was here. Then you complain about me flirting with a guy at your party. Then you sleep with me again, then—-nothing! What is going on? I'm confused. Did I do something?"

"No," he said, sitting down. He took a swig of his drink and then another. He was clearly searching for the words.

"Just tell me, Joseph. Please! Why are you treating me like this?"

"I'm not trying to treat you badly, Kat. I'm just trying to..." He hesitated and looked down at his brown liquor, swirling the liquid around the glass.

"What? You're just what?"

"I'm trying to keep my distance. Isn't it obvious?" He looked at me, his eyes filled with frustration.

"Yes! That's my point! Clearly you're trying to keep your distance, but why?" I asked, almost whining.

"Because I need to—okay!"

"Why? I don't understand!" It was like pulling teeth. He stood up and went to the bar. He grabbed the bottle of liquor sitting in front of him and filled his glass. He took a big drink of it and stood facing away from me. I stared at the back of him, waiting. I could tell he needed a minute, but I was determined to get answers. He walked around the bar and opened a drawer. He took a joint and a lighter from it, lit the joint and took a hit. He was struggling with the conversation. He gestured to me, offering me the weed. I shook my head. "Just tell me the truth."

"I need to keep a distance so I don't let things..." He swallowed half of his drink and took a long hit of his joint.

"Let things... what?" I stood up, went to the bar, and stood across from him.

"I need to keep things how they are in my life, Kat." He looked around the room, avoiding my eyes. "You come around and I get— mixed up!"

"Mixed up about what?" I asked.

"You make me feel things I don't want to feel. I get caught up. My mind goes back to Mark— to you and me and Mark, to nights we spent together— to that last night. It makes me feel anxious and sad and..."

"And what?"

"And fucked up! I feel my heart getting involved and I don't want that shit. It makes me feel guilty and mad at myself and mad at you. It pisses me off and it fucking scares me. I don't want to be in a relationship and I don't want to be...."

My breath caught at the word relationship. I just stared at him, desperate to hear more.

"Fuck!" He drank the rest of his drink, poured more, and put the joint out in an ashtray.

"You feel like you're having romantic feelings for me?" I asked, gently.

"No! Maybe—sometimes! I don't know what I feel. But the more time we spend together the more difficult it is to keep my thoughts straight. Don't you get it?"

"Yes! I do! I do because I have feelings for you. I had feelings for you before Mark died. I thought maybe you did too. I've been trying to understand what was happening—why you act so strange. I miss you and you're the only person I can really talk to about everything. The only person who knows the darkest parts of my life and you don't judge me for it. There's so much going on and I feel so alone."

"I don't want you to feel alone, Kat. I really don't. But—Mason..."

"Mason? What about Mason?"

"He seemed to have some feelings developing for you and I didn't want to get in the way."

"I don't want Mason! Even if I did, which I don't— I couldn't be with Mason knowing what I did, keeping a horrible secret like that, having to be so careful about what I say. The guilt was terrible being around him. I don't have feelings for Mason."

"I don't want to be in a relationship, Kat. I can't put myself in that situation. Not now. Not with all this going on— and when I'm with you—I feel guilty."

"Why?" I asked.

"Mark! You were his and I was his best friend... and after what happened, it just feels—wrong! It's wrong!" Joseph walked around the bar and stood in front of me. "I'm a fucking asshole! I don't deserve to.."

"To what? Be happy?"

Shit no! I definitely don't deserve that, but I don't deserve to just—to just take over where he left off with his girl! It ain't fucking cool!"

"Take over where he left off? How is that what you're doing? You were there! You and I had something. I felt connected to you and I know you felt something for me. Calling me his girl is a stretch! He didn't love me."

"Mark was unconventional, but you were his." Joseph's tone softened and he reached out and adjusted my collar.

"Joseph, you were his best friend. You and Mark had a special friendship. You know his darkest secrets. You know what he did to me that night and I..."

"What Rex did! You mean what Rex did!"

"No! I mean what Mark did. He let it happen. I came here to talk to you that day. He was here and he was fucked up. He didn't tell me to go. He didn't warn me. When Rex showed up he told me to sit in the living room and be quiet. He could have told me to get out of there. Then he came in with Rex and tried to drug me. He stood there while Rex carried me kicking and screaming into that room." I pointed to the room where it happened. Joseph's eyes scanned to the room and he just stared as I continued. "Rex threw me on the bed! He choked me and hit me! He raped me and Mark just disappeared! The only thing he did was tell Rex not to be so rough. Then when it was all over—when I was all used up, he tried to come and comfort me. He tried to tell me he had no choice. I don't know what he owed Rex, but he should have done something! He should have helped me! But he didn't." Joseph's eye's looked sad as I recapped the night. "I will never forget that night, Joseph! I never meant to hurt Mark. It was an accident—a horrible accident and I feel so guilty and we did a very bad thing, covering it up. Poor Mason will never know what happened to his brother. I feel so awful about it—all of it, but we have to move on, Joseph. Confessing won't bring Mark back and it won't make us feel better. We have to move on."

Joseph reached up and pushed my hair off my forehead with his fingers. He looked me over, tracing my face with his eyes, until his eyes landed on mine. It felt like he was speaking to me without words. There was a magnetic pull between us. He leaned in to kiss me. He hovered just a few inches from my lips and then turned his head and moved away.

"Joseph?"

"What?" He was facing away from me.

"Please kiss me," I begged. He just stood there, so I walked over and stood behind him. I touched his bare back. "Please!" He turned to face me.

"Kat, every fucking cell in my body wants to touch you right now. I am fighting with everything I got to stay away. Why do you insist on making it difficult for me?"

"Because every fucking cell in my body wants you to touch me, and it's how I feel every time I see you." I was telling him how I felt and begging him to touch me. I looked down to his chest and stomach. I touched his stomach with my fingertips and dragged them slowly up to his nipples and lightly ran my fingertips over them. He quivered, but he didn't move. I pulled my shirt over my head and dropped it on the floor. I rubbed my hands up his chest and over his shoulders, leaned forward and kissed his pecs. His breathing told me that he was struggling and the erection in his sweats told me he couldn't resist. I reached into his pants and stroked him. He closed his eyes and let out a deep breath. I went down to my knees and pulled his pants and boxers down. I put his erection in my mouth. He buckled a little and moaned, as I moved him in and out of my mouth. He put his hand in my hair and massaged my head. I cupped his balls in my hand and pulled lightly as I massaged him with my mouth. His moaning intensified.

"Oh fuck! Kat! What are you doing to me?" he groaned. I just kept going, trying to make him come. "Oh shit! Your mouth feels so fucking good."

I swirled my tongue around and pulled with my lips, allowing him to touch the back of my throat with the head. I loved the sound of his moaning and heavy breathing. Then suddenly, he grabbed my arms and lifted me to my feet and kissed me hard and deep. He squeezed my breast as he kissed me. Then he grabbed my wrist and walked me quickly to the couch. He ripped my pants and panties down rough and pushed me back onto the couch. He dropped to his knees and drove his face between my legs. His tongue moved back and forth and flickered around frantically. I gasped and grabbed his head. He pushed my knees to my ears, giving himself full access to my clit. He licked and sucked. I cried out loudly. I fought against him one minute and then squeezed him against me the next.

"Oh God Joseph! Oh God!" I whined. "Please!" I almost screamed as I came and then as it was almost over he stopped only to pull me down on top of him, on the floor. He slammed me down on his cock and I took over sliding up and down, curling my hips and shaking, as my orgasm still rolled through me. First he was looking down at my body moving up and down on him, but then he lifted his eyes to meet mine and we stared at each other as we moved, until Joseph had to close his eyes because he was coming. His orgasm was strong and long and I felt him shooting into me. I loved the look on his face as he came. I fell on top of him and laid my cheek against his chest. He wrapped his arms around me and I was relieved.

We laid there quietly, just breathing, for a while. Then I rolled off him and rested my head on his shoulder. His embrace felt warm. He dragged his fingers up and down my upper arm. I watched as his erection disappeared, laying off to the side, across his hip.

"I really needed that," I whispered. He sighed and squeezed me close. I didn't say it, but I really needed the embrace, as much as the sex. Joseph had become my safe space.

"You drive me crazy, woman," he sighed. We lay quiet for a few minutes, before he spoke again.

"What happened with the stalker thing?" he asked, after a long pause.

"It's still going on."

"What do you mean?"

"I actually had the police at my house tonight." I told him. He rose up and looked at me.

"I thought that shit was over. What happened tonight?"

"I spoke to him. He was outside my window. I couldn't see his face, but I saw his shadow, so I cracked my window and asked him to stop. He didn't speak. He just stood there, listening to me—glaring at me. Then I got spooked and called the police, but as usual, he was long gone by the time they arrived."

"Kat! What the fuck are the police doing? I thought they were on top of it!" Joseph stood up and pulled me to my feet. He put his sweats on and I grabbed my clothes.

"They can't do much. They search for him. They have more patrol cars in the area. They had an officer parked in front of my house for a few nights. They talked to my neighbors. They talked to me about safety and I changed my locks. I check the locks every night, several times. He disappears. He's like a damn ninja. He breaks in with no sign of force and he gets away with no one seeing!" I caught myself before I mentioned Noah's car. I didn't want to let Joseph know I had slept with Noah, at least not yet.

"That's crazy. You need to stay here." he said, with a delicate tone.

"Um, I don't know. I mean, I wouldn't mind it, but how long? Last time didn't change anything and you had a hard time with me being here. I wouldn't want you to feel uncomfortable."

"I wouldn't tell you to stay if it was going to make me uncomfortable. And if you stay for a while, maybe he will give up." Joseph sat on the couch while I put my pants back on. He watched me. I stood in front of him trying to read his face. I wondered if he really wanted me to stay or if he felt like it was just the right thing to do. He reached out to take my hand and gently pulled me down next to him. He stared down at my hand as he held it.

"You don't have to do this," I told him.

"I know that." He looked up and his eyes met mine. "I want you safe. I didn't realize it was still happening. I can't let you stay there alone. Please stay with me." His intense, hazel eyes looked honest and heartfelt. I knew he meant it. He was struggling with his feelings for me. It was obvious, but he wanted me to stay, so I agreed.

"What now?" I asked.

"It's late. You can sleep in one of my tee shirts and go get your things tomorrow," he said, stroking my arm, still holding my hand.

"Okay." My heart leapt in my chest, as I finally felt some of the connection we used to have coming back. Joseph had always been so sweet to me before and we always had great sex. He was also funny and playful, but I figured Mark's death had killed some of that and it would take a while for that side of him to return.

"Should I sleep in the room I stayed in last time?" I asked. He gave me a look that said 'Don't be stupid'.

"My bed is fine—unless you prefer the other room."

"No. I like your bed just fine," I answered quickly. He smirked.

"Well, make yourself at home. I need to return some emails, so I'll be in my office." He stood up and headed for the office.

"Joseph!" I stood up. He stopped and looked back at me. "Thanks." He smiled and went around the corner.

Later that night, lying in Joseph's big cozy bed, I was wide awake thinking, when I heard him coming up the stairs. I don't know why, but I pretended to be asleep. I watched through a tiny slit in one eye, as he came into the room. He plugged his phone into his charger and laid it on the dresser, before coming to bed. He stood at the foot of the bed and looked at me for a minute. I wondered what he was thinking, as he stared down at me. Then he stripped naked, underwear and all, went to the bathroom where he quickly showered and then crawled into bed, still naked. He slid in behind me and spooned me close. He wrapped his arm around me and I nuzzled my butt into him. I was in my panties and a gray t-shirt I had found in his closet. He felt so warm and safe. I was happy there, in his house—in his bed—in his arms.

I felt his cock pressed up against my ass, as it grew. I tilted my hips to rub against him and with that...he pulled down my panties and pushed into me from behind. I gasped and whimpered as he fucked me. He reached around and grasped my breast, squeezing and massaging them. It only took him about five minutes and he was coming. He turned me on my back and fingered me. He slid in and out slow and steady. I could hear the squishing from how wet I was. It felt so good to have his hands on me and in me. As he made me come, I thought about the words he spoke earlier. He had feelings for me. He didn't want to be in a relationship. And yet, here I was staying at his house for an unspecified amount of time, sleeping in his bed, fucking him. It felt like a relationship to me.

The whole time I was with Mark, I tried to make him care for me—to make him fall in love with me, but he never did. The sex was amazing—absolutely, fucking amazing, but I could never have anything more than that and maybe a friendship. With Joseph the sex was just as amazing, but he cared for me too. It was everything I always wanted. The only problem was he didn't want to have those feelings for me. It caused him pain and guilt to be with me. I wondered if he could move past it. I was going to do everything I could to help him get over it. I wanted him to have feelings for me. At that moment, I knew it was exactly what I wanted— because of what I was feeling for him.

Joseph slid his fingers out of me as my orgasm ended. I rolled onto his chest and cuddled up against him. He curled his arm around me and kissed my head. I was in heaven, as I fell asleep, warm against his bare skin. I woke up several times through the night, relieved to find him still there, sound asleep next to me. I listened to his even, deep breathing. I wanted to fuck him again, but I decided to let him rest. We had plenty of time.

The next day, I went home to gather enough clothes and personal items to last me a couple weeks. I had no idea how long I would be staying at Joseph's house. In a way, I hated to leave my house unattended. The idea of the stalker roaming through my house looking through my things made me feel sick, but I also thought how wonderful it would be to spend this time with Joseph, just the two of us. I filled a large bag and locked up the house. As I was packing up the car I noticed Linda was getting groceries from her trunk and I decided to head over and talk to her.

"Hey Linda! How are you?" I called, walking over. She looked startled.

"Oh hey, Kathren." She looked around and then gave me a tight smile. She was nervous about something. Her arms were super full, so I took a bag from her. "It's okay. I've got it." She reluctantly let me take a bag.

"Let me help you," I pleaded. "Linda, what's going on with you?" I followed her to her porch, carrying the bag. She turned and looked at me. "I know somethings wrong! Did I do something— or say something that upset you?"

"No. You didn't do anything. I just..." She put her bags down on the porch and took the extra bag from me.

"What is it?"

"I just don't want to be a bother. I have a lot on my plate and my husband wants me to do better with my duties at home." It always annoyed me to hear Linda say things like that. "He doesn't want me bothering the neighbors."

"You don't bother me, Linda. I miss our talks." I reached out and squeezed her arm.

"Well, I appreciate you saying that, Kathren. I really do. But I know I get in your way sometimes and I just want peace in my marriage, so I'm doing the best I can to keep him pleased. And it's going well. We've been doing a lot better."

"Well, that's good then, I guess. I mean, as long as you're happy, Linda."

"I am." She stood there, holding the bag, smiling at me. The smile was fake. I knew she wasn't happy, but I didn't know what to say. She seemed like she was anxious for me to leave.

"Well, I just wanted to let you know, I won't be home for a while. I'm leaving now and if you need me, you can call me—anytime."

"Oh, where are you going?" she asked.

"I'm staying with a friend for a while. So if you see any activity at my house, please call the police. Call me too."

"How long will you be gone?"

"Not sure. Maybe a couple weeks—or more."

"Wow! That's a long time?" She seemed surprised. "Is it because of the issues you've been having over there with the intruder?" She looked over at my house.

Yeah. I just need a break and I don't know, maybe if I'm gone for a while, he'll get bored and give up."

"Well, let's hope so. I think that's a good idea," she said. This time her smile seemed real. "I hope you enjoy your time away."

"Thanks, Linda. It's good talking to you." We stood there in silence for a few seconds and then she turned and put her key in the door. I went to my car. She gave me a wave as I pulled out of the driveway and headed towards Joseph's house.

Chapter 14

OVER THE NEXT SEVERAL days, I enjoyed my time with Joseph. It was as if something had changed and he was comfortable with me. I began to feel like we were a couple. We slept together every night. We ate breakfast and dinner together. We watched movies and talked. It was wonderful. I avoided talking about our relationship to keep pressure off him and let it just happen.

After about five days of living together, I was feeling calm and safe. One night, I came in from work and found Joseph in the kitchen cooking.

"Hey. How was your day?" he asked, stirring something in a pot.

"Good. Smells great in here."

"Are you hungry?"

"Yeah. I don't know if I've ever seen you cook," I said, dropping my purse on the floor. I walked over and stood next to him. "Spaghetti?"

"And meatballs," he added, smiling down at his sauce. He leaned down and kissed my hair. His affection had me in a state of euphoria. I felt like I was living in total bliss. I leaned into him and then excused myself to clean up and change into comfy clothes. Later we were sitting across from each other, eating spaghetti, and talking.

"I'm impressed. This is delicious," I told him.

"Thanks. I can cook several dishes," he said, smiling across the table at me.

He watched me as I ate. A noodle slipped out of my mouth and draped across my chin. Joseph leaned over and wiped the sauce from my face. The simple act sent a chill through my body. Something was clearly happening between us and I was loving it.

"I'm a messy eater," I admitted, taking my napkin from my lap, and wiping the spot he had touched.

"That's okay. Spaghetti is messy."

We chatted a bit more, finished our meal and I helped him clean up. Afterward we went to the living room to watch television. I went for the remote, but Joseph jumped in front of me.

"Oh no! We're not watching anymore of your chick flicks," he announced, as he reached for the remote. I reached past him and grabbed it.

"What?" I held the clicker out of his reach. "I want to finish the series." We had been watching a show on Netflix for three nights in a row and I was enjoying it. It was a romantic comedy and we only had two episodes left. Joseph had been watching with me, but he usually fell asleep halfway through. I would have to fill him in the next night on what he slept through.

"It's been three nights in a row. We're watching something I like, tonight." He grabbed at my hand, but I turned and pushed my backside into him. He pulled at me and we began to wrestle for the remote. I laughed and grunted as he playfully fought me to the ground. He tried to pin me but I managed to tickle him and he buckled, allowing me to crawl out from under him. He grabbed my ankle and slid me back. I screamed and tossed the remote across the rug, as he went for it. We were both laughing.

"You little..." He tried to crawl toward the remote. I wrapped my arms around his waist. He dragged me as he crawled. I started to tickle him again and he collapsed. I went for the remote when he grabbed me and pinned me to the floor. My hair was in my face and I was out of breath, still laughing. Finally, Joseph had me— pinned down, my arms over my head, him laying on top of me. He leaned in and kissed me. His tongue moved softly in my mouth. As he rose up, his mouth opened, as if he was about to say something and then hesitated. He moved my hair out of my face and smiled at me. "Okay. You win. We'll watch your show."

"Actually, I was going to say we can watch something else— or we don't have to watch anything tonight," I said, staring up at his sexy face.

"Oh. Well, what should we do then?" he grinned. I slid one of my hands out of his and rubbed down his chest and reached into his pants. I wrapped my fingers around his cock and stroked him. My desire to make him come was constant. I wanted to make him come every day, all the time, even more that I wanted him to make me come.

I knew that Joseph had been with many women and had many experiences, but he seemed to get off so easily with me: from my hand, my mouth, and my pussy. He never seemed bored. He seemed to have to fight not to come most of the time, so that he could give me the time I needed to orgasm. And he always made sure I orgasmed— usually more than once. Sex with Joseph was amazing. He knew what he was doing. But he was more than just sex. He was funny, smart, and charming. I was so into him.

"Wait! Don't make me come yet," he gasped, pulling my hand from his pants. Then he pulled my shirt up and started kissing my tummy. He slid his hands over my breasts and squeezed them. I dropped my hands over my head and melted into the tingly warmth of his mouth on me. He lowered my pants and undies and dropped down between my legs. He kissed and slowly licked me, getting in no hurry. I breathed deeply and moaned with pleasure. He pushed my knees, opening my legs wider. Then his fingers glided across my thigh and he pushed two of them inside of me. He pumped in and out slow and steady, while still licking me slowly, and after a few minutes I came—deeply and fully through my body.

"Oh my God. You're going to have to give me a couple minutes here. I wanted to make you come and you just sucked all the energy out of me," I told him. He laughed as he kissed up my tummy to my breast, then laid next to me, propped up on his elbow.

"You don't have to get me off every time, baby."

"I know, but I want to. And I like it when you call me baby," I told him. Joseph grinned.

"I wanted to talk to you about something," he said.

"What?" I was nervous. Was this the moment he was going to profess his feelings for me?

"I am having some people over tomorrow night." As the words fell out of his mouth, I had a sudden pit in my stomach. We had been alone in the house together for days and now he was telling me he was having one of his parties. I sat up and reached for my underwear. He sat up beside me and studied my reaction. I didn't want to let on that I was upset.

"Oh, a few or..."

"Not sure. It's been planned for a while. My buddy Matt is in town and we always get together and have some fun, so I invited some of the other people he knows and a couple he doesn't."

"That's cool," I said, putting my clothes on. "Do you need me to disappear? I could go home for the night or stay in the spare room." He reached out and touched my shoulder.

"Is that why you think I was telling you?" he asked.

"I don't know. It's your house. I don't want to make anything uncomfortable or whatever." He narrowed his eyes and tilted his head. I gave him a reassuring smile. "I mean, whatever you want."

"Kat?" He closed his eyes and smirked, shaking his head a little, then looked at me. "I wanted to talk to you about ground rules."

"Ground rules?"

"Yeah. Like what we expect from each other."

"Expect from each other?"

"So there are no misunderstandings," he said.

"Oh. Okay."

"What do you want from me?" he asked.

"I don't know. What do you want?"

"I think I would prefer that you don't hook up with anyone. I mean—You can do what you want, of course. I'm not telling you what to do, but if I'm honest, I don't want to see you with anyone else and I'm willing to do the same if..." I threw my arms around him in mid-sentence. He hugged me back. "So, I take it this is okay with you?" he chuckled.

"It's okay with me," I said, squeezing him tight.

"So, we have an understanding?" he asked, as I let go.

"Yes! We have an understanding." I was beaming.

We went to bed that night and made love for hours. That's what it felt like, now—making love. I mean, it was hot and wild and dirty, but it was also sweet and romantic. We fell asleep in each other's arms and I was happy.

THE NEXT NIGHT, I FOUND myself standing in front of the huge mirror in Joseph's master bathroom. I couldn't decide what to wear. I didn't want to look too sexy, but I wanted Joseph to be turned on. I wondered how he would want me to dress. Suddenly, I turned to find him standing in the doorway.

"You scared me!" I gasped, putting my hand to my chest.

"Sorry." Joseph grinned. "What are you doing?"

"Trying to decide what to do with my hair and what to wear." I told him. "Do you have a preference?'

"Me? I like your hair up or down. You always look beautiful."

"You're so sweet." He always said the right thing. "But, do you want me to look more sexy— less sexy?" I asked.

"Whatever you want. Dress how you feel comfortable. If you want to dress up—cool. If you want to wear jeans, that's great too." I could tell he was being genuine. Mark had often told me how to dress for parties and even went as far as to pick out my clothes. He always wanted me to look as sexy as possible and attract attention. I had gotten used to it. It was refreshing to be told to decide for myself. I turned and moved to touch Joseph. He let me at first, but then as my hand slipped down toward his waist, he took my wrist and held my hand still.

"I don't want to right now," he said, "I want to spend the night wanting you and waiting."

I smiled at him, kissed him gently on the lips and went to get dressed. In the end, I decided on tight black jeans, a low-cut black blouse, and black heels. I put my hair in a tight ponytail. When I came down the stairs Joseph took a double take.

"Damn! You're trying to kill me," he said, looking me up and down. He made me feel sexy.

"Thanks. You look pretty damn hot yourself," I told him. And he did. He had a gray, button up shirt and black slacks on. His hair was neat and his short beard was closer to a shadow than an actual beard. We smiled at each other for a minute until we were interrupted by the doorbell. Joseph stepped from behind the bar, where he was prepping to make drinks and headed for the door. I went to the bar and took a wine cooler from his mini fridge. I heard many voices, male and female.

Over the next thirty minutes, the room filled with people, close to thirty. There were good looking guys and gorgeous women everywhere. A few men introduced themselves to me and started to flirt. I was friendly, but I didn't let anyone misunderstand me. I was Joseph's and I didn't want it any other way. Women were fawning over Joseph, as usual, and he was very good at handling it. He would occasionally look over at me and wink, as a woman tried to get his attention. There was an exciting vibe: an unspoken conversation going on between us all night, as we stayed on opposite sides of the room. His smile was gorgeous and his stare was making me wet. I couldn't wait to have him inside me. Thoughts of the first time I met him and the first time we fucked swirled through my mind.

Suddenly, I heard a familiar voice. I turned to see Noah standing across the room talking to another guy. He wasn't looking at me. I turned quickly and felt a small panic rush through my body. I hadn't told Joseph about our encounter and I didn't want to do it now. I moved to the back of the room and positioned myself behind three women. I looked over at Joseph to see if he was watching me, but he wasn't. He was talking to a couple, facing away from me. I peeked through the women, I was shielded by, and saw that Noah was scanning the room. I wasn't sure if he was looking for me or if he had seen me, yet. For all I knew he had no interest in seeing me either, since the unfortunate ending to our night.

I moved behind the women and carefully positioned myself behind people till I made my way out of the room and up the stairs. I didn't look back. I just darted into the bathroom. I stood there for a while, trying to decide what to do, but I couldn't just hide in the bathroom all night. I had to go to the party. Maybe, I thought, I could pull Joseph to the side and let him know the situation before there were any misunderstandings. I stared at myself in the mirror for a minute, adjusted my hair and reached for the door. I stepped out and bumped right into someone— it was Noah.

"Whoa!" Noah spouted, as I crashed into his rock-hard chest. "Slow down, gorgeous! Where's the fire?"

I backed up and smiled at him. "Hey! Noah! I didn't know you were here. How are you?"

"I'm good. How 'bout you?"

"I'm okay." I nervously smoothed my shirt and swooshed my ponytail behind my back." He leaned in and gave me a quick kiss on the lips.

"I've been meaning to call you," he said.

"Yeah, I've been busy, too. So much going on," I said, anxiously. I took a quick peek around him to make sure no one had followed him up the stairs. He noticed my behavior and gave me a funny look.

"Everything okay?" he asked.

"Yeah. Everything's fine. You've been doing alright?"

"I have. I've thought about you— quite a bit." He moved closer to me. I stepped back and avoided contact. "You seem nervous. You weren't expecting to see me tonight, I guess."

"I wasn't. But it's nice to see you. It really is. Did you get your car all fixed?" I asked. I reached out and rubbed his arm. He looked down at my hand, as I touched him and chuckled. "What?"

"I make you uneasy. Not sure why, but you are uncomfortable."

"No! I'm not uncomfortable. You just took me by surprise, is all," I told him.

"I was hoping I'd see you here, actually," he said, moving closer again. "I really enjoyed our night together." He reached out for me and caressed my arms. He leaned in for a kiss and I put my hands against his chest, pressing lightly. I didn't want to be forceful, but I was struggling to verbalize that I wasn't available anymore. He ignored me and pulled me to him. I turned my head, as he tried to slip his tongue into my mouth.

"Noah. I can't." I whispered.

"Why not?" he asked, still trying to connect to me.

"Noah. Please..."

"Hey, I think the lady is saying no!" Noah and I both turned quickly to the sound of Joseph's voice. He had arrived at the top of the stairs and was coming toward Noah.

"Hey man! It's not what it looks like!" Noah said, backing away from me. I moved toward Joseph and stood in front of him, between him and Noah.

"Everything's fine, Joseph," I said, rubbing my hand up and down his arm.

Joseph ignored me. "It looks like she's saying she's not interested and you're not getting the fucking message!"

"Joseph, please! It's fine."

"We know each other, man! It ain't like that." Noah said, standing his ground.

"You don't know her. You met her once." Joseph said and before I could stop it, Noah told Joseph how we knew each other.

"I know her, man. I know her very well, as a matter of fact. You get my drift?"

Joseph looked confused. He stared at Noah and then looked down at me. "What the fuck does that mean. What am I missing, Kat?" he asked. I opened my mouth, but couldn't say anything.

"We've hooked up before, bro. Not here. At her house! I *know* her!" Noah's words, although true, made my stomach burn. I don't know why I hadn't told Joseph about me and Noah, but at that moment I really wished I had. I could tell Joseph felt betrayed. His eyes were filled with disappointment.

"Oh, my bad, dude. I didn't realize," Joseph said, apologetically. He backed away from me and gave me a look. I had embarrassed him.

"Joseph, it's not like that. I swear I..."

"You swear what?" I'd never seen him look at me like that before. He was angry and he was hurt. He looked back at Noah and apologized. "Sorry, man!"

"No problem, man. I respect you trying to look out for your friend," Noah told him.

"Yeah, I just don't want anyone feeling uncomfortable," Joseph said, "So... you guys go ahead and talk...or whatever. I'll leave you alone." He backed up and turned toward the stairs. Then he added, "If you need privacy, there's a few bedrooms up here," before he started down the stairs.

"Joseph!" I called, as he disappeared downstairs. "Damn it!"

"So, what was that? You guys together?" Noah asked.

"Well, if we were, you didn't help things between us!" I barked, turning toward him.

"Well damn! He was acting like I was trying to assault you or something! You didn't say much to defend me," he scoffed back.

He was right. I put both of them in an uncomfortable situation. "You're right. Sorry." I sighed and leaned against the wall.

"You should have told me you had something going on with him."

I looked at him and gave him a small, closed mouth smile. Noah sighed and shook his head.

"I guess I'll leave you alone. I don't want to get in the middle of—whatever this is." Noah gave me a twisted smile and went down the stairs.

I stood there for a minute thinking through what I should say to Joseph. I started down the stairs to find him, but before I could make it to the bottom, I was hit with the sad reality of what my night was going to be like. Joseph was walking into the downstairs bedroom with a sexy blonde. My heart sank.

I stood there for a minute and then I decided I wasn't going to accept it. All the progress we had made wasn't going up in smoke over a misunderstanding. I stormed down the stairs and burst into the room. Joseph and his guest looked at me with shock on their faces. He was standing against the dresser and the woman was sitting on the bed.

"I need to talk to you!" I squawked.

" Kat! What the hell?" He put his hands on his hips. The woman looked at him and then me.

"You ever heard of knocking?" she sneered.

"This doesn't concern you," I said, barely looking in her direction and then I continued with Joseph. "You need to give me a minute to explain. Ask your friend to leave." I demanded.

"Nothing to explain. It's fine. Everythings good," he said, trying to act as if he wasn't bothered.

"Then why are you breaking the rules?" I asked.

"Rules?" the girl scoffed.

"This doesn't concern you, bitch!" I shouted at her.

"Bitch!" The woman stood up and stepped toward me. I moved in her direction, but before we could take it any farther, Joseph was between us.

"Alright! Stop! Kathren, calm down. Jillian, please excuse us."

"Me? Ask her to leave! We were in the middle of something!" The woman insisted.

"Jillian! Please excuse us." Joseph asked again, politely, but firm. The woman made a face, mumbled under her breath, and walked out. I pushed the door shut behind her.

"What the fuck , Kat."

"Me? You were just about to fuck someone else after you told me you wanted us to be committed to eachother for the night! So, yeah, what the fuck?" I stared up at him, anger and hurt in my voice.

"You made me look really stupid upstairs, just now," he said. "That's the shit I don't do. I ain't getting caught up in no bullshit!"

"I didn't mean to. I was going to tell you about Noah. It just didn't really mean anything and I never found a moment to bring it up. It wasn't planned. I ran into him at a bar. I was a little tipsy and you weren't talking to me. I was lonely and it happened. It was one time. I didn't expect to see him tonight. That's why I went upstairs. He followed me. I didn't mean to make you feel stupid." I reached out and touched his chest. "Please! Don't let all the good... everything we've been through these last days get messed up by one misunderstanding."

Joseph stared down at me and sighed. He pulled me to him and hugged me. I wrapped my arms around his waist and relaxed into him. "Were you really going to fight Jillian?" He asked.

"Were you really going to fuck Jillian? That's the question."

"No," he answered. "I wasn't. I was going to talk to her for a while and make you jealous."

"That was mean," I said, smacking my hand against his back.

"Sorry. I got embarrassed and I didn't like it. I told you; this shit is hard for me."

"It's hard for me too. I care about you so much Joseph. I wanted to follow the rules tonight. I wanted it more than anything." I spoke softly. He squeezed me tighter. Then he lowered his head and began to kiss me. He was gentle and passionate. His lips were soft and his tongue was slow. I knew, at that moment, I loved him.

"Let's get you out of this room," he suggested. It was the first time I had gone in that room since that night. We went back to the party.

Chapter 15

AFTER SEVERAL DAYS with Joseph, playing his live-in girlfriend, I was running out of clothes. I was beginning to wear the same outfits to work every few days and I felt it was probably becoming noticeable to my boss. It had been a couple weeks and I needed to go home. I had been driving by after work to get my mail out of the box and take a look from the outside. From the street everything was peaceful, but it was time for me to go inside. I didn't want to leave Joseph, but we had not discussed how long I would stay or how things would be when I went home—if I went home. I had joked a few times that he was probably getting tired of me, but he always assured me that he was enjoying my company. Nothing had been mentioned about me moving in for good. Seriously, if he had asked me to, I would have said yes, at that point. I told Joseph I was going to stop by my house after work and take care of some things.

I pulled up in the driveway and got out of the car. I noticed right away that my grass needed to be mowed. My yard was small and it usually only took me an hour to do the whole yard, but I didn't want to allow the sun to go down on me, so I put that chore off for the time being. I unlocked the door and quietly opened it. The creek was so loud. It was still light outside, but all the blinds were closed, so the inside was dark. I flipped the light on, entered and shut the door behind me. It was quiet. I felt my anxiety increasing as I stepped a few feet into the house. Everything seemed to be in place.

When I realized I was holding my breath, I exhaled and headed for my bedroom. I went into my bedroom and looked around. The bed was messy. I couldn't remember how I left it. I went to the closet, pulled some clothes out and tossed them on my bed. As I opened the dresser drawers, I stopped and I felt my heart skip a beat. I did remember how I left my drawer, the way I always left it. Typically I rolled my panties into little balls and lined them front to back. My bras were lined up with the cups fitted one into the next. I glared down at the mess— bras and panties mixed together. It looked as if every pair had been pulled out and just tossed back in. Someone had been there, going through my underwear. I took a deep breath and closed the drawer. I went to the bathroom, where I found my hamper emptied and a few items of clothing laying on the floor. Someone had been going through my clothes in the hamper. A chill crawled down my spine. I went back to the bedroom and stood in the doorway looking around. I could see him in my mind, going through everything, laying in my bed, making himself at home, as he violated my privacy. I quickly threw some extra clothes into a bag and headed for the front door. I needed to get out of the house. I had no idea when the intruder had been there or how many times, but I felt sick to my stomach and I didn't feel safe.

Back at Joseph's house, I felt a sigh of relief as I closed the door behind me. I walked into the living room and was thrilled to find Joseph sitting on the sofa. He was still in his dress clothes, reading some papers. He was wearing reading glasses, which I rarely saw him in and he looked sexy as ever. He looked up at me from over the rim of his readers and smiled.

"Everything alright at the house?" he asked.

I dropped my bag and headed toward him. "He's been there," I answered. Joseph lowered the papers and his smile turned to a frown.

"You're fucking kidding me?"

I plopped down next to him and leaned into him. "My drawers were messed up and the clothes in my hamper were thrown on the floor. He was in there at some point, going through my underwear and who knows what else."

"Did you call the police?"

" No. What's the point? What are they going to do?"

"Yeah, but maybe at this point they could take prints or something. I mean, you need to tell them, Kat. They gotta get this guy. This is crazy. You can't just ignore it." Joseph leaned forward and slid his papers into his briefcase, which was sitting on the floor, near his leg. He laid back and cuddled me into his arms. He smelled good and his embrace was warm.

"Maybe I need to move," I said. The idea hung in the air.

After a noticeable silence, he asked, "Is that what you want? I thought you loved that house."

"I mean, I like it, but it's a rental and I never planned to live there forever. I don't know. I don't think I will ever feel safe there again." I waited, very curious to hear his response. He was quiet. He stroked my arm and although I wasn't looking at his expression, I knew he was thinking.

"Do you want me to help you look?" he asked, after a few seconds. It wasn't the response I was hoping for. I stood up and went to the bar for a drink.

"I pulled a beer from the mini fridge. "I can do it," I said, leaning against the bar. Joseph leaned forward. He was studying me.

"Well, you know you can stay here as long as you want."

"What does that mean, exactly?" I asked.

"It means just what I said." He stood up and came to the other side of the bar. "As long as you want."

"That's nice of you. Thanks."

He lowered his brow. "Why do you seem upset?"

"I'm not upset. I appreciate your hospitality." I took a swig of my beer and turned away from him.

Joseph came around the bar and stood in front of me. "What is this weird energy? Talk to me."

"Nothing." I started to walk away, but he stopped me and made me face him.

"No. Be honest. What are you thinking?" He stared down at me with those beautiful, hazel eyes that always made me want to stop talking and just kiss him.

"Do you want me to leave?" I asked.

"What? I just told you to stay as long as you like." He looked confused.

"When should I leave? I guess that's a better question."

"I don't understand."

"Yes you do." We just stared at each other for a minute and then his expression changed as he realized what I was asking.

" Are you saying you want to move in?" he asked, in a low voice.

" What do you want?" I asked, apprehensively.

"Am I not being clear?" The corners of his mouth curled into a seductive smile.

"I mean, not really." I lowered my head, sheepishly.

He touched my chin and raised my head, forcing our eyes to meet. "I said I want you to stay as long as you want— as long as you want." I just stared at him. "Do you need me to say the words?"

"Yes." I blinked up at him, begging him to say it, with my eyes.

"Kathren, do you want to move in?"

I exhaled and wrapped my arms around him. "Yes." I breathed into his neck. He hugged me and lifted me onto my toes. I was elated. I kissed his neck and worked my way to those succulent lips. He slipped his tongue into my mouth and lifted me off the floor and walked me to the stairs. He wrapped my legs around him and climbed the stairs carrying me the whole way. When we reached the bedroom, he dropped me on the bed. He was already panting from carrying me. He tore my clothes from my body. He unbuttoned his shirt, exposing that beautifully chiseled physique. He dropped his dress pants and the muscles flexed in his strong thighs, as he climbed on top of me. Then, those heavenly fingers were between my legs, making their way into my folds, stroking my clit, as he kissed me. I gasped for air, as his lips moved from my mouth to my neck and my body shuddered from the combination of his lips on my neck and his fingers moving from my clit to inside of me, smooth and easy.

Joseph knew my body. Maybe he just knew a woman's body, period, but every move he made was perfect. As I got closer to exploding, he kissed down my stomach to my mound and switched from his fingers to his tongue at the perfect second. As he licked me, he used his hands to get his boxers down. He knew exactly how to make me come and he knew just when I was about to. His plan was flawless. He would make me erupt into orgasmic convulsions and then pull his mouth away with one final suck of my clit. Then he would slide his delicious cock into me and begin to pump his hips, making me quake and shiver as he pleased himself with his forceful injections. He was never in a hurry and never stingy. My pleasure always came first.

Once I regained some strength, I pushed him to his back and positioned myself on top of him. As I lifted and dropped myself onto his throbbing cock, he held onto my thighs and grunted, trying not to come sooner than he wanted. I let my hair fall into my face as I closed my eyes and thrusted faster and faster. Finally, his fingers dug into my thighs and his eyes squeezed shut, as he erupted and poured his hot nut into me. He moaned and then whimpered and shot several times. I felt his legs shaking under my ass, as his hot blasts tickled my insides and made me come again. After that, I collapsed on top of him.

"I love you..." I wasn't sure who said it at first. The words were going through my mind, but it wasn't my voice. It was his. He actually said it. He said it first. I lifted my head and looked up at him. His eyes were closed.

"I love you too." My voice was shaky, but absolute. I meant it and I had felt it for a while. His eyes opened, he smiled and stroked my messy, sex hair out of my face. As we looked at each other with tenderness, there was clear uncertainty, as we considered the line we had crossed. These three simple words, while they said everything I had been feeling and he had been fighting against for weeks, they also exposed our vulnerability and scared us both.

I laid my head back down on his chest and pressed my body into his. I couldn't get close enough. He loved me. He really loved me. He was mine. I was his. Every bad thing left my mind at that moment. The peace that filled me was amazing. Joseph rolled me to my back and leaned over me. He stared deep into my eyes like he was searching me for any doubt.

"I haven't said those words to anyone in a very long time," he said, soberly. "I'm feeling a bit raw, right now."

"I know, Joseph. I have been in love with you for longer than I would like to admit. I'm scared. I don't want to be hurt either."

"I won't," he whispered. The way he looked at me— I knew he meant it. I touched his face and ran my thumb across his lower lip. "You're safe with me," he whispered.

I felt tears filling my eyes. "You're safe with me too."

He kissed me softly and I took the moment to say it again. I love you. I really love you, Joseph."

He laid on his side and pulled me into him. I was thrilled. The smell of his skin was like melatonin and I slept like a baby.

The next morning, I woke up alone in bed. I called out to him, as I walked down the stairs. But Joseph was gone. Before I could head to the kitchen to get my coffee, there was a knock at the door. I was caught off guard. It was quarter to nine and I had never answered Joseph's door. It crossed my mind that it was no longer only Joseph's door. He had invited me to move in and I had accepted, so I figured it was my door too. After the second knock, I walked over and opened the door. There was a delivery person, holding a long box.

"Kathren Thompson?"

"Yes?"

He handed me the gold-colored box.

"Thank you. Is there a card?" I asked.

"Probably in the box." he said in a monotone voice. "Have a nice day." He turned and walked away. I closed the door and headed for the kitchen. It was clearly flowers and I opened the box, excited to see what gift Joseph had sent me. He was so thoughtful. I opened the box to see a dozen beautiful, red roses. I took them from the box and pressed them to my nose. They smelled so fresh. I tried to find the card, but as I shifted the paper around in the box I realized there was no card.

"No note?" I mumbled to myself. I took the flowers to the sink, found a vase, and filled it with water, then arranged the flowers and set them on the table. I stared at them as I drank my coffee, thinking about the night before. The amazing sex followed by the words I'd been waiting to hear. I wondered what it meant for us. Would we be together forever? Would he ask me to marry him one day? Would we have children? I thought about the fact that anytime someone asked us the story of how we met, we would need to hold back most of the details. Then I wondered what Mark would think. If he was still alive, would he be angry? So many thoughts swirled through my mind. My cell phone rang and I rushed to retrieve it from my purse. As I found it, it stopped ringing. I had just missed it. Actually, I had missed four calls that morning, all of them were blocked numbers. There was no message left. *Weird?*

Later that evening, after work, I decided to head to my house to gather some more things. I grabbed a few boxes from the back room, at work. We were lazy about recycling our cardboard. I pulled up to what appeared to be a quiet, undisturbed house. I carried the boxes in and shut the door behind me. I didn't plan to be there very long. I figured I would grab the rest of my clothes and personal toiletries. I emptied the remaining contents of the fridge into the garbage and put my pantry items in one of the boxes. I took the garbage cans to the street and went back inside to finish boxing up the bedroom. I pulled the last bit of clothes from the drawers of my dresser and turned to get started in the bathroom, but to my shock, I bumped right into someone. I looked up, but before I could speak, I was hit in the head and everything went black.

Chapter. 16

"KATHREN? CAN YOU HEAR me?" I didn't recognize the voice. I tried to open my eyes, but I was blinded by something. Everything was dark. As the cloudiness left my mind, I tried to comprehend what was happening. My head was throbbing. Something was over my eyes— a blindfold. I tried to move, but I was bound. I was clearly lying on what felt like a bed. My hands were over my head and my legs tied tightly to each corner.

"Where am I?" I asked. My voice was hoarse. "What's happening?" I could feel some sort of bandage on my head, over my right eye.

"How's your head?" the voice asked. The voice was deep and quiet. I felt the bed indent as someone sat next to me.

"Who are you?"

"I didn't want to do this, but I didn't know how else to..." The stranger stopped mid-sentence and sighed. "You left me no choice?"

"What are you talking about? Who are you? What's happening?" I was terrified.

"I've watched you for so long. I know you saw me," the voice said. The voice was calm and low.

"What are you talking about? I don't know who this is! Please uncover my eyes!" I started crying.

"Don't cry. I will uncover your eyes, soon! For now, I need you to stay calm and listen to me."

It was him— the stalker. He'd finally done it. He had taken me. Where? I wasn't sure. I recognize the smell. It was musty and stale. I could tell I was in a bed, but it wasn't mine. I knew that much. I could see very dim shapes and the movement of the man, but it was too dark to make out anything. It occurred to me that I wasn't fully dressed. I was in a shirt. My bra was gone and I could feel that my legs were bare. My panties were still on.

"Please! Don't hurt me! Please let me go! I won't say anything," I begged.

"I wish I could, Kathren. I really do." he sighed.

"You can! I promise I won't tell."

"You left," he said, his tone sounding bitter. "You went to that party house with that devil and didn't come back. What was I supposed to do? You were going back for good, weren't you?"

He knew where I was? He had been following me everywhere?

"I don't know what you want, but I promise if you'd just let me go..."

"Stop talking. I have to think. I didn't want to do it like this, but..." He stood up and seemed to be pacing back and forth. "I tried to give you time. I tried to be patient. You kept provoking me with your clothes, walking back and forth past the windows and then having sex with men when you knew I was watching— making me watch you share yourself with men who don't deserve you ."

"I swear, I didn't know. I didn't know you were watching."

"Bullshit!" he yelled. I jumped. He sat back down and touched my shoulder.

"I'm sorry. I didn't mean to yell. But I can't have you lying or playing games—not anymore. We're done with all that now. Did you get my flowers?"

"Flowers?" They were from him, not Joseph. "Yes. They were beautiful." I tried to stay calm. My mind was racing. I didn't want to upset him. If I was going to get out of the situation, I needed to stay calm and most importantly, keep him calm.

"I know what you deserve, Kathren. You deserve respect and love. You deserve to be taken care of and to be admired. None of those pigs you let have you, respect you, especially not that devil—Joe. He uses you like a whore. He always has. Same as all the others."

I was confused. It seemed like this man knew Joseph in some way. He seemed to know some of our history.

"Have we met before?" I asked.

"That doesn't matter. What matters is that we're together now. We are supposed to be together, Kathren. I've known for a long time. I just had to get you to accept it. You weren't ready before. I didn't want to rush it. But with you moving your stuff into his house, I had to act fast. I couldn't let you move in with him. It would make things much harder for us." His voice was quiet and shaky as he sat down on the bed, again, and leaned over me. I tried not to flinch, but I was horrified.

"You're so beautiful. You smell so good. Your skin is so soft." And I recoiled as he stroked his fingers down my cheek. I shook as he caressed me—my face and then my neck. He moved his fingers over my chest and slid them around the bottom of my shirt. I could feel his breath as he leaned in close to me. I turned my face away from him, but it didn't deter him. His mouth was on me, sliding down my neck. He moaned as he licked my collarbone. I didn't want to die, but it occurred to me that I may not be able to avoid an assault. I pulled at the rope that held my wrist together over my head.

"Please! Please don't!" I whimpered. He stopped and stood up. There was silence for a few seconds and then he turned and left the room, slamming the door behind him. "Please don't leave me here! Let me go!" I shouted, but I could hear his footsteps as he walked down what sounded like a long hall.

I called out a few more times, but it was no use. I began to squirm and twist, pulling against my restraints. This guy was obviously obsessed and clearly nuts. It was very likely that he would kill me. It occurred to me that since I was blindfolded and hadn't seen his face, yet, he could still release me and not get caught. I thought that was a good sign that he may plan to let me go. I tried to stay calm and make a plan, even though I wanted to scream and cry and beg for help. If I played into his game and made him think I wanted him, I was sure to be raped, but if I showed my disgust and fear, that could send him into a fit of rage.

I lay there for what seemed like hours. Then finally I heard something—footsteps. He was coming back. I was so afraid. The door opened and closed. I heard shuffling and clinking noises.

"Are you hungry?", he asked. His voice was sober.

"I'm thirsty. And I have to use the bathroom." I heard him sigh.

He sat down next to me and lifted my head. He pushed a bottle to my lips. I sipped the water. A bit spilled down the side of my face. He wiped it with the back of his hand.

"Okay. If you don't want me to bring a bedpan, you are going to behave when I get you up to use the bathroom. Do we understand each other?"

"Yes. I'll behave." I tried to smile. It was hard. I've never been a good actress. He rose up and I heard noises, what sounded like metal clanking and a cabinet door squeaking open and shut. I felt him putting what felt like handcuffs on my wrist, then the sound of a chain dragging over metal. One restraint was removed, but another was there and he was pulling it tight. Then he was releasing my other hand and cuffing that wrist, too. The chain made noise again as my hands were pulled together. Next, my legs were freed.

"Now stand up and don't try anything. Don't remove the blindfold or it's the bedpan. Got it?"

"I got it." I stood and I stumbled as he pulled me across the room. The floor was cold. It felt like cement.

"Careful. Here. To your right." He took my hands and pulled them down until I felt something in front of me. It was a toilet— not a regular one. It was portable. I didn't go into a bathroom. I never left the room. It was a portable toilet sitting in the room, like hospitals use.

"There's no door?" I asked.

"Sorry, but this is all you got, so go ahead. There is toilet paper on the shelf, on the wall to the right."

"I can't go in front of you." I whimpered.

"Yes you can! And that's the only choice. Go now or...."

"I know. The bedpan. Okay. I'll try."

"Do you need help with your panties?" he asked.

"No." I was so scared and disgusted. I didn't want to go in front of him, but I had to go so bad and I realized I had no choice. I turned and tried to pull my panties down, while covering myself with my shirt, as I sat on the toilet and started to pee. It was humiliating. When I was done, I felt for the paper and ripped a piece and wiped, quickly. It was hard to pull my underwear up with my hands cuffed together. I had to get out.. I couldn't last for long in that hellhole. He led me back to the bed and laid me down, securing me back the way I was. I felt so exposed.

"Can I ask how long you are going to keep me here?" I asked, timidly.

"Depends."

"On?"

"You."

"What can I do?" I asked, almost begging. He didn't respond. I focused my eyes, trying to see him through the blindfold, but I could only make out his dark figure.

"You really are so beautiful, Kathren." he whispered. And again, I felt his hand on me. His fingers brushed my hair away from my face and around the edge of my ear. He brushed his fingers down the side of my neck and across my collar bone. Then he moved over my shirt to my breast and let his fingertips find my nipple. He rubbed lightly, bringing them to a point. It was involuntary. I wanted to tell him to stop, but I stayed quiet and let him do it. I felt nauseous as he caressed my breast through my shirt. I could hear a low moan under his breath. Then he moved lower, dragging his fingers down my stomach. He pulled up on my shirt and exposed my navel. The room was cold and I shivered. I could hear his breathing get deeper and shakier as he looked at me, not that I could see him, but I felt it. Then I felt his lips on me. I jerked. He dragged his lips across my belly and then his tongue. He was licking my stomach. Suddenly I became aware that he was moving. The bed was rocking, slightly. He was stroking himself.

"Please..." I stuttered, fearful that he was about to force himself on me. He ignored me. He brought his mouth down to the edge of my panties and pressed his face into my mound, as the rocking grew harder. He was jerking off, as he blew his hot breath through the thin material of my panties. He moved his face against my pelvis as his masturbation finally brought him to climax and he groaned into me, as he came. I didn't move. I didn't speak. He lifted himself and I could hear the sounds of him cleaning the come from the bed and putting himself away. He was quiet and still. I wondered if he was ashamed. It was frightening to hear him unable to control himself, getting off from rubbing against me, like a young boy who couldn't control his lust.

Then finally, he got up and left the room. I was alone again. I began to cry as the tension and fear released from the place I was holding it, trying not to upset him. I let out my emotions for a while, but then it was time to figure a way out. There had to be a way. I hoped that he left clues behind, at my house, when he abducted me. It was unlikely, though, considering all the times he had entered and exited and disappeared without a trace, leaving the police baffled. Then I thought of Joseph. I wasn't sure how long I had been gone. I knew he had to be worried. I wondered how quickly he would go to the police and let them know I was missing. I couldn't understand how this guy had gotten me out of the house without anyone seeing. This had to be my punishment for my sins. I thought that maybe I deserved it. I just didn't want to die. I wanted to see Joseph again.

Later, I was awoken by the sound of someone talking. It was him. He wasn't in the room with me. He was outside the door. There was only his voice... he was on the phone. I strained to hear.

"Yes... I know.... I will talk to you about it later... Just do what I told you... Enough..." That was all I could hear, then he opened the door. I waited for him to speak. I could tell he was putting a bag down on a surface, next to the bed. He was moving things around.

"Are you hungry?" he asked.

"No...Thank you." I tried to be polite.

"You need to eat," he insisted.

"I'm not hungry."

"I know you're upset and this is not ideal, but I need you to eat and drink." *Not ideal?* He made it sound like I was in a resort and my room faced the parking lot, instead of the ocean view. I smelled something. He had brought food.

"It smells good. What is it?" I asked.

"Just a burger and fries from Maxwell's. You like that place, right?"

What the fuck? How long had he been following me around? It had been months since I had gone to Maxwell's. I felt sick, but I stayed calm...outwardly.

"Maxwell's is good." I answered. I listened as he unwrapped the burger and then he touched it to my lips. I took a small bite. He wiped my mouth with a napkin.

"Here." He gave me the straw of a soda, next. I felt like a child, being fed.

"Can I have one hand free, maybe....to feed myself?" I asked, softly.

"Not a good idea," he mumbled, offering me the burger again.

"I promise, I will behave." I spoke sweetly and submissively, trying to give him confidence that he was in control. I mean, he was in control, but I needed to gain his trust and make him believe that I was too timid to ever try something.

He sighed and then after a minute he began to free my right hand. "Don't make me regret this."

"I won't. Thank you." I smiled and rubbed my right wrist with my bound hand. He sat the burger, in its wrapper, in my lap. I picked it up and took another bite.

"Your drink is on the table to your right," he said, standing up. I reached over and felt around the table. I found the cup and took a drink. I could feel him watching me, as I ate my meal. I tried to appear relaxed and content. If I could get him to allow me to keep my one hand free, I would be one step closer to escape.

"What can I call you?" I asked. He didn't respond. "I know you won't tell me your real name, but is there something I can call you... a nickname, maybe?"

"Why?" he asked, indifferently.

I wasn't sure how to respond. I couldn't tell him that I was trying to connect, so he wouldn't kill me and possibly drop his guard and let me go. "Just think I would feel more comfortable. I can't see you. It makes it hard. I don't know who you are or where I am. Sitting here in the dark all day and night is very—lonely and—scary. If I could just have a way to feel like I'm not alone." He was quiet for a minute and then he spoke.

"Call me— Mark."

What? I stopped breathing. I stayed frozen, but my mind was in chaos. *Was this a sick joke? A coincidence? A message?*

"What's wrong? You don't care for the name Mark?" he asked, coldly. I couldn't speak. I lowered my head. I took the burger from my lap and sat it on the table next to the drink.

"Who are you? What do you want?" I asked, defeatedly.

"I am a real man, not one of the twisted bastards you are accustomed to and I want you to understand that. You want to call me something? Call me Sir!" He came over and started to restrain my wrist again.

"Please! Don't. Just let me have one free!" I begged, but he didn't listen. He locked me up and walked out. "Please!" I screamed, but he ignored me. I listened as his footsteps disappeared and he left me there. I started to pull and jerk at the restraints again. I thrashed and fought. I pulled and pulled until my wrists were killing me. Finally, I gave up and laid limp on the bed.

Chapter 17

IT HAD BEEN, WHAT SEEMED like several hours, when my kidnapper returned.

"I need to use the bathroom!" I announced, as soon as the door opened. I was about to pee my pants.

"Okay," he answered and began removing my restraints and cuffing my hands together in front of me. He freed my ankles and helped me up from the bed. He moved me across the floor to the toilet.

"Can I have privacy? Please..."

"I'll turn around."

"That's not privacy," I argued. "Can't you just stand outside the door?"

He thought for a minute, then said, "Don't take off the mask. I'll be just outside. I will come in when you flush. Don't take too long."

"Thank you. I'll try to hurry." He left the room and I sat down on the toilet. As I started to pee, I immediately lifted the mask to get a quick look at my surroundings. The room was dimly lit by a small lamp on an old table next to a bed in the middle of the room. The sheets looked clean, thank God. The floors were concrete and the walls were brick, with no windows. The door was solid steel and it was opening. I quickly lowered my mask. "I'm not done." I called out.

"One more minute," he ordered. He left the door cracked this time. I hurried to finish. I quickly stood, pulled my panties up and flushed the toilet. He came back in and grabbed me by the arm. He walked me back to the bed and laid me down.

"How long am I going to be here?" I asked as he connected me to the bed again.

"I don't know. However long it takes."

"However long, what takes?" I asked. He didn't answer.

"I can't stay here. I need a shower. I need to be able to eat and drink and use the bathroom when needed. I haven't brushed my teeth. Please. I'm begging you. Just let me go. I won't say anything." He got up and walked out. "Please! Sir!" I screamed. I cried myself to sleep.

The next time I woke, it was to the sound of him moving things around in the room. Suddenly, he pulled my mask off. Instinctually, I squeezed my eyes shut. I was afraid to look at him. He sat down next to me and started removing my restraints and cuffing me in front like he did when I needed to use the toilet. He dragged a chain across the floor and connected it to my ankles. Then he disconnected them from the bottom of the bed.

"Open your eyes," he said. I hesitated. "Open them." He insisted. I peeked out and saw a masked man sitting in front of me. He had a full mask on his face. It was black, with a slit in the mouth and a weird, shaded material over his eyes, so he could see out, but I couldn't see him. It covered his entire head. Not even a strand of hair or inch of skin was exposed. He wore a black long sleeve turtleneck shirt and black pants and boots. Only his hands were exposed. He was white and thin, medium height. That's all I could tell.

"What's happening?" I asked.

"I heard what you said yesterday. I don't want you to be so uncomfortable, especially if you're going to cooperate. There is a shower in the next room and a sink. I bought you a toothbrush and paste, some soap and shampoo... the kind you use. I have a change of clothes and towels in there. Now, we are going to try this. The first time you test me, it's over! You'll be back on the bed, spread eagle with a bedpan— and I will hurt you! Understand?"

"Yes. I'll be good."

"Now you can stand up and go to the bathroom when you want and eat and drink as you want and when I am here, you can shower and clean up."

I looked around. There were a couple cases of water on the floor, against the wall, a bag of chips, peanut butter, crackers, and bananas on the table. I could move around on my own, now...sort of. My feet were chained together with about a foot of slack. There was another chain attached that he would use to control me and keep me locked to the bed. My hands were cuffed in front, but I could see... no blindfold.

"Let's go shower." He stood me up and walked me to another room just outside the room I had been trapped in for, I don't know how long. I could only take short steps. I definitely couldn't run from him. There was a hall with a few doorways and, what looked like, a few steps leading up to another level, at the end of the hall. I couldn't see beyond that. The room that he led me to was just to the left outside of mine. It was big and empty with a couple shower heads sticking out of the wall. It reminded me of what you would expect in a shitty prison or a mental hospital in a scary movie. It was cold and old. I looked at him and then back at the showers.

"No curtains?" I asked.

"No."

"Are you going to step out?"

"No."

"But..."

"Don't say anything else!" he barked at me. " I've seen you, Kathren. I know what kind of things you've done. You've exposed yourself to so many men—fucked so many men. Don't play shy and innocent." I didn't argue. But I wondered who the fuck he was and how he knew these things.

"Are you going to uncuff me so I can undress?" I asked. He pulled out a knife. I shuttered away from him. He stepped toward me and pulled at my shirt. He sliced it with the blade, cutting it from my body. Then he pulled at the strings of my panties and cut them off. He stripped me naked and then turned on the water. The pressure wasn't very strong. He stood there, next to the place I needed to stand, watching me. I moved toward the water and let it soak me. At least it was warm. He took a cloth and squeezed soap into it. It was the soap I normally use. He started to wash me.

"I can do it," I told him. It was a statement, but also a request. He didn't respond. He just continued to wash me. He cleaned my back and bottom. He squeezed the cloth and let the suds run down my body. Then he moved to my front. He began to bathe my breast and stomach. His sleeves were getting wet, but he didn't seem to care. He wore the mask, but I could tell he was staring at my breast as he caressed them. I could hear his breath quiver as his hand slipped around, over my soapy breasts. He rubbed over my nipples again and again until they became hard. He moved the cloth down to my legs and pushed between my thighs. He moved it back and forth, to clean me, but he was doing more than just cleaning me. His fingers were covered by the rag, but he was moving in a way that was obvious. He was watching me closely. I didn't react. I just looked away.

"Rinse off," he said, when he realized I wasn't getting aroused and he went to the doorway. He watched, as I finished washing. Then I took a towel from a ledge and wrapped it around me. I brushed my teeth and turned to look at him.

"Let's go," he moved aside and motioned to the room with the bed. I walked back to my new prison and sat down. He connected the center chain to the base of the bed and then stood there, staring at me.

"What now?" I asked.

"Lay back."

"Please... don't..." He moved toward me and I submitted. I laid back, my towel still around me. He lifted the cuffs over my head and connected them to the head board. "I thought you were going to let me move freely, if I behaved!"

"Shhh..." He opened my towel and exposed my nakedness. He just stood there, breathing deeply, ogling me. Then he reached down and touched my thigh. I didn't speak. I tried to stay calm. He moved his fingers up and down stroking my legs and then he pushed them apart. I was so bare and unprotected. I waited for the assault. I was sure I was going to be raped again, but like last time he pulled his cock out and began to stroke himself. I looked away. He just stood there, staring at me, masturbating, and touching my leg, until he came. He shot onto my leg and then he reached for a napkin and wiped it off. He put himself away and without a word he freed me from the headboard and left. I was still cuffed, but I could get out of bed, now. I closed my towel. He didn't allow me to dress. There was a shirt, pair of shorts and underwear at the foot of the bed, but with my hands still cuffed and ankles shackled, I had no way to put them on. At least I had a towel to cover me.

I stood and walked around the room, taking a good look at everything. I took a water bottle from the case and drank. It worried me to see so many bottles— enough for a week, at least. I tried the door and to my surprise, it was open. I couldn't believe it. I thought it may be a trick. Maybe he was testing me. Maybe he was still there, waiting to see if I would try to escape. I closed the door and sat on the bed. I inspected the cuffs. I turned my wrist in different directions to see if there was a way out of them, but then I thought I should work on my ankles. If I freed my hands and couldn't get my ankles out, he would know I tried to get out. I had to be sure I could free myself before I attempted an escape. So, I started on my ankles. I twisted my feet until they were sore. After several hours, I grew tired and fell into a deep sleep.

"HOW DID YOU SLEEP?" I opened my eyes to find him standing over me. I was sound asleep when he came in. I didn't even hear him. I had barely been sleeping for days and now that I could actually move and lay in different positions, I guess I needed a good long rest. I wondered how long he'd been looking at me. And, when I realized I was uncovered, I assumed it was a while. I grabbed the towel and covered myself.

"I slept better. Thank you for letting me move around." I smiled at him. It was hard. As I said, I'm not a good actor, but I had to gain his trust. He had a bag in his hand. "What's in the bag?"

He tossed it on the bed. I reached inside. When I pulled the box from the bag, my jaw dropped. It was a vibrator. I stared at it and then looked at him.

"I want to watch you," he said. "You saw me, now I want to watch you do it."

"I can't." I whispered.

"Yes you can. I figured it might be difficult under these circumstances, so I bought that. That makes it easy for you, if you're nervous. No woman can use that and not finish. I'm certain of it. I want to watch you. Please do what I ask." He was asking, but it wasn't a request. He took the box out of my hand and opened it. He hit the button and it came on. "It has a charge," he said, turning it off and handing it back to me. He reached down and unshackled my ankles, so that my legs could open. He sat on the edge of the bed and waited, staring at me from behind his dark mask. I wondered if he felt shame from masturbating in front of me and this was his way of evening things.

I wanted to refuse, but I had no power. I knew there would be consequences. So, I backed away from him a bit, turned it on and opened my legs. He pushed my towel away. I didn't know how I would be able to come, in this situation. I thought I would have to pretend. I lowered the vibrating wand to my pussy and pushed it against my flesh. He watched and leaned closer to get a better look. I felt ashamed. It was strong. I held it there, thinking it would do nothing for me, but the thing was powerful and I began to tingle and my breathing quickened. He began to rub himself over his pants, as he watched. I closed my eyes and tried to shut him out and think of something arousing. And, suddenly, I saw Joseph and Mark. They were touching me... fucking me and I began to grind against the vibrator. It only took a couple minutes and I was panting and my leg was shaking. Then, I gasped and released a quiet moan, as I came in front of him. When I opened my eyes, I saw that he was panting hard, too. I don't know if he came in his pants, but he sounded like he had, still stroking himself slowly. I stopped the toy and laid it beside me. The shame was awful..

"How much longer, until I can leave." I asked, still labored, crossing my legs, and raising my cuffed hands to hide my breast.

He got up and walked out, slamming the door behind him. He was only there for about ten minutes. I covered up and pushed the vibrator to the floor. Then, it occurred to me, he left my legs free. I stood up and looked around. I went to the folded clothes, still laying on the bottom corner of the bed. They were my clothes. I put the underwear on and the shorts. It felt better to be partially dressed. I still couldn't put on the shirt with my hands bound, so I wrapped the towel around me and tucked it tightly, over my breast. I ate a banana, some peanut butter and crackers and drank some water. After waiting a while, letting some time pass, I went to the door and tried it. It was still open. I listened hard, but other than the sound of the door's creek and my breath, it was quiet. I took a deep breath and stepped out. Passing the invisible barrier, between obedience and betrayal.

It was now or never. I wasn't sure if he was gone or if I would make it all the way out. It could have been a huge mistake, but I knew that things would eventually escalate and I could be risking my life whether I stayed or tried to escape.

I moved down the hall, slowly, looking in each room as I went. The rooms were mostly empty, except for some trash and a couple old filing cabinets and chairs. I made my way to the end of the hall and stopped at the bottom of the short staircase. I leaned forward without moving my feet and listened. There was an echoing noise, I can't explain. Sort of the sound of a big empty space. I walked up the stairs and came into a big area. It looked like a small warehouse. There was another stairway to the right that looked like it led up to an office. There were two large garage doors that had locks on them and to the left...a door. I moved quickly through the space, to the door, and turned the knob. It was locked. At first, I panicked, but then I realized there was a bolt lock. I turned it and tried the knob again. It opened! The light from outside blinded me and the fresh air smelled like freedom.

Holy shit! I was free! I squinted, trying to see my surroundings. I was in a parking lot, sitting back between two large brick buildings. I rushed through the lot and looked both ways down the street. I had no idea where I was. I headed right, to the closest intersection. I held the towel around me, my wrist still cuffed. It seemed to be later in the afternoon, but the streets were very deserted. The area looked somewhat industrial with some abandoned buildings. I made it to the corner and looked up at the street signs...Weber and National. I didn't know Weber, but National was a street that ran through several towns including mine. I had to find people, quickly. I was scared that my stalker may drive by, on his way back and recapture me. Finally, a car was coming. I took a chance and stepped out onto the road and waved my hands. It was a woman in the car. She slowed to a stop next to me and cracked her window.

"Do you need help?" she asked.

"Yes! Please! I was kidnapped! I escaped! I need the police!" The emotion of the situation and the danger I had been in began to overwhelm me. I burst into tears.

"Get in, honey." she unlocked her doors and I walked around to the passenger side and got in. I was safe. I sobbed, as she called 911.

A COUPLE HOURS LATER, I was sitting in a room at Mt. Blessing Police Station. They gave me a gray tee shirt to put on and a blanket to stay warm. It felt so good to have my hands and feet free. I found out that I had been missing for four days. I still hadn't had a chance to call Joseph. There were police at the location where I was being held. It was an old, abandoned warehouse in Mt. Blessing, a town about an hour from my house. I wondered if they would have evidence to catch him, now. I was just so happy to be free and safe. They had questioned me for about an hour, about what happened and everything I could remember about him, which wasn't much. I knew his height, his build, and his race. And I will never forget his voice. It was awful having to explain what he did to me, but they needed to know everything. They even tried to get some DNA from my leg where he had ejaculated, even though he wiped it off. Suddenly, the door opened.

"Kat!" It was Joseph. He rushed over to me and I reached out for him. He scooped me up, into his arms and I burst into tears, again.

"How did you know I was here?"

"Casteel called me as soon as he got word you had been found. Thank God you're alright." He leaned back and looked at me, "*Are* you alright?"

"I'm okay now." I buried my face back into his chest.

"Did he hurt you?" he asked, stroking my hair.

"Not really. He hit me in the head when he took me." He looked at the small gash in my hairline and kissed it.

"That motherfucker. He better hope I don't get my fucking hands on him."

"I just hope they find something that helps them catch him." I said, wiping my tears.

"Jesus, I thought I lost you." He squeezed me so tight. "This has been the longest four days of my life." It felt amazing to be back in his arms and to hear him being so protective. I wanted to be in the safety of his arms, in his bed, where I felt the safest. I loved him. It took a while, but finally they let me leave and Joseph drove me home.

Chapter 18

"YOU WON'T BE GOING back." Joseph said, as I stepped out of the shower.

"What?"

"Your house. You're not going back. I'll get the rest of your stuff. We'll get a moving company to get your furniture and we'll store it, but I will pick up your personal things." He stood at the doorway, looking at me. I loved the authoritative way he told me what was going to happen. I smiled at him as I dried my hair with a towel. He looked so beautiful, standing there shirtless, in his blue jeans.

"Sounds good to me." I sighed and walked toward him. He opened his arms and I pressed into him.

"I bet you're tired," he said, stroking my hair.

"I am."

"Come on." He led me to the bed. "Do you want pajamas?"

"Why?" I normally slept naked and he had never asked me that before, so I was confused.

"Just... After everything, I thought..." He paused. I reached up and kissed him. I wrapped my arms around him and let my towel drop.

"Are you sure?" he asked, while I kissed him. "Kat..."

I stopped and stared at him. I didn't say anything. I unbuttoned his jeans and reached into his pants. He gasped as I took him in my hand. He closed his eyes and tilted his head back, as I massaged him.

"I missed you," I whispered, kissing his neck and chest.

"I missed you, too," he moaned. Then he reached down and pushed his pants down. He hoisted me up and held me, wrapping my legs around him. I could feel his rock-hard cock under my ass, ready to slip in. He began to kiss my neck. "You want me?" he breathed, his voice was low and filled with desire. I didn't just want him. I needed him.

"Yes," I mumbled.

"Yes, what?" he demanded.

"Yes, I want you. I want you so bad." He dropped me down onto the bed and as he thrust inside, I squealed with pleasure. His strokes were smooth and slow at first. My pussy squeezed tight. He kissed my shoulder and collar bone massaging my breast and every nerve in my body was on fire.

"Fuck! You feel so damn good, baby!" His rhythm grew faster and his thrust was harder and harder. He grunted, as he fucked. It was almost as if we were fucking away any remnants of what had happened to me. I needed it. He did too. He pushed into me with such force that my body was jolting and sliding up the silk sheets and he was climbing along, to stay with me and stay deep. I moaned louder, as I got closer to orgasm. The sound of him grunting was driving me crazy and then finally we both came...hard. It was an explosive release and it made everything right in my world, for the moment.

Later that night, as we lay holding each other, my head on Joseph's chest, I could tell, by his breathing, that he was awake. Usually, when Joseph couldn't sleep and we were taking a break from the physical, he would retreat to his office, but I knew he didn't want to leave me and something was bothering him. I felt it.

"What is it?" I asked, softly.

"What?"

"What's on your mind?" I knew it was something. He sighed. I rubbed his stomach and pulled at him, signaling for him to come out with it. "Tell me."

" You were gone for four days. What happened?" he asked.

"I told you. He kept me chained up like a prisoner."

"But, what—what did he do to you?" he sounded, almost afraid to ask. I looked up at him. His eyes were concerned.

"He didn't rape me."

He exhaled so much relief. "Thank God. He didn't touch you. I'm so glad, Kat."

I didn't want to upset Joseph and I didn't want to talk about the weird things that happened while I was being kept, but I didn't want to lie to him, either. I dropped my head and took a deep breath.

"Hey. What is it?" He touched my chin and lifted my face to meet his gaze. He could see it in my eyes. "You're not telling me everything."

"It's hard to talk about. I didn't say he didn't touch me. He— He touched himself while he— looked at me. He rubbed his face and tongue on me while he touched himself... and he gave me a shower and he wouldn't let me do it myself... and he... he..." Joseph shushed me and pulled me into him, close.

"That fucking sicko. I'm so sorry, baby. I'm so fucking sorry. I should have never let you go to that house alone. I don't know what I was..."

"No! Don't you dare! This isn't your fault. And I'm okay. Nothing's hurt that won't heal."

You can't say that, for sure, Kat. You've been through so much the last year. It doesn't make any damn sense. Most people don't experience one of the fucking horrors you've gone through in their whole life. I mean, shit! I can't believe you're handling it so well. I can't believe you're even able to let me touch you."

I cupped his face in my hand. "Joseph, your touch heals me. I am safe when I'm with you and I know it. I never feel more safe. I know you would never hurt me. I trust you... and I love you. No matter what happens in my life, when I am here..." I caressed his chest, over his heart, " I'm okay." I stared deep into his gorgeous, hazel eyes, right into his soul. He stared back, his breath trembled. He leaned in and kissed me, softly. We fell asleep and slept deeply through the night.

OVER THE NEXT WEEK, the Mt. Blessing police interviewed me again and Joseph arranged to get my belongings from my house. I took a week off work and Mr. Lewis was more than fine with it. He kept insisting that I might need more time, but I told him I would go crazy if I didn't get back to my life soon. He agreed that I would come back in a week. Joseph tried to convince me that I should go to therapy, but I refused. It's not that I've ever had a problem with therapy and I agreed that I could probably benefit from it, but sitting and talking with a stranger about all the shit I was dealing with, in my mind, just didn't make sense to me. How long would it take for something about Mark and what happened to him to accidentally slip out? It wasn't an option—not for me.

It was about midway through the week and Joseph came into the kitchen, where I was sitting, scrolling through my phone, and drinking a cup of tea. He sat down across from me and rested his elbows on the table, folding his arms. He looked like he needed to tell me something.

"What is it?" I asked.

"How do you feel about a trip?"

"A trip?"

"Yeah. We could get out of town for a while... a few days in Florida. Truth is, I have a business thing. I need to go and I want you to come with me."

"When?"

"We'd leave Sunday. Come back Wednesday."

"I can't. I start back to work, Monday." I told him.

"Tell him you need a few extra days."

"I can't."

"Sure you can. He'll give you more time."

"Yeah, but I don't want to do that. He's been without me for over a week already. I need to get back to work."

"I don't want to leave town and leave you here alone," he said, anxiously.

"I'll be fine here at your house." I assured him.

"Kat! Listen, I don't want to freak you out, but that bastard's still out there. You said he followed you and he knew things about you. He could follow you here. He might already know that you're here. He could be watching our coming and going. I can't leave you here alone. I just won't feel comfortable."

I really didn't want to go on a trip. I wasn't up to it. "Joseph. I appreciate your concern and I get it. I'm not thrilled about the idea of you leaving and I would love to take a trip with you sometime, but now's not a good time for me and we have to live our lives. We can't let him win. I don't want to live my life scared or running away. You have an alarm system. I won't go out at night. I'll watch my back. I really want to go back to work. Please understand."

Joseph looked frustrated with my request, but he wasn't going to force me. I may have been making a huge mistake. I probably should have stayed stuck like glue to Joseph, but I didn't want to overdo things, either. Joseph was so wonderful and he seemed to really love me, but it wasn't too long ago that Joseph was telling me he didn't want this and he was sleeping with lots of women. If he never got a chance to breathe, away from me, I feared he may get sick of me and retreat. I didn't want to lose him.

"I don't understand... but, I do. I just don't like the idea of leaving you here alone. He already got close to you more than once, and the last time, he fucking took you. Kat... If he ever gets a chance to get his hands on you again, he'll make sure this time you can't get away. I need you to realize that."

"I do, Joseph. I know the risk. I promise I do. I will be safe." I could see the concern on his face. He was genuinely worried and I understood why. Truth be known...I was worried too.

Later that night, I laid in bed awake. Joseph was asleep next to me. My mind was racing. I was remembering how things were when Mark was alive. I missed the relationship between the three of us. It occurred to me that I may never have the feeling of more than one lover at a time and the thought bothered me. I pulled back the covers and got out of bed, quietly. I crept across the floor and gently opened the drawer of Joseph's dresser. There was the photo of Joseph and Mark. I leaned against the wall near the french door, letting the moonlight shine in and illuminate the image. Mark was so gorgeous. Those eyes... That body... That dimple...

The way thoughts of Mark still consumed so much of my desires bothered me. One thing about Mark, I didn't think of very much, was that he had a violent side and he was beginning to let it show more, the days before his death. He could be so manipulative. Mark always said he was just helping me realize and accept my hidden desires, but sometimes I think he was creating them. I didn't know they were there before I met him. Sure... I wanted passion and heat in my life, but the darker stuff was never there before. The problem was, now that I had moved past it all and Mark was gone and Joseph loved me... I still wanted it. I wanted that excitement.

My stalker said something when he had me. He insinuated that I wasn't as innocent as I might like to portray and that I had done nasty things with many people, so my requests for privacy and reluctance to be exposed were phony. *Were they? Was he calling me a whore and was he right?*

"What are you doing?" Joseph's voice startled me. He was sitting up in bed, staring at me.

I quickly put the picture back in the drawer and closed it. "Sorry. Did I wake you?"

"It's ok for you to look at that picture, Kat."

I didn't know what to say. I just went back to bed and sat next to him.

"What's wrong? You missing Mark?" he asked.

"Um, sort of. I mean, I'm thinking about him. Really, I am thinking about us— the three of us, the things we used to do together." I felt ashamed to say it out loud.

"You miss those things?" he asked, lowering his head to catch my gaze, in the dim room.

"I don't know... I..."

He adjusted himself, so that he was in front of me. I was sitting cross legged and he was leaning on his elbow, in front of my lap. "You what?" He smiled, a bit seductively. He was curious.

"I don't know."

"Yes you do. You know exactly how you feel. You just don't want to admit it. It's okay. Tell me." He swept his fingers in a circle on my thigh.

"Well, yeah. I do miss the things we did. Some of it." The muscles between my legs tightened as he caressed me and my thoughts went back to an intense moment between the three of us.

"Do you fantasize about it?" he asked.

"Yes."

"What do you remember?"

"All of it." I don't know why I was so shy to talk about it, but I could tell he was aroused and wanted to hear me say it. "I think about that first night the three of us were together, you watching me from the chair in the corner. I was so nervous and you promised me you wouldn't move until I told you to."

"I remember that night. You were so sexy." He moved his fingers under my panties and I inhaled sharply, as he grazed the edge of my lips. "You wanted me then, but you couldn't accept it, at first. We really had to work with you to get your guard down. You were so timid. You drove me fucking crazy. It was all I could do to keep my ass planted in that chair."

"I was a little tense."

"A little? You were shaking like a leaf, but you were fucking excited. There's nothing quite like that feeling, huh?" he said, stroking the lips of my pussy. What else do you think about?"

"You...watching me and Mark. Mark really got off on you watching. Then when he was done, you asked if you could move. I was so nervous. I couldn't even look at you."

"But you said yes."

"I did. And you walked over to the bed and stood over me. The first touch almost sent me through the roof."

Joseph rose up and began to slide my panties off. Then he pulled me down. He opened my legs and laid them over his lap. My ass was propped up so that my pussy was tilted up, facing him. He ran his hands up my tummy to my breast and lifted my top. He pinched my nipples and played with me, teasing me. "What else?"

"I remember Mark watching us. You put my hands on you, so I could feel your body. It excited me so much. You touched my..."

"Your what?" He slid his hand down between my legs and parted my lips. He began to brush circles around my clit, slowly. It sent shock waves through me and I started to shake. "Here? Did I touch you like this?"

"Yes..." I whimpered.

"Then what did we do to you?" he breathed. He was driving me crazy. I could hardly speak. He bit into his lip as he watched me. "Tell me what else we did to you."

I put my hand over my face. I panted and squirmed, as he teased me. In my mind, I was back there... back in that room, that first night with both of them.

"Did we make you come?" he asked, as he lowered his boxers and released his beautiful, stiff cock.

"Yes." I purred.

"How?" He positioned himself at my opening and shoved it inside. "Like this?" he grunted, as he began to fuck me. I cried out in pleasure and pain. I wasn't the only one who was aroused by envisioning that night. Joseph liked to be watched, too. He was really worked up and he fucked me, hard. There was so much intensity. It was so incredibly exciting.

"Fuck! You feel so damn good!" he mumbled, between his moans. We were both in that moment, that moment with Mark. I could hear Mark's voice saying "Come for me, baby." that always drove me wild when one of them was pleasuring me while the other whispered in my ear. I loved it when they talked to each other about what they wanted to do to me or how tight I was, or how wet.

"That night we fucked you together, both of us in you at the same time—you were like fucking puddy, sandwiched between us. You came so fucking hard." He thrusted deep as he spoke through his moaning. "Come for me now, baby! Come hard for me!" he growled, and I did— we both did. We orgasmed, in a euphoric explosion, together. It was electrifying.

Joseph collapsed on top of me, almost hyperventilating from the workout. It was so perfect and exhausting.

Chapter 19

SUNDAY ARRIVED AND it was time for Joseph to leave on his trip. He had tried to convince me to go with him, every day. I declined, though. I wanted to go back to work. I wanted my boss to know that everything was going to go back to normal and my trauma wasn't going to affect my job.

I had been through a lot over the last year. Joseph was right about that, but I am tough. I was stronger than I ever thought. Mark taught me that. I was a bit nervous about being all alone in Joseph's big house, though. I usually felt safe there, but I had never been there alone.

"Don't hesitate to call the police if you see or hear anything. Do you understand?" Joseph insisted.

"I promise. I will." I assured him. He showed me how to use the alarm system and double checked that I had it down. He kept looking around, as if he was afraid he had forgotten to show me something.

"Call me if you need me and I will call as soon as I land." He was so sweet.

"Don't worry. It will be fine. He got lucky last time because I underestimated him. I won't do that again." I hugged him tight. I was going to miss him and his body. He kissed me deeply, reminded me to lock the door and he left. I was alone. Joseph's house was big, around thirty-five hundred square feet, and with him gone, it felt like an empty museum. I didn't like it.

Later that night, Joseph called to check on me. I let him know that I was safe and I missed him. We chatted for a while and then I went to bed. It felt so strange to wander around the house as if it were my own. It occurred to me that if I left Joseph or he tired of me, I would have nowhere to go. I only had a few months left on my lease before it was time to renew it and I felt a bit uneasy about letting the house go. I had lived there for several years. But, I was enjoying playing house with Joseph.

Monday morning, I went to work and as I expected, Mr. Lewis was being overly attentive and caring.

"How are you? Are you sure you're okay to be here? It's not too soon?" He was being so sweet, but he was driving me nuts.

"Mr. Lewis. I really appreciate all your concern. I do. I am okay, though. Really, I am. If I start to feel like it's too much and I need to leave, I promise I will tell you, but honestly, it feels good to be back at work and back to normal." I smiled at him and waited for the exhale that told me he was okay with me being there.

"Okay Kathren. Well, I'm glad to have you back. I've been so worried about you. And I want you to call me when you arrive in the morning, so I can come to the door and I am going to walk you out at the end of the day." His tone and requests was like a father's.

"Okay. That sounds good." I smiled and looked at my desk and then back at him.

"Let me get you caught up." He grabbed some papers off his desk and brought them to me and I got to work. The rest of the day went pretty normal. I was very busy and it was great. Mr. Lewis walked me to my car at the end of the day, as he said, and I headed home... to Joseph's. I still didn't feel like it was my home. I wondered if I would ever. Something about it felt temporary.

Later that night, I sat in the living room, after locking all the doors and setting the alarm. Every time I looked toward the stairs, I saw Mark's body and I felt guilty...guilty that I pushed him... guilty that I was living there... guilty that I was lying about everything... guilty that no one would ever know what actually happened... and guilty that I still fantasize about him. I couldn't help it. As amazing as sex was with Joseph, the experiences I had with both of them were unforgettable. Mark hurt me. He manipulated me and destroyed my life, but I was crazy about him, at the time. He was so sexy and so unpredictable. And he was a master in bed.

Suddenly, the phone rang. I picked it up, expecting it to be Joseph. It was a number I didn't recognize.

"Hello."

"So you've moved in with him..." I knew the voice. I couldn't speak. "You thought you escaped on your own. Silly girl. I let you go. I took you when I wanted to and I released you when I wanted to. And I can do it again whenever I want." He sounded angry.

"Why won't you leave me alone?" I asked with as much strength as I could muster. "I don't understand."

"I thought it was their fault, but maybe I was wrong, Kathren. Maybe it's all you. Maybe you can't be saved. Maybe you are just a little whore. Well, if you want to be treated like a whore—I can do that..."

I hung up. My heart was racing. I dialed the police. Ten minutes later, they were there, at Joseph's. Detective Casteel came in about five minutes after the first two cops.

"He knows I'm here. He knows I moved in." I told him, in a panic. "What am I going to do? He won't stop."

Detective Casteel looked at me, consolingly. "You don't know him...you're sure?" he asked.

"I don't. I will never forget his voice and I know his build, but I have never seen his face."

"This guy is determined. That's for sure. We checked the number. It's a burner phone."

"You'll never catch him." I said, defeated.

"Yes we will, Ms. Thomas. We'll get him. I'm sure of it. He's going to mess up. They always do. Just like with Mark Sander's disappearance. It might take time but I will find out what happened."

I just stared at him. A cold chill ran down my spine. I really wished Joseph was home. I didn't want to be alone. Detective Casteel told me an officer would hang out for a while. He would stay in his cruiser in the driveway. That gave me some relief. When they left the house, I set the alarm and called Joseph. He was so upset that I didn't come with him.

"I knew it was a bad idea for you to stay behind. I wish you had listened to me. I need to see about canceling my meeting. I 'll come home."

"No Joseph. Don't miss your meeting. There's a cop parked out front. I have the alarm on. I'll be okay."

"Well, I am going to get an earlier flight. I will leave right after the meeting tomorrow night instead of Wednesday morning. Damn it. This is so fucked up. I feel helpless down here. What did he say to you?"

I didn't want to tell him. I didn't want to alarm him. "He just said that he let me escape. It wasn't an accident and he called me names and he said he knew I moved in with you." I tried to pretend that I wasn't scared. I was, though. I really was.

"What did he call you?" he asked.

"A whore."

He was quiet for a few seconds and then he said, "That mother fucker!" Joseph stayed on the phone with me for a long while, until I was falling asleep. He didn't want to leave me alone. I was glad to have him there, even if it was just over the phone, but finally, I had to make him hang up and go to sleep. He had a busy day the next morning. I, on the other hand, barely slept that night. Every little noise startled me. I repeatedly double checked the window to make sure the police officer was still there. He left, sometime between four and five am. I was glad to have him there most of the night. Joseph called me in the morning and let me know he had changed his flight and he would be getting in around nine o'clock. I couldn't wait for him to get home.

I got to work and I called my boss so he could watch me walk in. I felt better to be with Mr. Lewis. I felt safer when I wasn't alone. Life felt sort of normal when I was there, focusing on my job. The day stretched. I couldn't wait to feel safe in Joseph's arms.

That afternoon, I told Mr. Lewis about the phone call. He was very worried for me. He asked me if I would like him to reach out to a friend of his, who was a private investigator. I agreed to speak to him, but I couldn't afford to pay for an actual investigation. At the end of the day, Mr. Lewis was walking me out and my phone rang. I didn't recognize the number and I gave Mr. Lewis a look.

"Answer it. I'm here," he encouraged me.

"Hello." I stood next to my car with Mr. Lewis standing in front of me, watching my reaction.

"Kathren? It's Linda." I exhaled and smiled at Mr. Lewis.

"It's okay. It's my neighbor, Linda." I told him.

"*Okay. See ya tomorrow.*" he mouthed.

I got in the car and locked the door. "Hi. Linda. How are you?"

"I'm okay. It's been a while. So, you've moved, I guess," she said. Her voice was fragile sounding.

"Yes. After what happened, I decided not to come back. I'm sure you heard that I was abducted by that crazy person." She was silent for a minute. "I'm okay, though. I'm staying with a friend now."

"Kathren...would you come over? I'd like to talk to you."

"What is it? Is everything okay?" I asked. I could tell something was wrong.

"I would just like to talk to you in person. Can you come?"

"Sure, Linda. I'll be there in a bit. I'm just leaving work."

"Okay. See you soon."

Driving over, I was a little nervous. I hadn't been back since my kidnapping. Not even to get mail. Joseph had my mail changed over for me and picked up what was in my box until they stopped delivering. I did feel bad, though, about how I had left things with Linda and I knew something was going on. She had been so hesitant to talk to me the last couple of times I saw her and I knew things had been difficult with her husband. He didn't treat her very well. I tried to call Joseph, but he didn't answer. I wanted to tell him that I would be at Linda's house for a while and let him know I would have her watch me when I left. His voice mail was full. I assumed he was still on the plane. I knew he would call when he landed and I could tell him then. I couldn't wait to see him.

As I drove onto my street and pulled up in front of Linda's house, I got an eerie feeling. Would he even come around now that he knew I was living with Joseph? Maybe he was hanging around Joseph's street, now, watching for me, there. I had become accustomed to watching my rear-view mirror when I drove and I felt confident that no one was following me. I looked over at my house. There was an emptiness hanging over. It was dark and abandoned looking. It made me angry. Not that I wasn't happy to be living with Joseph, but I didn't like that someone had forced me out. It made me feel weak. I didn't want Joseph to feel obligated. Granted, he asked me to move in before the kidnapping, but if he ever had second thoughts, he might feel like he couldn't say anything because I had nowhere to go, now.

Linda's front door opened and she appeared in the entryway. I felt secure to get out of the car. I waved as I walked up the driveway. She smiled, keeping her arms folded as if she were cold. The wind was picking up and the weather report on the radio was predicting a storm on its way. She looked tired. I walked up the steps to greet her.

"Hey there." I greeted her as she moved to let me enter. Something seemed off. "You okay?"

"Yes. I'm alright. Have a seat. Can I get you something?" she asked, closing the door, and locking it behind us. Linda had always been a bubbly person, even with her marital troubles, but there was a darkness in her now—a sadness and what I could only interpret as worry.

"Sure. What do you have?" I asked.

"I have some coffee in the kitchen."

"That sounds great."

"Sugar and milk alright?" she asked, disappearing around the corner.

"Perfect," I answered, peering around her living room. I had never been inside Linda's house before, other than the front doorway. It was clean and sort of empty. I was a bit surprised. I expected lots of decor and figurines. Linda struck me as that type, but this was not warm and friendly, like her normal personality. This was cold and kind of sad, like a man's place.

"I just realized this is the first time I've been in your house. It's cute." I called to her in the kitchen. She didn't respond.

"I can't remember. How long have you been here, now?" I asked, trying to make conversation. She still didn't respond. I wasn't sure if she could hear me. "Linda? Can I help you with anything in there?" Still nothing. I stood up and took a few steps toward the kitchen. "Linda?" Still nothing...

I walked to the entrance to the kitchen and as I came around the corner there was a man standing at the counter, facing away from me. He was making the coffee and Linda was sitting in a chair at the table, her hands folded in her lap.

"Hello?" I said, softly. Linda looked up at me, her expression was contrite. She didn't speak. The man turned and looked at me. He smiled and held out the coffee. It was Paul, her husband. I had never been very close to him, but I had seen him from a distance enough to recognize him in the moment. I took the coffee from his hand.

"Hello Kathren." As the words left his lips, I gasped and my coffee cup fell from my hands and crashed on the floor.

Chapter 20

I KNEW THE VOICE! I could never forget that voice and suddenly the structure of his build and shape of his hands— it all became crystal clear! It was Paul! Linda's husband was my stalker! I backed away and looked at Linda. She dropped her head, in shame and fear.

"Oh, look what you've done." he said, in a calm voice. "Hunny..." he gestured to Linda. Linda quickly stood and pulled paper towels from the counter and kneeled in front of him, wiping the mess.

"What is this?" I asked, sharply! I felt the terror rising from my stomach, into my chest. I looked at the doorway, the voice in my head telling me to run.

"Let's just stay calm and quiet and have a seat," he instructed. He pointed to the living room, the opposite way from the front door. I stood against the wall, frozen, not moving in any direction, but then he said my name in a louder, more commanding voice and moved toward me. I flinched as he stepped toward me and hurried to the couch and sat down. I sat on the edge, stiff as a board. He came and sat beside me. I recoiled, as his elbow touched my arm.

"You? You're him? It's been you this whole time?" I mumbled.

"Kathren, give me your phone, please." He held his hand out. I pulled it from my pocket and gave it to him, reluctantly. "I know you may not believe it, but I am trying to help you. You don't make good choices." he said, swiping my hair behind my shoulder. I cringed at his touch. I didn't look at him. Linda came around the corner and looked at us. She looked like a scared puppy. "You can go to your room now, sweetheart," he told her in a very flat tone. She nodded and started for the hall.

"Linda?" I pleaded. She looked at me with shame and so much timidness. "Go on," he ordered, in a firmer voice and she disappeared around the corner. I called for her one more time, but she didn't respond.

"What is this? I don't understand?"

"Kathren. Do you not remember me?" he asked, staring at me with his dead eyes.

"Remember you? From where?" I didn't know what he was talking about. He shook his head and huffed.

"Wow. There's been so many, you don't even remember. Don't you feel embarrassed? Are you not ashamed?"

"I don't know what you're talking about!" I insisted, letting the frustration seep out.

"No! Of Course you don't! Cause you're a whore, aren't you?" He spoke with disgust and venom, clenching his teeth.

I backed away. "What have I done to you?" I asked in a softer tone, trying to calm him.

"You don't remember me. But I remember you. I remember you from the first time I saw you, at that house— that den of sin with those devils and whores! You didn't belong there. I knew it from the second I saw you. You weren't comfortable. You were like an angel standing in a fiery pit. I wanted to rescue you then— you were so beautiful and innocent. But that...savage... he was determined to destroy your innocence and to prostitute you to anyone who wanted a taste! It made me sick. I couldn't understand why you let him treat you that way— to use you like that. Those other women... they were harlots, but you were different." He glared at me. I realized that Paul had seen me a year ago, at Joseph's house... with Mark. I couldn't believe it.

"You're talking about Mark." I spoke quietly, afraid to upset him more. "You saw me with Mark?"

"He was sick! A pimp! You weren't meant for someone like him! Then..." He sighed and acted as if he could barely stand to say the next part. "He took you to that place. I watched you and I wanted to snatch you away, but you— you started behaving like the rest of them. I would have never... but you made me... You acted just like the others—like a whore!" He grabbed my arm tightly, squeezing me hard. He was seething over what he thought I did!

I started to cry. "I don't know what you're talking about! Please! I don't understand!" I pulled away from him. He released me. I wondered why Linda didn't call the police or go for help. She had just disappeared into a back room, and her husband was clearly insane.

"That sex club! You went there with him! You let some woman touch you! You let him violate you while everyone watched! You were disgusting! I would have never done it if you hadn't done what you did!" He was sweaty and practically foaming from the mouth.

"I don't know what you're talking about. I don't remember." I really didn't.

"I wanted to take you out of there. I stood there watching everything and then you reached for me. You looked up at me and pulled at me. I tried not to do it, but you grabbed me and I couldn't help it!" He stood up, suddenly, and paced around the room. "I'm just a man! I can only take so much!" His voice was loud again. "What was I supposed to do? You were begging for it! You made me do it!" He leaned down and shrieked in my face. "You made me! He was pointing in my face, spit flying!

I suddenly remembered. Mark had taken me to a swingers club. I was high. He had given me something and I was out of it, but things happened. I messed around with people. Mark told me, at the time, that I was instigating it. I was angry because he gave me a drug I had never tried before. He did it before taking me there, and I ended up having sex with people, even though I didn't want to. There was a man... I remember. *Oh God! Was Paul that man?*

"We had sex?" I asked timidly.

"You know what you did!" he insisted. "Don't play innocent now!" He was shouting in my face! I backed away, cowering at his aggression. It began to storm. I could hear thunder rumbling outside, as the evening turned to night. Then, I noticed my phone buzzing from Paul's back pocket. I wanted to get away. I regretted going to Linda's and not texting Joseph to let him know where I was.

"I was high at that place. Mark drugged me. I didn't mean to." Then, all at once, Whack! He hit me across the face. My head jerked sideways. "Are you saying it was my fault?"

"No," I sobbed. I clutched my cheek. He kneeled down, immediately, and began to pull my hand away and caress my face, a look of guilt in his eyes.

"Oh Kathren. I didn't mean that. Forgive me." His eyes darted back and forth. He was insane and I was in serious danger! He patted my hair and rubbed his hand down my face to my neck and shoulders and began massaging me, as his breath trembled. My phone was buzzing again. He ignored it. His eyes panned down to my breast and he squeezed my shoulders and arms, still kneeling in front of me.

"Please..." I mumbled.

"Please...Please what?" He leaned in close with his mouth close to mine. "Do you need to lay down?" He started to push me back onto the couch. I hesitated, but obeyed. He scooped my legs onto the couch and placed me in a laid-back position. He leaned over me and stroked my hair, his eyes moving from my face to my body. There was a deep moan coming from his throat.

"Paul? What about Linda?" I asked, trying to distract him from what I was afraid he might do next.

"She won't bother us. She'll do as she's told. She always does." He leaned in and kissed my mouth. I cringed, but tried not to be obvious that I was disgusted. He licked my lips. "Open your mouth, angel." He lowered his hand to the bulge in his pants. His breath was shaking. I did as he told me. I was terrified. His tongue was in my mouth and he lowered his other hand to my stomach and pulled up my shirt, only exposing my belly button. He dragged his fingers against my skin, as he stroked himself over his pants and kissed me. I was rigid from head to toe.

I turned my face away. "We can't do this to Linda," I begged. His eyes became dark with rage.

"Linda? We can't do this to Linda?" He stopped touching himself and backed away. "You never worried about other people before— not with him! You didn't care who saw you or heard you!" He stood up, looking down at me.

"But she's not just some woman. She's your wife... she might get jealous." I tried to connect to the part of his twisted mind that seemed to think he was a good man...some sort of hero. My phone kept buzzing.

"Shut up!" he screamed, pulling my phone from his pocket, and throwing it against the wall. I flinched and turned my head away.

"Paul...please. Can we just talk for a while? I'd like to know more about you. I want to understand. Please. Maybe if we could just talk, we could help each other."

"Help each other? I'm not the one who needs help!" he growled.

"Then maybe it can help me... if you'd be willing to talk, I mean." I prayed he wouldn't catch on. He seemed crazy enough to think I really wanted his help. "I think you're right. I didn't want to do those things. Mark made me... Mark and Joseph. They manipulated me and tried to turn me into a whore. I was a good person before all of this. I know I don't act like it, but I am glad that someone sees the truth..." I leaned up slightly, as his stare softened. His breathing slowed as I spoke. "I'm so messed up, Paul. I've been so lost. Please, I do need your help. I want to be a good person again."

Paul chewed at his lip, looking at me with skepticism. He came back close to me and kneeled down again. I tried with all my might not to flinch and I tried to force a small smile. I didn't know if it would work, but I tried to push through his uncertainty. He began to stare adoringly again, but I knew at any moment that could spin back into his sick and twisted lust or rage.

"I can help you." He smiled, but his smile was disturbing. "Stand up."

I stood in front of him. Paul was slender, pale skinned and his hair was dark brown with a slight receding hairline. His face was boney and his dark eyes seemed sunken. He looked like he might not be that strong and I wondered if I could overpower him long enough to get out of the house. I remembered, though, that when he abducted me, he seemed to be very strong. Of Course I was handcuffed. This time my legs and hands were free, but I tried to bide my time and wait for my moment.

"Go!" he said, directing me to the hall.

"Where are we going?" I asked, worried now that he was moving me into the back of the house, away from my way out.

"Just walk." He held me by the arm and pushed me toward a back room. "Here." He stopped and turned me toward a closed door. He pushed the door open and inside was a bed and a strange-looking contraption. It looked like a long, skinny, padded table, with restraints attached to the bottom of the legs. I tensed and he had to shove me into the room. There were belts and whips hanging from the closet door.

"Paul, please! I want to go back to the living room." He pushed me again and I stumbled into the edge of the bed. He shut the door behind him and turned a bolt lock. As the sound of the lock jolted into place, I instantly felt like a trapped animal. I backed away, to the other side of the bed. Paul opened the top drawer of a dresser that stood next to the door. He reached inside and the moonlight shining in from the window reflected off the item he pulled out. It was a gun! I gasped and backed up even farther into the wall! "Paul! Please! Whatever you're thinking...please don't!"

"Take off your pants," he ordered in a quiet, sinister voice.

"Paul..."

"Shut up! Don't speak! Do what I say! Do you understand?"

I just stared at him and the gun dangling at his side.

"Now— do what I said and take off your pants!" This time he said it louder. "Do what you're told!"

I sighed, every part of me trembling in fear. I unbuttoned my pants and pushed them down. I stepped out of them and pushed them away with my foot. I cupped my hands over the front of my panties.

He looked me up and down. "Your panties too," he mumbled, licking his lips. He was rubbing the gun against the outside of his leg and his other hand was starting to move toward his groin again. I hesitated and he lifted the gun. I quickly pulled my panties down and began to cry. He came toward me and I winced and turned my body away, finding nowhere to go. I was cornered. He took my hand and pulled me toward the contraption. I resisted, but the gun was forcing me to comply.

"Please Paul! Don't do this." I cried.

"Bend over, " he said, gesturing toward the table. "Bend over the table!"

I tried to stall, my mind racing, trying to think of a way out of this, but I couldn't. "Bend over the table!" He yelled this time, jerking my arm down. I grabbed the edge of the table and laid my body over it.

"Please don't hurt me!" I begged, now in a full-blown cry.

"Stop crying!" he demanded, pushing the gun against my side. "Now!"

I tried to control my sobs. Tears and snot were dripping from my face.

"Put your hands through the restraints." I slid my hands through and he bent down and pulled the straps tight, locking me in. He placed the gun on the floor next to me and moved around to the back and fastened the straps around my ankles. I was bent over the table, my body lying on it with my hands and feet strapped down. I was completely exposed and helpless. At that moment, I wished that I had tried to fight my way out, when I had the chance. He moved around me. As he passed my face I could see him unbuttoning his pants.

"Paul! Please don't do this! I know you don't want to hurt me! Please let me go!" I begged him, but he just kept telling me to be quiet. Then I felt him lifting the back of my shirt, uncovering my back. I felt the coolness of the air against my skin. A chill ran up my legs and back. Was he going to rape me, like this? He could do anything he wanted. I was powerless and terrified.

"Are you sorry for all the bad things you did, Kathren?" he asked. His fingers were raking against my flesh on my back. His voice was low and shaky. I knew his other hand was on his cock. "Are you?"

"Yes."

"What are you sorry for?" His nails grazed my back slowly toward my ass.

"Everything!"

Smack! He slapped my ass hard. The shock of the hit caused me to yelp and my legs jerked from the sting.

"What are you sorry for?" he asked again, louder, and more stern.

I tried to catch my breath from the shock of the spanking. "I... I'm sorry for doing horrible things." I tensed, preparing for another possible slap.

"What kind of horrible things?" He was almost whispering now. I could tell he was aroused by the quiver in his voice.

"The sex... and the parties."

"What did you do at the parties?"

" I did bad things."

Thwack! Again, he struck me hard! This time it was with a belt. I cried out. It burned and stung like fire. My breathing was labored. I was almost convulsing from the fear of another hit. My knees tightened and then gave out over and over, as I pulled against the restraints.

But, he began to gently stroke my ass, as if he was trying to sooth the sting.

"Tell me the things you did, Kathren. If you don't want to be punished, you must confess it all." The shake in his voice was the sound of a man fondling himself and getting off. "Confess."

I swallowed hard and tried to remember.

"I let Mark fuck me."

"How?"

"However he wanted."

" What else?"

"I put his cock in my mouth, while Joseph fucked me. I fucked different people. I let people see my body. I let Mark and Joseph touch my body at the same time, and... I fucked them both— at the same time." I tensed, as I listened to his panting. I expected a smack at any second or to feel him put his cock inside me.

"And what did you do to me?" he asked, breathing hard. I knew what he wanted to hear.

"I tempted you. I made you fuck me."

"Yes! Yes you did! And you liked it— didn't you?" He was worked up. His voice was almost a whimper.

"Yes. I liked it!"

"Did you climax when you made me do that?"

"Yes..."

Smack! Smack! Smack! Three hard whacks in a row, with the belt. My ass was on fire. I winced and gasped, jerking and thrashing, unable to go anywhere.

"Are you a whore?" he snarled and moaned as the question stammered from his mouth.

"Yes!" I cried and he smacked me again and again and again...four, five six times, until I screamed out. He moaned, as he came. The sick fuck was getting off on beating me, making me talk dirty to him. He grabbed a mound of my ass, as he finished coming and began to whine down. His breathing was heavy and strained, as he squeezed my ass and my flesh blazed with pain. I let my legs go weak and let the weight of my body hang on the table.

He was quiet for a while and I didn't speak. I just waited, wondering what came next. Then there was a soft knock at the door. He stopped breathing for a moment and then unlocked it and barked "What!"

"I need to talk to you." I heard Linda's voice. She was quiet and submissive. I wanted to call out to her for help, but it was clear she was under his control. I knew Linda had issues with Paul, but I never could have imagined anything like this. I wondered if she suspected him when I told her about my stalker, but she was the one who told me she saw a man that first time and wouldn't she have recognized her own husband? *They're both fucking nuts!* I thought to myself.

I stared at the gun, still laying on the floor, about a foot away from my restrained hand. I had to try and get my hands on it. It might be my only way out of this. Although, in the position I was in at that moment, still tied to the table, it was a lost cause. I had to convince him to release me. He had left the room, closing the door behind him. I could hear him speaking harshly to Linda. His voice was loud and angry, but I couldn't hear what she was saying. I was able to catch a few words from Paul, though...

"When I'm ready..."

"You just do what you're told..."

"Shut up! Don't make me punish you, again!"

That was all I could make out. He was a fucking monster— a crazy, twisted, sexually deranged psycho! One wrong word could send him over the edge. My jaw was still sore from the hard slap, earlier and my ass was throbbing. He seemed to be ashamed that he had sex with me at the club, all those months ago. I couldn't really even remember it, but he didn't like that I said I was drugged and didn't want to. It was like he needed to feel that I seduced him— that he was innocent in it. He got off on hurting me— punishing me, and that scared me more than the idea of him raping me. He wanted to degrade me. He was a freak.

The door shut and locked, again. He was back. He came over to me and picked the gun up. It scared me when he had the gun in his hand. I could see the lower part of his body and could see him tucking the gun in the back of his pants. I exhaled, relieved that he wasn't holding it. That meant my brains weren't about to go splat, but still anything could happen to me at any minute.

" How does it feel to have confessed?" he asked. His voice sounded more at ease.

"It feels good," I answered, assuming that's what he wanted to hear.

He sat down on the floor beside me, where he could look at my face and see my eyes. I hated looking at him. He pushed my hair back from my face. "You really are very lovely," he said. I mustered a smile. "I'm proud of you. It didn't take that long to get you to tell the truth. That's good." He kept touching my hair and caressing my face. It was making me feel queasy. I hated his touch. I couldn't let it show, though.

"I wanted to tell the truth— to get it off my chest. It's been such a burden. I've carried all of it around for so long— the shame—the bad memories. I want to be good again." I was giving the performance of my life. I hoped it was believable.

"I don't know, Kathren. You're living over there in that den of vipers. And it wasn't that long ago, you had different men in and out of your house: that devil... the one with the long hair, and the one with the fancy car. I taught him a lesson. I saw the tantrum he threw when he saw what I did to his precious car," he chuckled. "But that wasn't that long ago. You didn't have to move in with him." His expression turned hard, again.

"I— I didn't really want to. I was scared. I didn't know who you were and I thought... I don't know. I just felt scared over here, all alone." He just glared at me. "Paul? Do you think you could let me out of this thing. now? Please. If I could just sit up... on the bed, maybe?" I leaned my face into his caress stroking my cheek against his touch. It made me sick, but I needed him to feel empathy and close to me. I tried to be submissive. He seemed to need that. He stared quietly for a minute longer and then he began to undo the straps around my wrist. It was working! He was feeling pity for me and granting my request.

"Don't make me regret this," he warned.

"I won't. I promise, I will be good."

He freed my hands and then moved behind me and began to release my legs.

"Stay still, until I tell you to move," he demanded. He undid the final strap and stood up. I stayed right there, frozen still, waiting for him to tell me I could stand.

"Okay. Get up." He stayed behind me. I put my hands on the table under my chest and slowly pushed myself up. My legs felt weak and my bottom was still tender. I balanced myself as I stood facing away from him. "You can put your panties back on."

"Thank you, Paul." I walked gingerly to where my panties lay on the floor and slid them back on. I was so thankful to be able to cover back up. I reached for my pants.

"I didn't tell you to do anything else!" he barked at me. I flinched and dropped them.

"Sorry. You're right. My mistake." He seemed edgy, like he wasn't sure what to do next. *What was he going to do next?* It wasn't like he could just let me go. He knew I would go right to the police. I knew who he was now and where he lived. His wife was hidden away in another bedroom. He couldn't keep her locked up forever. And, he knew Joseph was going to be looking for me and it was only a matter of time before someone came knocking. He didn't have a lot of choices. I mean, a crazy person doesn't think things through, but at some point he was going to realize that he had to do something, and my fear was that it might mean a fight for my life.

"Sit down on the bed." he ordered. I complied and sat on the foot of the bed, staring down at the floor. I folded my hands in my lap. I could see them trembling.

"Paul. I'm so sorry." I offered an apology. I had to work on his unhinged mind and convince him that I had seen the light and he didn't have to see me as a threat.

"Sorry for what?" His voice was unsure, but definitely softer than it had been.

"What I've put you through." I looked up at him, trying to appear regretful and affectionate. "I didn't realize how my bad behavior was affecting you. You saw me— the real me, from the beginning and you wanted to help me. All this time... I see it now. You just wanted to help me. I made things so hard for you. It must have been so difficult... watching me act so terrible. I'm such a disappointment. I don't deserve your help, but you gave it anyway. I wish I had noticed it in the beginning, before I let those bad men..." I dropped my head into my hands as if I couldn't bear to continue. Paul quickly sat down beside me. He put one hand on my back and gently pulled my hands from my face. He looked at me with affection, his eyes filled with empathy.

"Kathren, you still have time to change it. That's why I'm here. I'll help you." He leaned in to kiss me and I let him. I fought every impulse to squirm away. I lifted my face and kissed him back. His breathing shook, as he moved his tongue around, in my mouth. I wanted to vomit. Then he laid me back, laying his body on me. He took my breast in his hand. I touched him back. I put my hands on his shoulders and caressed down his arms. I moaned, as he squeezed my breast, making him believe I wanted him. I slid my arms around him and stroked his back.

"Oh Kathren! Sweet Kathren. You're so beautiful—so soft—so dirty." He moved his knee between my thighs, opening them. He was going to fuck me or kill me, maybe both. I had to act. I reached down to his waist and pulled the gun, still tucked into his belt, and shoved him with all my might.

"Get off of me, you bastard!" I shouted, as I jolted from the bed. He had fallen to the floor when I pushed him and he hurried to stand. He was about to lunge toward me, but stopped when he realized I had the gun pointed at him. "Back up mother fucker! I'll blow your fucking head off!" I was shaking like crazy, but I was determined to get out. I realized that it was possible the gun had no bullets when I made the choice to go for it and he could have attacked me, knowing the gun was empty and that he wasn't in danger, but clearly that wasn't the case. He backed up, his hands out in front of him.

"Kathren— listen... Give me the gun!" he tried to speak with authority, while obeying me, at the same time. It was exhilarating to finally have the power.

"Shut up, you sick fuck! Unlock the goddamn door! Now!" I waved the gun, just enough to gesture toward the door. He shimmied to the door and unlocked it. "Open it!" He did. "Now move!" He walked backward; his hands still lifted in a protective way. He was the submissive now!

"Kathren. I wouldn't hurt you."

I scoffed. "Wouldn't hurt me? You already hurt me, you sick bastard! But that's over! You're going to prison, you psycho!" We moved through the hall into the living room. My eyes scanned to the floor to see the pieces of my phone scattered everywhere. "Where is your phone?"

"I don't know."

"Bullshit! Where is it!" I screamed.

"I'm not lying. I don't know where it is," he insisted.

"Kathren?" I turned to the voice behind me. It was Linda. Right then, Paul lunged forward with a loud roar and plowed into me, knocking the gun from my hand, and tackling me to the floor! I fought him as hard as I could, swinging wildly, screaming in anger and terror! He lifted me by the collar and punched me in the face! I tasted the blood in my mouth immediately, as my head hit the floor. I swung and clawed, but he straddled me and got his hands around my throat! I scratched at his grip, when suddenly a loud boom shook the room! We both startled to attention and found Linda standing with the gun pointed at Paul! Her whole body was vibrating!

"Baby..." Paul stood slowly. "Give me the gun, baby."

"Stop..." Her voice was a whisper. She looked unsteady and her eyes were wide and lost looking. Her face was wet with tears.

Paul reached toward her. "Sweetheart. It's okay. Just give me the gun. Everythings okay now." She stepped back, shaking her head, almost in a convulsive way. She still had the gun pointed at Paul. I pushed up on my palms, slowly. She looked at me and then back at him.

"You have to let her go, Paul," she told him. I scooched away, backing up into the couch.

"Linda. Listen to me. I can't let her go. She will have them take me away from you. You don't want that do you? Give me the gun. Let me get her back into the punishment room and you and I will sit down and have a long talk. I love you so much, baby. You know I do. I just need to teach her. You get it...right?" He was inching closer to her, his hand extended toward the gun.

"Linda..." I spoke in a soft voice. "Linda, please don't give him the gun." I begged. She looked down at me. Her breath quivered. She was so broken.

"Linda! Give me the gun!" Paul raised his voice. He was becoming impatient with her. She flinched at his loud command. Paul's eyes darted at me quickly, but then back to Linda, who was swaying, still pointing the gun at him.

"Linda, please. You're my friend. He was going to hurt me, Linda. He was going to rape me!" I pleaded.

"Shut up!" Paul shrieked at me.

"You're crazy!" I bit back.

"Lying whore!" Paul shouted. Then, enraged, Paul came toward me. Linda fired! Paul spun to his right! He almost went to the floor, but he managed to stagger back up onto his feet. He was holding his shoulder. She had shot him in the right shoulder. He looked shocked at his wound. He looked at Linda, infuriated and then turned and went for the front door. He unlocked it and bolted out!

I exhaled, in relief. Linda walked calmly to the door and looked out. I struggled to my feet. I walked toward Linda, every part of my body hurting from Paul's assault. I wiped the blood from my mouth.

"Linda...Thank you." I sighed.

Linda turned to face me. The look in her eyes was pure shock, but there was something else. She raised the gun again, this time facing me. I lifted my hands and backed up.

"Linda? What are you doing?"

"This is your fault," she said. "You did this."

"Linda! Please! You're in shock!" I tried to ease her. She looked like a mad woman with her hair a mess and teary mascara running down her pale face. "Linda, please don't do anything you'll regret."

"Regret? I regret moving here! I couldn't understand why he wanted to move here. I liked our old house. I should have known when he insisted we move all of a sudden. I should have... He was doing so much better. He was acting like a regular husband. We were happy again... and then you... You had to flaunt yourself in front of him! Triggering him... just like last time."

"Last time?" I asked, still backing away, trying to spot a way out. She was blocking the entrance.

"Yeah! Oh, did you think you were the only one? Don't flatter yourself. There have been others. You're not special!"

Linda *was* nuts! She was traumatized from her husband's sickness and it had turned her into a fucking crazy person, too. I had to find a way to get her to drop the gun.

"Linda. Listen... I am so sorry for what you've been through and I accept my fault in all of this. You're the victim of all of this! You're such a good person. You don't deserve to be treated this way." I forced a sympathetic smile. "Linda, I always valued our friendship, even though it may not have seemed like it. I was just fucked up and I didn't realize how I was treating you or how I might be causing Paul to..."

"You caused him to ignore me! You took him back to that place he worked so hard to heal from!" She screeched. "I knew it when I saw you that first time. I knew why we moved here. He was watching through the window and you just traipsed around in front of him— never closing your blinds. Walking around in your yard with those tiny shorts. You wanted his attention. Then when he started coming to you— you acted so surprised— so scared. Meanwhile, I'm over here doing everything I can to please him— to get his focus back. I thought, maybe if I become friends with you— maybe if I told you my marriage is struggling, you would stop. No! You just kept it up. You kept tempting him! Now look at what's happened! Everything's a mess— because of you!" She raised the gun.

"Linda please!" I begged.

"Kathren!" Joseph's voice bellowed from behind her! Linda turned. I heard two other voices yell, "Drop the Gun!" and then... shots rang out! I covered my eyes and dropped to the ground! It was so loud, but just as quickly as it happened... it was over and there was silence— except for the storm raging outside! I kept my eyes squeezed shut and I didn't move. Then, after a few seconds, I felt hands on my shoulders and heard the sweetest voice.

"Kathren?"

"I opened my eyes and looked up to find Joseph squatted down in front of me. Behind him two policemen stood over Linda, who was laying on the floor, a puddle of blood growing from her side. I heard one of the officers calling for an ambulance. I looked back at Joseph and reached for him. He pulled me into him and his embrace, at that moment, might have been the best thing I ever felt.

"Jesus! Are you okay?" he gasped. I just cried. All the stress poured out of me, as I realized for the first time that night that I wasn't going to die.

Chapter 21

I STOOD THERE, IN LINDA'S front yard, watching as the paramedics loaded her into the ambulance. She was alive, thank God. Linda might have killed me, but I felt so bad for her. Paul had really screwed her up and she needed help. The storm had calmed—both storms!

"Man, you never know about people, I guess." Joseph said, squeezing me close. "All this time, it was your neighbor. No wonder he got away so fast when the cops came. He just snuck right back into his house— that sick mother fucker!"

"And Linda knew... She knew the whole time." I added.

Detective Casteel was approaching us, having just arrived on the scene. He looked at the ambulance and then back to me, consolingly.

"Well..." He exhaled, "I guess we should have looked more closely at your neighbors."

"You think?" Joseph scoffed.

"Are you okay, Ms. Thom... Kathren?" he corrected.

"I am."

"The other officer said you're refusing medical care. I really think you should go get checked out."

"The paramedics looked me over. Just some bruises and a cut lip. It doesn't even need stitches," I assured him. I did not want to go to the hospital and have to explain the causes of the injuries, especially not the bruises that I was sure had begun to form on my ass. I just wanted to get out of there. I wanted to get to the safety of Joseph's house.

"We have a lot of questions, Kathren. Would you be willing to go to the station?" he asked.

"How about in the morning?" Joseph answered for me. "I think she's had enough tonight. Can't it wait?"

"Well, the more info we get while it's fresh, the better."

"I already told the other officers what happened. I mean, you know who he is now. There's no more mystery." I said.

"I just can't believe the wife tried to shoot you." Casteel shook his head in disbelief.

"Linda has been dealing with abuse from Paul for a long time. From what she said, I am not the first woman he has obsessed over in their marriage. She convinced herself that he was in love with her and that he had changed. She's going to need some help." I told Casteel.

"I'm concerned that Paul Davenport is still out there," he voiced.

It was the first time that I had heard Paul and Linda's last name. Well, it was possible that Linda had told me, but I didn't remember. The truth is, I never paid a lot of attention to what Linda said most of the time. Maybe if I had been paying closer attention, I would have picked up on something.

"Yeah. I am too. Hopefully now that you know who he is, it won't be so hard to catch him." Joseph said.

"We'll get him." Casteel assured us. "Can you come in tomorrow morning?"

"Sure." Joseph and I left and headed home. I couldn't wait to get out of there.

Later that night, I was in the shower, washing off the remnants of everything from my horrible night. My jaw was swollen and sensitive to the touch. The inside of my lip stung from the gash. My throat was tender and I had aches in other areas from injuries I couldn't identify, just the general onslaught of attacks. As I washed over my rear, I felt a deep throb in the tissue. Joseph opened the shower door and stepped in with me. He took the soapy sponge from me and gently washed my back and shoulders.

"Are you okay?" he asked.

"I am now." I smiled.

"Really... Are you okay?"

"Physically, I'll heal. Mentally...it might take a while," I confessed. It was an honest statement. I had been through so much and yet I didn't feel as damaged as I thought a person would from such chaotic and terrifying events. I wondered if something was wrong with me. *Had I become so desensitized, that I couldn't react naturally to trauma? Was it all going to hit me later and bring me to my knees?* The thought of things bubbling to the surface later, caused its own stress in the back of my mind. I elected to keep that concern tucked away for now. I needed to get past it all and the fact that Paul was still out there, somewhere, was weighing on me more than I wanted to admit.

"Those look painful," Joseph said, looking down at the red welts that had formed an artistic design across my ass.

"Yeah. It doesn't feel good," I answered.

"What a sick son of a bitch." Joseph shook his head and clenched his teeth. "I shouldn't have left you."

I turned to face him. "Don't," I insisted. "It's over. I should have gone with you, like you asked." I wrapped my arms around him and consoled him, rubbing a gentle circle around his back. Although I was the victim, I knew Joseph was blaming himself and I couldn't stand the thought of it. We finished the shower and retreated to the bed, where we curled up together and slept hard until morning.

"Kathren!" Joseph's voice woke me. He was standing at the edge of the bed, holding his phone. "Detective Casteel wants us to come in, now."

"Alright." I looked at the clock. It was ten. I hadn't slept that late in a while. We got ready and headed to the police station. I wasn't looking forward to rehashing everything, but I knew it was important for them to ask questions so that they could have a better chance of catching Paul. Sometimes it's the little details you don't think are important that crack the case... at least that's what they say on all the police shows I have watched.

As we walked into the station, I noticed Casteel was behind the counter. He looked up and seemed relieved to see us finally there. He waved us to the back. He seemed amped up.

"Come on. I've got some great news," he said, holding the door open, leading us to a room.

"Did you catch him?" Joseph asked, as we found our seats in the small room.

"Not yet. We will. But that's not why I wanted you to hurry in." He sat across from us. "I know why you haven't answered your phone. It was destroyed," he said looking at me and then he turned to Joseph, "But why haven't you answered yours?"

"What do you mean? I answered as soon as you called this morning." Joseph looked confused.

"Mason Sanders has been trying to reach you since last night. Mark Sanders has been found!" We both looked at eachother. Sadness wafted over me.

"I don't know how that's good news," Joseph frowned. "Where did they find his body?"

"No! You're not hearing me... Mark Sanders is alive!"

My face distorted and the air left my lungs. Joseph looked at me and back at the detective.

"What?"

"Yes. He called Mason last night. Mason's been trying to reach you both since he heard from him." Casteel's eyes swayed from me to Joseph, waiting to see our relief.

"I don't understand," I uttered, my voice shaking. "How? Is he sure?" Surely this was some kind of sick joke. It wasn't possible. Joseph and I knew it wasn't possible. My mind couldn't conceive what was happening.

"He's sure. Mark was injured and as crazy as it sounds, apparently, he was unconscious for several days, in some cabin, with a woman, who found him. She never contacted the authorities. I know... Don't ask. I can't wait to hear this ladies story. I know it sounds ridiculous, but he had injuries that made it hard for him to get to town and his memory was hazy or something. It's crazy! I know! He called Mason as soon as he was able. Mason's on his way to get him and bring him home."

Joseph just stared at the detective. He was in shock, I think. I tried to act relieved. I sighed and brought my hand to my chest.

"This is such a relief. We had begun to give up hope if you want to know the truth." I told him. Joseph just looked at me. I struggled to hold back tears.

"I can see that. Mr. Brooks, you look like I could knock you over with a feather, right now." Casteel laughed. I smiled and put my hand on Joseph's arm. I squeezed a little, trying to snap him out of it. Finally he blinked and swallowed.

"Um, yeah... I didn't expect to hear such good news. When will they get to California?" Joseph asked.

"Oh no... Mason's not taking him to his home. He's bringing him here." I felt Joseph's arm tighten. His eyes were like saucers. At least now he was blinking.

"When?" I asked.

"They should be here tomorrow. I can't wait to hear what happened to him." Detective Casteel said, shaking his head. "What a story he must have."

"Yeah... what a story," I repeated. I nudged Joseph, who was still looking like he saw a ghost.

"So, considering the fact that you're already here, I guess we should talk about what happened yesterday." Casteel said, pulling his note book from his pocket. "Why don't you start at the beginning?"

I did my best to explain everything, from Linda's call to the cops shooting her, but honestly the events felt a million miles away, now. All I could think about was Mark. Later, as Joseph and I exited the station I tried to remain calm, but as soon as we got in the parking lot....

"What the fuck!" I practically choked.

"It's not possible," Joseph whispered. "He was dead."

"Is someone fucking with us?" I asked.

"I don't know," he said, opening my car door. Joseph walked around and climbed in the driver's side.

"Wouldn't Mason know his own brother's voice?" I asked.

"Yeah... he would." Joseph pulled out his phone and saw that there were about a dozen missed calls from Mason. "I didn't answer. With everything going on last night, I turned the ringer off, so we could relax."

"Joseph... I think it's time to tell me— where did you put his body?" I stared at him as he just glared out the windshield, still sitting in the parking lot.

"There's a guy. He does things. He told me that he put the truck in a lake and threw his body down a ravine three hundred miles from where he sank the truck." Joseph looked at me. His eyes looked

dazed. "I checked, Kathren— He wasn't breathing."

We just stared at each other for a minute and then Joseph started the car.

"Well, someone's going to be here, with Mason...tomorrow..." I said, as we left the station and headed home.

I looked out the window and whispered under my breath, **"So... *I'm not a murderer...*"**

Don't miss out!

Visit the website below and you can sign up to receive emails whenever Marie Carr publishes a new book. There's no charge and no obligation.

https://books2read.com/r/B-A-KGUZ-GBQNC

BOOKS 2 READ

Connecting independent readers to independent writers.

Also by Marie Carr

Twisted Flowers: Book One: Spiraling
Twisted Flowers: Book Two: DUPLICITY

Milton Keynes UK
Ingram Content Group UK Ltd.
UKHW040653140923
428670UK00001B/121